Praise for Abby Lane

"A shape-shifting lord and a princess with snakelike powers battle a witch's curse—and a potentially fatal attraction—in this debut fairy-tale romance."

Kirkus Reviews

"Borrowing inspiration from modern and classic authors of the genre, yet creating a magnificent new world all her own, *The Scarlett Mark* is an impressive start to an immersive and lavishly written series."

Self-Publishing Review

"Makes me nostalgic for all those old epic fantasies that first got me interested in writing. It has strong ties to fairy tales that many readers will recognize, but it isn't a strict retelling of any. Rather, it stands on its own, with a richer backstory than most fairy tale retellings and with powerful, fascinating characters."

Jo Niederhoff, Manhattan Book Review

"Lane creates a colorful tapestry: a story of a cursed nobleman and exiled princess, of dark and light, good and evil; a tale in which many things are not as they seem at the first glance."

J.F. Kaufmann

"Rich prose and intriguing characters make for an engaging story."

A.M. Westerling

"This is a fabulous blend of romance and fantasy. Lane had it right calling it a Romantasy!"

Katie O'Connor

the Scarlett Mark

The Scarlett Mark

A Medieval Romantasy

ABBY LANE

A REIGN OF BLOOD & MAGIC

BOOK ONE

Published 2015, 2020
ISBN: 978-0-9959680–8-0 (Print edition)
ISBN: 978-1-7770699-0-2 (Kindle edition)
ISBN: 978-0-9959680-9-7 (Other digital edition)

Design and cover art J. Caleb Designs
Copyediting by Karen Crosby of Editarians
Line editing by Ted Williams

The Scarlett Mark is dedicated to the memory of my grandparents, Ernest and Ellen Brewster, who shared many stories during my childhood. Perhaps my joy of writing novel-length fiction was first established at their kitchen table, a place where Grandpa was known to share tales that inspired joy and laughter for the family. My grandparents taught me that regardless of the storm, hope is always waiting to be found.

Preface

The Scarlett Mark was an abstract idea during the summer of 2012, in that a story hadn't taken shape yet. At that time, I was employed as a bookseller at Indigo Books & Music, and though I had written several manuscripts, I wasn't writing at this time. In fact, I'd given up on writing a book, let alone publishing one. Yet, I worked in the bookstore for years, waiting for inspiration to bear words. Participating in Harry Potter's and then Stephanie Meyer's book releases, always waiting, *hoping*, the muse would strike again.

And then: The first season of *The Game of Thrones* aired on HBO. The story hooked my imagination to such an extent, I was soon reading the series: *A Song of Ice and Fire*. I appreciated George R. R. Martin's writing style, especially the way he shared his prose, offering up one character at a time. Now, some readers might be upset by a character's demise, and I certainly was too, in some cases, but history proves that humanity is unkind, so what I see as a realistic approach to characterization or being true to one's narrative, is what I admire most about George.

And then, *bam!* My imagination sprouted a seed of an idea.

A Reign of Blood and Magic (not the original series title) began with Scarlett, Ruby, and Rose. One day at work, I'm in the lunchroom and three names pop into my head. I'm mindful of the color red, from the beginning. It isn't long before I'm writing their story. This story.

My favorite character to conceive is Cynara. The story begins with her and if she ever dies, the series will end with her, too. I love her capacity to act. To not accept strife from anyone. To go where no other woman has gone before, regardless of the consequences.

I published the first edition in 2015. An early reviewer and close friend said this book seemed as if it was written from a childhood heart, and I think that's true. The author in me who love's fairy tales, especially *Sleeping Beauty* and everything Disney, wants to connect with real life heroes and heroines in a fantasy way, wrote this story.

I hope you enjoy it!

Abby Lane.

Acknowledgments

I thank friends and family who have supported my writing career. I especially wish to express my gratitude to the love of my life, my husband, Wayne, who has supported me and encouraged me in my ambition to publish.

I also thank my adult kids and their partners, Carrie and William, Shawn, and Alicia and Trevor, whose belief in me inspired this story to be written.

I thank my mom, Inez, who believed in my writing gift and encouraged my craft through reading when I was a young girl. My favorite book was a gift from my mom, and children should read it: *A Child's Garden of Verses* by Robert Louis Stevenson.

The business of publishing is a work in itself, and I appreciate the support and wisdom received from my writing colleagues' Katie O'Connor, Jennifer Howard, and Brenda Sinclair. Brenda offered excellent critical advice. Thank you, ladies!

I am also grateful to Karen Crosby for copyediting the

revised edition and Ted Williams for a final line edit. Their editorial contributions and careful eye for detail have polished *The Scarlett Mark* to perfection!

Much thanks as well to Jake for an amazing cover!

Each of you has encouraged my dreams to morph into goals, which I can now hold in the palm of my hand. Thank you for your contributions!

Prologue

CYNARA

The eye of the storm circled toward Drum Manor, *her* resolve surrendering to wickedness. Gale force winds blew cold, threatening to topple the oak trees as if their brine-soaked trunks were no more than thin sticks. Lightning flashed white, rippling between gray clouds, and thunder roared and crackled. Mother Nature brewed a warning of evil entering the forest, but a witch's wrath could not be stilled and the settling of scores persisted.

Cynara Musadora conjured the storm.

She'd prepared for this night and wore the ceremonial robes of her coven, a black cloak flecked with silver that swirled around her legs. The fabric itself seemed to breathe an insidious life. She didn't care. It was her destiny to wield darker arts, but until this moment, she hadn't used her gift for nefarious purposes; and no one, man, woman or child, had been hurt by her art, even so, no human had harmed her emotional well-being like Nicolai Graydon.

In her life, she'd encountered many ignorant sards. Childhood friends, young adults, the odd household lord or lady, too. But after one cruel handling by a rake, she'd taken enough abuse and wasn't suffering further exploitation. Not from anyone. There were consequences for manipulating a woman like her, and punishing the offender seemed appropriate.

After all, Hell hath no fury like a woman's scorn and Nicolai's rejection had been the worst. The betrayal had weakened her, causing feelings of shame, sadness, and grief. Losing his love, or what had seemed like love, had broken her spirit. She couldn't overcome her grief and like a weakened fool, for weeks, couldn't stop crying.

She'd loved the man!

But his betrayal had crushed her heart and torn it into two bloody pieces. Where a heart muscle should beat strong, now, only sorrow, silent rage, and two black stones beat weakly inside her chest. As far as she was concerned, it wasn't unreasonable that a man should suffer a similar fate and cry at sorrow's door, too.

Yet in light of new ambitions, she was calm. Peaceful. She stepped from behind a tree, finding the pathway that led to the mansion and the man who had hurt her, shunned her, and forced their relationship to end. She'd hiked this pathway so many times before, it almost disappointed her that this would be her last visit beneath these trees.

The forest was full of old, gnarled oak. In the darkness, the trees were hauntingly beautiful and she treasured them. She swept aside their branches as if the limbs were her web, and she the spider skittering across the silk. Lord Nicolai, unaware of her pursuit, struggled on the line. She felt him. Heard him. The thrum of his heartbeat pulsed. *Thump—Thump.* She approached it, to wrap him within her curse to punish him for his crime, a love crime that drove her closer to his home.

Long jet-black strands of hair whipped into her mint-green eyes, and though cold air spat against her face and nipped at her hands, her desire for revenge did not abate.

"Soon, Nicolai," she cackled. Lightning flashed and thunder boomed a second time. "Very soon, I will have your heart. Lady Alexandra cannot have what is mine."

If she could not have the man she loved—or rather, had loved—if Nicolai could not see *she* was his other half, *his better half*, then she'd curse the bastard to the Netherworld.

As the forest gave way to a clearing, Cynara trudged through tall grasses that swished with the breeze, marching toward the ridge, whose rocky embankment traversed the path between the land and the sea. The tide was stronger than usual and though the waves crashed beneath the cliff, surging against the rocks, the ugly roil did not lessen her pursuit.

Drum Manor waited on the other side of the meadowlands. Candlelight flickered on the other side of the dormer windows, drawing her closer. The light illuminating her footpath to the manor. Nicolai was inside that house and she knew where the lord entertained his company. In the great hall with his bride-to-be.

Though the thought of the pair caused Cynara to scream with rage, amusement soon creased her face. A matrimonial affair was not happening. *No woman would wear his ring, nor share in his impassioned bed.* She would find them, curse their future, and snuff out their passionate flames forever.

Lord Nicolai Graydon

Lord Nicolai stood near the banquet table, dressed in a rich black vest accentuated with silver brocade, holding a tankard of ale in his right hand. He grinned, swirling the amber fluid, acknowledging the fact he had reached a once unattainable goal—amassing his fortune through a betrothal commitment, and in so doing, returning his family name to its proper status. He considered this milestone while scrutinizing the gilt-edged hall. A windfall of capital presented itself in the form of wealthy guests. He contemplated men and women who were engaging in conversation, dancing to classical string music, feasting on finger foods, or stealing away to private chambers to share in more intimate pursuits. Drum Manor hosted the best of the best and he was grateful the wealthy were in attendance.

He watched them. Counts and viscounts discussing parliamentary issues. The Lord High Marshall, in company with members of the king's privy council, droning on about military matters to nattering diplomats and stewards. Lords and ladies presenting their stylish daughters in the hopes of finding a suitable husband. He watched the drama unfold with a keen intellect, understanding that everyone who could make a difference in his future was sharing his home at this betrothal celebration. Lord Nicolai Graydon had risen in status, too, and he felt like he'd won a lavish prize. *Gratefully*, his life goals could mature due to this makeshift measure.

What more could a man do than celebrate his success and sip his ale? He supposed he could thank the woman who brought this influence into his life. Alexandra, the daughter of an earl; from the start he'd known she'd make the perfect wife. Yet, some aristocratic men considered their pairing a selfish pursuit of material gain, since her dowry advanced a required coin into his pocket.

He didn't care what anyone thought about his actions. His debtors had demanded their funds, a manor required refurbishment, and his life needed a face-lift. He couldn't wait to be wed to realize the wealth. And her delicate features, blonde hair and celestial blue eyes, provided the perfect genetics should their union bear children. Dressed in a pale blue surcoat threaded with silver, she shimmered like the metal. He should probably love the woman for all she brought to his life, but what did Nicolai know about love?

He had never considered the question of *love* until a hunting lad had enquired about his matrimonial motives, motives that could never define a lover's true purpose. He had skirted the issue with a response long in coming.

What is love, anyway?

He sipped his drink and contemplated the question. The poets wrote about this notion of love as if its essence were a heady desire or a dark spell that *squeezed* at the victim's heart, rendering them helpless. The minstrels sang of silly infatuations with high-pitched voices, imparting an intense lust and sudden couplings of the heart.

"Huh," Nicolai recalled, chuckling under his breath. He had a fondness for a good song, but felt that *love* was no more than an incurable malady, an arthritic condition; a chain that threatened to drag its victims into a life of servitude. He did not care for such an affliction, but he did covet the monetary elements that came with commitment—the money a marriage would bring.

Someday, he might care for Alexandra, perhaps love her as well, but if not for his needs, he would never have chosen her for a bride. Despite her beauty, she feared his advances, shied away from conversation, and cringed at the slightest touch. Frankly, they entertained little chemistry. Bedding the woman might prove to be a chore.

Lord Nicolai, or Nick, as the more brazen ladies chose to refer to him, was not accustomed to a shy lady like Alexandra. A daredevil of a woman had been more to his liking. He licked salty ale from his lips as Cyn came to mind—a dark-haired vixen who had joined him in raucous exploits. He heated, recalling their affair, but their sex-play had ended when the marriage banns were announced. Perhaps he could find her again, take her as his mistress, and enjoy seductive pleasures on the side.

"I think not," he whispered to himself, swallowing his ale in a choked gulp. Removing the woman from his life had been a wise decision, as their last encounter had ended horribly. Cynara had fought the news of his upcoming marriage. She chanced to be a take-all or take-naught sort of woman, a wanton warrior who would crush a man's genitalia if he didn't pay close attention to her needs. A regrettable cost he couldn't afford to pay.

The time had come to announce the engagement, so Nicolai placed his empty mug on the table and went in search of Alexandra, finding his betrothed where a dutiful daughter should reside; at her father's side, behind her mother's skirt.

"There you are," he acknowledged, reflecting on her beauty while crossing the space between them. "You're dressed like an angel in your pale blue gown. Lady Alexandra, I swear, your eyes are glowing with an inner light."

She curtsied, dipping daintily. "Thank you for your kindness, my lord."

He extended his gloved hand toward her. "May I have your hand, my dear? It's time to make the betrothal announcement."

Alexandra breathed deeply, sighed, then placed her petite hand atop his palm, lowering her gaze. "Yes, Lord Nicolai."

Gently, he pulled her to him. A tiny, fragile bird, she appeared ready to flee while flitting to his side. He felt the fright in her quivering hand.

"Alexandra, my dear," he whispered, ushering her away from her father, and escorting her toward a raised platform. "You must not quiver with fright. Soon, I will be your husband."

"I'm not frightened of you," she mumbled, taking a deep breath. "Lord Nicolai, if I'm to be honest with you, I'm not ready for marriage, or this betrothal."

He studied her sedate expression, fingering her shoulder. "I know our engagement is sudden, but it's a good match for our families. Surely a beauty, such as yourself, yearns for a husband? Isn't that why your mother brought you to court a fortnight ago, to find you a suitable partner?"

Unresponsive, the angelic woman glanced at his fingers. He listened to her stiff breathing and perceived a weak heart-beat pulsing beneath his touch. Her fear was obviously expressed. Was she concerning herself with the possibilities held within their bedchamber? He removed his hand.

"I confess, I was excited to explore the idea of marriage," she confided, nibbling at her lip. "Nevertheless, I didn't imagine I'd find myself betrothed so quickly. And to— a rake of a man."

Surprised at her temerity, he grasped her hand and whispered words only she could hear. "A rake of a man?" Nicolai chortled, leaning closer, grazing her earlobe with his lips. "My reputation precedes me. I assure you, my dear, I am a gentle-man, and as such will treat you with the utmost respect."

"I don't doubt you will respect me, my lord. However, I've heard tell your standing rule with women is one of mutual affection."

"I'm uncertain as to what you imply, but I imagine in time you'll assert your position."

"You know," she said, blushing, "your clandestine rela-tionships with the opposite sex."

Nicolai shook his head. "Will it go easier for you if I promise to love only you?"

"Do you mock me? Am I wrong to want a loving commitment? A man who will share his flattery with only one woman. With me?"

He broke their contact and faced her, assessing her expec-tant mien. One white lie; what did it matter if he shared a mistruth? "I see how this matter concerns you, so to aid in putting worry behind us, I promise to bestow my fragile heart upon your good graces. Perhaps, in time, some affection, too."

He studied her wary expression, then attempted to lead her toward the podium. She glanced at her parents and her former life with concern, then paused, seeking his observation again.

"Are you toying with me?"

"I assure you, where matters of the heart are concerned, my courtesy extends further than the physical pursuit of a gentle-born lady. I make you this promise: to take proper care and consideration of you. Come now, we have an announcement to make."

He extended his right hand toward Alexandra, and he watched her studying his palm, perhaps considering whether she should accept his offering. He worried when an awkward silence stretched. "Alexandra…"

Nicolai winked when she placed her hand in his. "I'll trust you then, my lord, to keep your word."

He squeezed her fingers, then commanded the orchestra to stop the music. The conversations drifted away to silence. "I am honored to announce my betrothal to Lady Alexandra von Kampen, the beloved daughter of the earl and countess, Lord Victor and Lady Anna von Kampen. We will be wed in the private gardens of her ancestral home in a fortnight's time. We thank our friends and family for celebrating this occasion with us. All we ask is that you support us in our journey to the altar."

Lightning streaked white inside the great hall, and the thunder boomed so loud, the entire chamber quaked. A gust of wind struck the manor house with such force, the double doors at the end of the hall surged open and banged against the wall. The woman who had entertained Nicolai's earlier thoughts stepped inside the room, dressed like a nymph risen wet from the sea.

Nicolai cringed. Alexandra staggered backwards. The angry mien shadowing Cynara's facial features caused his heart to skip a precious beat.

"What do we have here, a party?" she hissed, assessing those assembled in the great hall. She swept a black hood from her head, detached her cape, then let the material slide from her shoulders to form a large stain on the flooring. The fabric of her silver-patterned dress molded to her feminine figure and outlined the curvy hips Nicolai remembered well. She walked across the hall to meet him with the grace of a serpent accustomed to the constriction.

"Rude of you not to include me, Nicolai."

He cleared his throat. "What has brought you to my home, Cynara? You're no more than a lowly woman and have no right attending this celebration. Furthermore, you were not invited."

"I have every right to be here," she rasped, pointing at him. "I should be standing beside you—not her!"

"What do you insinuate? Accept your lot in life. You were not invited to stand anywhere near me, Madam."

Once quiet as a dormouse, Alexandra squeaked, "Nicolai, who is this woman?"

He glowered at Cynara's minty eyes, wishing he could answer that damnable question. For a certainty he knew her and remembered her, but after their last meeting, he had thought their paths would never cross again.

"Her name is Cynara," he growled, taking one uncertain step forward. "But the 'Cyn' nickname was more to my liking."

"Nicolai, you ignorant sard," the witch spat. "I should have known you'd be a terrible life partner when you couldn't appreciate my name. The 'Cyn' assertion is disrespectful. It gives the impression of a bad seed and I'm nothing of the sort. I promise you this, you'll never forget the ring of Cynara again."

"Don't throw your empty threats at me. You're not an innocent in this affair. Surely you know, we were never meant to be more than bedmates," he called out, unmindful of his guests. "I respect your lot in life. I do. A pity you can't accept mine."

"That comment will cost you dearly."

"Cynara, my affairs no longer concern you. Our relationship is over. Accept it. Retrace your steps, collect your cloak, and leave my home."

Whatever her purpose, Nicolai's demands did not deter her movement. She appeared to sadden at first, and he almost felt sorry for her, but then her face contorted with anger and she progressed closer. So close, he could see the fiery sparks in the whites of her eyes. *Should he be afraid?*

She paused meaningfully. "*Cynara*, Nicolai. Always remember it was Cynara who put you in your place."

"What's the meaning of this intrusion, Madam?" Alexandra's father bellowed.

Nicolai groaned, watching his soon to be father-in-law, a know-it-all blatherskite, pace forward across the hall. The blighter stepping into the fray wore a belt under his girth to hold an overly large tummy. No hope from this quarter—the man gave the impression of a fool as he slobbered further with his prattle.

"Who are you to walk uninvited into this hall? This is my daughter's day, Madam, and you will not dishonor it. Do what has been asked of you and leave this place."

"This should have been my day," Cynara howled, waving his words away as if he were a fly, and turning her attention to Alexandra in an unnatural way. Nicolai saw the hate in Cynara's expression as his fiancée stepped backward in response, toward the natural protection of her father.

"Soon, your daughter will wish she had never been born," Cynara spat, moving closer to the pair. "Perhaps she will also wish you had never sold her to this cat's-paw."

"My guests and I have heard enough," Nicolai raged, facing his former lover. He grabbed Cynara's arm and attempted to escort her from the hall. But she pulled free of his embrace, broke their contact, and raised her hands against him in an unnatural manner.

"Nicolai Graydon," she shouted, "you have wronged me!"

He tried to laugh, but the sound came out strangled. The situation grew more ludicrous as the minutes passed. At one time he had taken his pleasure from this woman, as most lords were inclined to do in the company of a common servant, but now she was embarrassing him in front of his guests.

"Cynara," he said, attempting to placate her. "A man cannot wrong a fallen woman. Saying anything more will only serve to embarrass you. You do not know your place and have entertained us long enough."

Nicolai searched the crowd of shocked guests until he saw his butler. "Bensen," he called to him, "escort this woman from the hall and have her away."

Cynara's face distorted and colored purple with rage. Her sudden scream echoed throughout the great hall. "I would ignore your master's instructions, if I were you."

The butler was not deterred by her caustic tone, and had not advanced farther than a few steps before she raised her hand, splayed her fingers wide, and directed a current of energy at him. Lightning sizzled from her fingertips and surged across the room. The candlelight flickered; the thunder echoed her anger and raged aloud.

Nicolai could not believe the scene he was witnessing. Black magic wrapped Bensen in a cocoon of light and lifted him off the floor as if he were no more than a rock, then catapulted him across the hall. He lay on the flooring like a beaten dog, whimpering, clutching the leg of a lounge chair. Helpless, all Nicolai could do was stare at him in shock.

"Who's next?" Cynara screamed, facing Nicolai while women cried in fright and ran from the hall in panic, with husbands, fathers, and servants following.

Alexandra tried to flee the melee, too and attempted to reach her parents, but a force held her in place. "Mother?" she said, whimpering. Her face contorted in fear and tears filled her eyes. She reached for her mum, but Lady Anna could not free her daughter from the evil.

Cynara's eyes pierced Nicolai with white-hot anger. "I hate you, Nicolai. I abhor you for using me. I curse you to the blackest depths of the Netherworld for as long as you shall live."

He didn't know how to respond. After witnessing her unnatural power against his butler, Nicolai didn't know whether he should laugh or cry. For the first time in his life, he was frightened. His only thought was to protect Alexandra. He grabbed her hand and tried to escort her to safety, but she had become affixed to the floor, rooted there like a statue.

What in the sarding nether land was he supposed to do?

"If you think to leave, my lord, you should be aware that a predator always gives chase."

Nicolai stepped away from his betrothed, sensing that standing near Alexandra would only threaten her further. He heard Cynara chanting in her witch's voice, loud and shrill, speaking slowly at first and then so quickly he couldn't understand the language.

What in God's bones was she muttering?

Though he didn't need to understand her foreign words to know lives were in danger. Cynara held all their fates in her hands.

White light blinded him and the thunder boomed again as if the storm was churning inside the hall. Dark powers were consuming his home and he couldn't protect himself, Alexandra, or any of the guests he had welcomed to Drum Manor.

And then Cynara wailed: "Within this hour, I bind thy power. To be mine for eternity, cursed with black poverty."

A celestial body entered Nicolai's chest and grasped his beating heart. Light energy squeezed his lifeblood and pulled him away from his betrothed.

"Cynara, please don't do this—" Nicolai begged of her, groaning in agony. He fought against the electric current burning him inside his chest. The powerful surge yanked him off his feet and slid him beneath her heated, maniacal gaze.

Strange laughter filled his head and pressed against living tissues; the pain so intense, he curled into a fetal position, clutching at his chest and excreting urine inside his pants. He begged for mercy, moaning in pain, but he could see from her crazed expression that a merciful escape would not be possible.

"You foolish man, I curse you to live in darkness for the rest of your miserable life. You have wronged me. And because of your ill-treatment, you will live in a black existence like a cat chasing a mouse, unable to hold the love *you forfeited* when you wounded me."

"Please, Cynara," Nicolai cried, writhing on the floor. "Please, release me…"

"Leave him alone, you monster," Alexandra shrieked, finding her voice.

Cynara shouted: "No more from you, little bird!"

Lightning flashed quick and silver and enclosed Alexandra within a cloak of crimson flames. For an instant, a beautiful angel stood inside a hateful light, appealing for help. She screamed in terror, her hands clawing, trying to escape the heated barrier. The fire melted and destroyed her flesh. The heat burned her so efficiently, soon only flames surrounding a woman's shape were visible. A million stars consumed her slender form and then simply burst apart like diamonds scattering in the air, falling to the ground, then dissipating. Soon, nothing remained. The space where Alexandra had stood was empty, not even an ash littered the planked floor.

Nicolai's betrothed was gone. Lady Anna screamed in

horror. Cynara did not appear to hear the mother's cries of distress.

"Consider your betrothal broken, Nicolai."

Earl Victor von Kampen, undone, stepped backwards, tears leaking from his eyes as if he could not believe what had taken place. He beheld the spot on the flooring where his daughter had fallen, and wailed like a baby, then grasped his countess's hand and rushed her away.

"What have you done?" Nicolai asked, incredulous, feeling the weight of his loss in the empty hall.

"What have *I* done?" she said, pointing at him, "What have *you* done, Nicolai Graydon? You brought this storm upon yourself, not I."

She approached him where he lay on the floor, and he knew she felt joy in his suffering. He saw she was a witch and did not care about the lifeblood lost. She reached toward his chest and her fingers squeezed into a fist. White light formed the shape of a hand and tore inside his chest, to squeeze his heart. "Feel this," she said, her tone calm and peaceful.

Nicolai writhed in agony. Pain twisted like a knife inside his gut. His world shifted, setting in motion a transformation. The witch shrouded him in her dark magic, but he barely heard the conjuring.

Make me strong where this man is weak, and give him little wisdom to seek.

Twist his heart into cold black stone, never to love again, for the pursuit of love will capture him alone.

Set on him a sharp ugly tooth—a black cat in the night, to feed on red ruins.

Before me now let him cringe in pain, never to enjoy the fruits of life again.

"Cynara," Nicolai cried, trying to breathe, tears streaming down his face. "Please, I beg of you. Have mercy."

"*Mutatio, mutatio*—" She invoked her spell, then lifted him off the floor and spun him in a circular motion, rotating him, faster and faster.

"Transform! Change! My will be done!"

Pulled off the ground, Nicolai knew something was wrong. Liquid fire shot to his veins and flowed to the tips of his fingers and toes, burning his blood vessels. His insides pulled apart and then molded back together, a whir of cells and molecules, separating and reforming, while his mass spun in the air. He convulsed, twisted and flexed, but he did not catch fire. Human flesh softened to workable putty and reshaped into a new form. Cynara relinquished her hold. The spell loosened its grip, and he fell.

He landed on the flooring perfectly intact on his feet—on *four* feet—knowing a wicked event had occurred. Cynara towered above him. He tried to talk to her, but only a snarl emanated from his mouth.

"Look at you, Nicolai," she cackled with ill humor. The evil cadence ricocheted in his head. He watched as the minty color in the matrix of her eyes returned to normal. "You poor, furry creature. You don't know what you've become."

He snarled again and leapt at her throat, swiping at the witch with thick black paws and extended claws, but she pushed him away as if he were no more than a gnat.

Her voice became serious, yet again. "You answer to me

now, Black Panther, and though your teeth are sharp and your claws are deadly weapons, you cannot use them against me, for I am your keeper, the situation no different than how you kept me. You are cursed with black magic, Nicolai. Cursed."

He growled. He stalked around her, pacing back and forth, searching for possibilities to attack, his huge black paw swiping through the air. He wanted to lunge at her throat. The hatred inside himself raged to fight, to taste her blood, but he could not attack. He roared in frustration and jumped against an impenetrable barrier.

Cynara returned to where her cape lay on the flooring, picked it up, and swept the silvery blackness around her shoulders, attaching her ceremonial robe at her throat. The hall was empty and they were alone. His butler had managed to crawl to safety, but Nicolai was not safe. He'd lost everything.

"It's not as bad as it seems. You won't hold this form for long. I promise you, you'll be a man again, but you won't enjoy the carnal pleasures of a woman beneath your loins," she said, snickering. "I will satisfy myself knowing that this black transformation will make you miserable for the rest of your dying days."

Unable to reply, he watched her saunter toward the double doors at the end of the great hall.

"Not that I care, but accept some words of advice. If you think to pursue *sex-play* with a woman, you will change into the panther, and when the darkness transforms you, I promise, carnal pleasure will not bring satisfaction. Your teeth are deadly sharp, your claws as well."

She grabbed one door and closed it, then paused while

holding the other. "Good night, Nicolai," she said with a satisfied grin, cackling with a shriek that grated his eardrum. "Black becomes you."

She slammed the door and escaped into the night. Nicolai wondered if he'd ever see her again.

Chapter One

PRINCESS SCARLETT

The logs on the hearthstone had been licked clean by fire and diminished to ash; even so, molten embers still flickered beneath its grate, weaving a pattern like a dying snake. The boisterous events from the previous hours had quieted as well, yet the name day celebrations continued into the evening hours within the great hall of Camden Castle.

King Rickard and Queen Cynara sat at the high table with their son, Prince Lowell, to proclaim his coming of age. They were not alone in their public declaration. Well-dressed courtiers attended the royal family from numerous territories in the Kingdom of Velez, and given the formidable history of this monarchy, a call to manhood was reason enough to throw caution to the wind. Laughter, raucous shouts, and tankards of ale slamming on tables resounded from blue-blooded nobles to lesser lords and ladies, who were already deep in their cups with drink. The only participants who gave pause to the occasion were Prince Lowell's three half-sisters, Scarlett,

Ruby, and Rose, who sat separate from the royal family at a lower secondary table.

Scarlett didn't appreciate this slight against their royal status, didn't like it at all.

"One would hardly know we share the same bloodline by comparing our wardrobe," Scarlett whispered to her sister, Ruby. "Look at our father, the king. He wears his finest ceremonial attire, an elaborate royal blue surcoat embroidered with golden thread and an under-tunic of the finest silk weave, while we wear rags."

"Surely you wouldn't describe your overdress in such a way, Scarlett?"

"I would. It's dull and old, and the white underlay is graying. It's atrocious."

"But your hair is pretty," Rose said.

Scarlett offered a half-smile to her youngest sister, regarding her red strands, and reflecting on her own auburn hair bound under a modest snood with tiny seed pearls. A snake circlet lay beneath and wound its way around her forehead to rest behind her ear. Only she knew the trinket hid there.

"Still," she mused, observing her kingly father with his thinning black hair streaked with gray. "That middle-aged man is dressed far better than I."

"He is the king," Ruby countered, as feelings of disappointment and jealousy creased Scarlett's brow. "Despite how you feel about the man, he must dress the part."

Scarlett observed her father's meaty hands, laden with grease and a huge sapphire ring, easing bite after bite of bird past his full lips, and washing the meat down with a jolly smile and more cups of wine than she could count. She supposed his girth could handle the excess.

"I hate his expressions of joy. See how he nudges Lowell sportingly on the arm? He's our father, too. I despise him for ignoring us."

Ruby sighed, taking a sip of her wine. "I understand your sadness, but we can't alter the social issue at hand. Our lot in life is to sit beneath our father. We must accept the situation."

"I will do no such thing. I am the rightful princess. I should be sitting next to that man. King Rickard needs to take notice of his daughters, and I will help him recognize the error of his ways."

Huffing, Scarlett reflected that one possibility lay hidden in a velvet handbag at her feet. The creature within it was shifting, searching for warmth.

Rose cleared her throat. "Sitting at a table higher than this one is unlikely while the witch occupies a seat beside our father. Be careful, Scarlett. She might hear you."

Scarlett contemplated Queen Cynara, ignoring the warning. "Look at her," she said, whispering, angering further. "She sits at the right-hand side of the throne, acting as if she's an extension of the king's authority. I bet she impacts royal decisions, too."

"I don't much care for her midnight hair or her dark clothing," Ruby stated.

"I'm frightened by the dark magic she weaves," Rose shared, her lip quivering, staring.

Scarlett gazed at Rose's pale blue eyes. *What visions did her sister see?* She wouldn't ask in case the information challenged her plan; instead, she returned her attention to the evil queen.

Cynara wore a royal blue gown trimmed in the same dark fur as the king's and a golden embroidered overdress with a gold snood spotted in white and black diamonds. "Behold her surcoat," Scarlett observed. "Where our father's surcoat appears as golden embroidery, Cynara's fabric shimmers and glows as if it were alive. The molten hues dance with the candlelight but seem to escape the notice of others."

Rose gasped, nibbling at her lip. "She's caught you staring."

Her statement forced Scarlett to look elsewhere. "I should have known better than to regard the mint-green spell of our stepmother's eyes."

"It's a rule not to take notice of the queen," Ruby berated, shaking her head. "Surely you know better than to break Cynara's rules."

"Do you think King Rickard has rules to follow as well?" Scarlett grumbled, staring at her empty plate. "Perhaps the queen is the reason for his negligence."

"Not that," Ruby sighed, appearing sad. "He has the son he's always wanted. We're just girls."

Jealousy seeped through Scarlett as she studied her half-brother. Girls? If only she'd been born a boy. Prince Lowell sat on the left side of King Rickard, tall and slender for his age with a dark mop of shiny black hair and eyes the color of a storming blue sky.

"He's dressed in clothing too fine for a boy who has just become a man, but I envy Lowell's royal position far more than his silver surcoat."

"I suppose if we had been born boys," Ruby suggested, acknowledging the truth, "we might have celebrated our coming of age as well, but we had the misfortune to be born girls, and it appears to me that in our father's opinion, girls matter not at all."

"Somehow," Scarlett vexed, sipping her wine, "I will show this man that girls grow to be women—and women hold power, too."

Rose whimpered, nudging her head in the direction of the queen. "That woman certainly does."

Scarlett paused her conversation as the servants entered the great hall yet again, carrying platters laden with fine delicacies. Cynara had spared little expense in the celebration of her firstborn and only son. Dish upon dish arrived at the head table. Seventeen soups and pottages in the first course; twenty meat dishes, including stuffed quail, roasted duck, and venison in the second; and twenty-three sweet dishes in the last. Scarlett turned away many helpings, choosing to pass most delicacies on to the lesser lords with a forced smile, as if she wanted to share. She knew she should be happy for her younger sibling, but in truth, jealousy grew like a disease inside her heart. She kept her opinions to herself, but she disliked her half-brother. While their sibling relationship was limited, he appeared spoiled, manipulative, and sometimes cruel. Lowell enjoyed privileges she yearned for: a father, a mother, and every royal indulgence.

When Scarlett had celebrated her fourteenth name day three years ago, the simple observance had occurred in the privacy of her bedchamber, with only her sisters and her lady servant in attendance. Without the recognition of her father, a mother, or even the court jester. She had felt like a peasant and had missed her father more than ever. The shun hurt now as much as it did then. She deserved more. She expected more.

Watching Lowell receiving the accolades of maturity served only to rub salt in her wounds.

How could she celebrate this name day, be happy, or proud of a brother she only viewed from a distance? He was more a stranger than a sibling. She sat beneath the head table, beneath the royal family, and the separation outraged her. Lowell had three half-sisters by the true queen, but as their blood by birth contained a different mix, they were raised separately.

King Rickard held the blame, having chosen this woman as his mistress. What had happened to her mother, the true Queen Regana?

When servants placed a dish of strawberry tarts in front of her, Scarlett couldn't help herself. She selected a particularly plump pie and bit into the delicacy, enjoying the tangy sweet flavor as red juice exploded in her mouth.

"At least the food is good," Scarlett suggested. "We'll probably not taste another sweet course in the near future."

"You speak true," Ruby agreed. "The queen doesn't often share simple pleasures with her subjects, and it's best we understand this."

Rose's eyes seemed to glaze over. "Oh no, trouble is coming," she warned, staring fixedly at Scarlett. "Don't do it."

Scarlett turned away from Rose, pretending she didn't know what her sister was talking about.

Two male heralds stepped forward onto the dais on either

side of the head table and played their trumpeting horns. The musical notes delivered a sign for attendees to quiet their conversations.

Once they completed their repertoire, the taller of the two spoke. "The people of Velez, all rise and hail for His Royal Majesty King Rickard, Her Royal Majesty Queen Cynara, and His Royal Highness Prince Lowell. Listen thee all now and heed the words of King Rickard."

The room quieted and chairs and benches slid backward. Men and women stood together, almost in unison. King Rickard slid his throne chair backward, stood, and addressed the royal assemblage.

"My Court!" his voice boomed, "I welcome you. Tonight we celebrate my one true son, who yesteryear stood before you as a boy, but on this night his name day, he takes his place in this kingdom as a man and a royal prince."

King Rickard placed his hand on his son's back and gripped his shoulders in a firm embrace. The sire appeared happy, proud. Lowell returned his father's affection with a beaming smile. Scarlett forced her attention away, saddened, angry, knowing she would never receive such a touch or look of admiration. The bag shifted at her feet.

"Now, let us stand together and raise our tankards high in tribute to His Royal Highness Prince Lowell and his beginning journey as a man. May he always feel the earth beneath his feet, the sun on his back, and the love of a good woman at his side," he said, chuckling. "To my son— to Lowell."

"Cheers," Scarlett toasted, glancing at her sisters who raised their wine goblets as well, freshly filled for their father's tribute. Scarlett scrutinized her brother and took the tiniest sip. Lowell returned her interest with the strangest half-smile. She couldn't be sure, but she thought Cynara herself appeared smug. The red wine tasted sour, almost bitter. The dryness puckered her tongue.

"Ruby," she whispered, nudging her sister gently in the side. "The wine tastes foul. Drink no more and tell Rose to do the same."

King Rickard's brow wrinkled as he stared at his own cup, but he seemed to put whatever misgivings he had aside and continued with his speech.

"A time of gift-giving will now take place. You may approach the head table in order of importance. We will begin with the presentation from the most honorable Marquess and Marchioness of Drury. The court may take their seats."

King Rickard returned to his throne chair and his people did the same as a robust man with balding hair approached the dais. The Marquess Fitzgibbon bowed to those seated at the royal head table and then passed a small package wrapped in burlap to a gentleman usher, who held it patiently, waiting until word was given to pass the gift to the prince.

"Your Royal Highness," Marquess Fitzgibbon said, "a wise man once said that like a bird of prey, a man must have a third eye and a keen sense for detail. This gift will help broaden your skills."

The king nodded, and the usher presented the gift to the prince. Lowell took the offering and unwrapped it with interest. It was a telescopic lens. He grasped the length and took a close-up look at the court, soon pointing the implement at Scarlett. She forced a smile in his direction.

"Thank you, my Lord Fitzgibbon."

Viscount Ramsay approached the head table next, bending at the neck in respect. "I gave careful consideration to this gift to celebrate your name day, but I thought a fine young prince, such as you, ought to own one of these. Be careful unwrapping the package, Your Royal Highness."

Lowell was eager, and the excitement shone in his eyes, but he heeded the warning and carefully unwrapped the second gift. A beautiful dagger with a ruby-encrusted handle emerged from a leather sheath. Lowell smiled in contemplation and waved the precious metal back and forth as if he was already fighting an imaginary battle. "Thank you, Lord Ramsay."

"You must be cautious when using the blade, Your Royal Highness. It was forged by a well-regarded master craftsman, and the steel is deadly sharp."

Satisfied, Lowell carefully slid the blade inside its sheath, then placed it on the table.

"Lord Ashburn," King Rickard called. "What gift do you bring my son?"

"Your Majesty, Your Royal Highness," Lord Ashburn said, bowing to the king and the prince in turn. He met their questioning gazes squarely. "Such a fine upstanding prince should have the very best, but my gift is too large to be wrapped. In the royal stables you will find a Frisian stallion by the name of Drakones. He's a rare beauty."

Prince Lowell grinned with excitement. "Lord Ashburn, you have given me the best gift yet. Is this stallion sure of leg and fast on his feet?"

"That he is, Your Royal Highness. Some say he runs so

fast, he could almost fly. I'd wager that few horses could keep up to his stride. He's magnificent. Strong enough to carry a knight into battle, and he stands nearly seventeen hands high."

Scarlett watched lords and ladies offering her brother the most extravagant gifts. She knew that gold chains, expensive tunics, and black stallions were meant to impress the king and to satisfy the black queen. Prince Lowell, his royal high-ass, did not deserve to receive a black stallion. She hoped he appreciated such a generous gift, but she imagined a horse like Drakones would be more valued by the lads who tended to him in the royal stables than by this unpleasant man-child. The stallion would be ridden hard to begin with, but a selfish boy would soon grow bored of the animal and move on to other games.

Scarlett had debated giving Lowell a gift. She knew she should not test him or his queenly mother, but test him she would—and likely live to regret her decision. She kept the gift safely stowed by her feet and waited for the appropriate time.

King Rickard interrupted her thoughts. "I have a gift for my son, a gift that will make him a man. Guards, open the doors. People of Velez, move aside and clear the floor for Mirabella the Lovely."

"What's this nonsense?" Scarlett gaped as a scantily clad woman with chocolate hair rippling to her waist appeared at the entrance of the hall. She was dressed in a jade brassiere adorned with golden bells that trailed the line beneath her breasts. A sheer silk skirt flecked with gold matched the bandeau and fell to the floor at her feet. Wound around her tiny waist and wide hips, and tied into a dainty bow at the side, the fabric did little to hide her naked hips and legs. With a fan clutched in her hand, she caught the attention of the boy who would be king when she snapped the silken bands open.

"My lady," Lowell said, clapping his hands together twice as if he had known this gift would come. "Show me your pleasures," he sniggered as drums and rhythmic music struck up a chord to play.

"I'll show you some pleasure," Scarlett growled under her breath. "Later."

The seductress entertained a few steps toward him and waved her hand-fan back and forth, her gaze never leaving his face. Tiny feet and slim hips twisted and gyrated to the rhythm. Liquid amber-brown eyes only stared at Lowell, and her red-stained lips lifted into a sultry smile as she waved the fan to cover her near nakedness. Her free fingers slid across her breast as if she desired his attention. She pouted as if the act of touching herself was unsettling, but then she smiled again with seductive pleasure and peeled the bandeau away, tossing it to the floor, leaving only the jeweled bells, tiny golden crowns affixed to her nipples, and little else to cover her bare breasts.

"Come to me, my lovely," Lowell urged as her hips swayed to the sound of the music, her fan now in front of her face as she stepped closer to the head table and to Lowell.

"She'll soon have her breasts in his face!" Scarlett said, amazed at what she was witnessing.

"He seems to be enjoying the entertainment," Ruby agreed. "In a moment the lad will be on top of the table."

But when Mirabella handed Lowell an end of the bow

from her skirt, requesting he unwrap the king's gift, Scarlett was repulsed beyond good reason and understood the true nature of the present King Rickard had sent.

Lowell indeed placed his hands on the table's edge and propelled himself over the table in one full leap, apparently not caring that his red wine spilled and left behind a red stain.

"Look how he kisses, full and sloppy on the mouth. Disgusting."

"He plays with her like a boy would play with his toy," Ruby said, shaking her head. "Roughly."

He released her from his sticky fingers, pushed her away to drink in her full appearance with his greedy eyes, and then grabbed for the ribbon at her waist.

"May I unwrap you?" he teased, grasping the bow. When Mirabella nodded yes, he pulled her close, then twirled her round and round, revealing more and more skin with each revolution and less and less skirt. Mirabella, for her part, merely winked, smiled, and giggled, permitting the fabric to flounce to the floor. Soon she stood before him and everyone else in the great hall with strung jewels beneath her navel and tiny gold crowns affixed to her nipples.

Lowell laughed and brushed one crown with his thumb and index finger.

"My lady—" he yelled so all could hear— "I want to crown you, here and now!"

Boisterous laughter erupted around the hall from the males, but Scarlett seemed certain that Queen Cynara was holding her tongue. If she didn't know better—and she knew better—the queen was angry. Scarlett dared not look her way.

"King Rickard, Father," Prince Lowell wailed in wild

abandon, pulling Mirabella into his arms. "May I crown this woman?"

The king chuckled, and slammed his hand against the table in debauched merriment.

"All men, even a king's son, must learn to ride," King Rickard grinned. "Save Drakones for another day and take this woman where you will. Mirabella, be kind to my son. He will one day rule Velez, and you will have danced with a king. Should you be doubly blessed, you will birth a king's bastard."

Mirabella smiled and escaped Lowell's arms to retrieve her jade fabric from the floor. She tied the silk around Lowell's waist. He grinned and laughed when she gave a sudden tug and pulled him forward to greet her breasts. His head nuzzled between the mounds until she urged him upward to kiss at his blubbery lips. She rubbed the growing bulge beneath his surcoat, and Scarlett imagined the young man gave way right then. He was the type who would.

"Would you look at that," Scarlett gestured at Ruby. "Mirabella leads Lowell away from the hall as if he were a goat."

Scarlett tried to ignore the humor in the situation, but she couldn't help herself from the hilarity of the scene. She giggled.

"Scarlett," Ruby whispered, giggling as well, "shh…"

Cynara abruptly stood. She raised her hand and motioned toward her son. The room went silent.

"Lowell, you are the Prince of Velez, and your tastes must be more discerning. You have had your fun. Now release the woman."

KING RICKARD

KING RICKARD FACED HIS QUEEN, anger wrinkling the lines on his forehead. "Cynara, you wound me in front of my son and my people. Woman, know your place."

At first he thought Cynara would listen to him as they were in the company of their court, but it did not surprise him when she stepped behind his person and placed her hands on his shoulders.

"My place is at your side, husband and king. But if you think to dishonor our son in this manner, you will rue the day." A sudden penetration of painful bee-like stings prickled his shoulders.

"My queen," he breathed, struggling to speak through the burning pain. "No harm can come to our son from Mirabella. Stop this enchantment you force on me."

She patted his shoulder; further pain shot to his nerves. "After all the years we have lived together," Cynara spat, digging her nails into his skin. "You'd think a man could learn to curb his behavior."

"Cynara, our son is single. Our situation is not at all the same."

"It's exactly the same, or will be, but I cannot fault you for your lesser values, husband, for the father before you taught you your careless ways. But you will not pass on your sexual misdeeds to our son. Lowell will learn to appreciate the fairer sex only when he takes a wife. He will never stray from her matrimonial bed, and no bastard lordlings shall be produced.

And should his eye ever think to stray from responsibility, he will lose his sight!"

"I don't doubt you would harm him," King Rickard growled, grasping the queen's hands and pushing them away from his shoulders. "You selfish woman, you think only of yourself."

"I'm losing my patience with you, Rickard."

He could see the citizens of his court sensed her control. Defeated, he crumpled toward the table while his evil queen stood taller and stronger than him.

"Cynara, were it not for this power you wield over me, I would kill you."

She smiled tightly, leaned toward him, and brushed her lips across the nape of his neck. "Don't worry my love, my king. In this world mortal hearts and physical structures crumble with time, and I promise you this: our union and our suffering will one day end, too. Now speak the words that need to be spoken."

She released her hold on him. He saw an ugly satisfaction marred her features where she stood behind the throne. He had no choice, and so he rose to his feet. He was unsteady and his fingers trembled.

"Lowell," he offered weakly, his voice quivering. "I'm glad you enjoyed your gift, but it pains me to tell you I only engaged the dance. Further interaction with this woman would be improper. Mirabella must return from whence she came."

At first Lowell held tight to Mirabella, but then he released her from his grasp and approached the head table. "But Father, I want to engage this gift more fully."

King Rickard regarded his son, his focus solely on him. "Such gifts must wait until a lady wife dances for my son, and though Mirabella is lovely, she cannot serve in such a role."

Lowell pouted. He kicked his right foot against the floor to show his disappointment and then stepped toward his mother.

"Mum, this is your doing. Why must you always interfere in my fun? I am a man full grown, and it is time you permitted me the rights of my adult life."

King Rickard knew this appeal would make no difference.

"Lowell, I would have stopped this sordid affair and saved you from public humiliation had your father's plans been known to me," Cynara harangued. "You are the Prince of Velez, and though others may fornicate with whomever they please, my son will not stoop so low. You will wait on your future bride for such pleasures, and sons or daughters who come into your life will not be born bastards. Royal children will be brought into the Kingdom of Velez only by your wife's royal hips. I apologize for your public disgrace, but the situation must be put right. Men must never ignore their responsibilities."

"But Mother," he cried, "I wanted this gift."

Her voice softened. "And a gift you shall have, my son. As you have said, you are a man full grown, a prince, and we celebrate your name day, after all. Since the man who sired you is good at finding attractive trinkets, we will charge him with the task of finding you a wife."

King Rickard saw that Lowell looked to him for fatherly guidance, but he had none to give. Defeated, he returned to his throne chair. Equally beaten, his son sighed heavily before continuing.

"Will she be pretty, Father, like Mirabella? And I insist she come wrapped as well."

"Indeed," King Rickard agreed, reaching for his goblet and taking a slug of wine as if his thirst depended on the liquid. "Wrappings," he muttered under his breath, "are the trappings of life."

PRINCESS SCARLETT

AFTER THE CONFRONTATION, the party continued as if nothing unpleasant had taken place. But Scarlett wouldn't forget the scene that had occurred between Queen Cynara and King Rickard. In fact, she knew she would talk about it later with her sisters in the privacy of their bedchamber, cuddled in their bed in their nightclothes. They would giggle and giggle over the gift that got away, but now the time had come to present her endowment.

Scarlett waited patiently until the dancing seductress had left the room. When Lowell returned to his seat, she carefully reached for the handbag lying beside her feet. It was tied with a secure knot but the contents shifted when she lifted it into the air and slung it over her shoulder.

Finally, the hour of reckoning had arrived.

Chapter Two

PRINCESS SCARLETT

A red velvet handbag, embroidered with golden thread, hung at Scarlett's waist. She touched the frayed edges, her fingers massaging the piece as faint memories of her mother suffused her thoughts. The heirloom piece had been left to her by the former Queen Regana, and though the bag revealed its age, the inner lining offered more than bright stitches. The intricate mosaic represented her mother's sigil, a golden vase with snake-like handles, holding sheaves of grass, daisies, and a sea of serpents portrayed as the ocean's waves. Her mother might be horrified to learn she intended to bring the dramatic stitchery to life and Scarlett didn't have to touch the outer layer to feel the life struggling inside the handbag.

The cobra continually moved, prodding her waist. She felt its backbone flexing like the weighted pull of a metal trap, threatening to release, but the animal's escape would not be permitted, and the conviction brought her a small measure of despair for the battle that must ensue.

Evil must be fought with similar conduct, and demons,

perhaps her own hidden monsters, must face the sting if change was to be effected. Scarlett understood the risks, the sacrifice she must take, and what could happen to her if she failed. Still, she was one with this animal and would be safe from harm as long as she kept the creature close.

She took a deep breath for courage, stood, and shifted the bench backward. Once she presented the gift to Prince Lowell, her true strategy would begin. The circumstances could not be changed, and her life on the morrow would be different. But her mother would be proud, and King Rickard would understand his daughter would fight for her future.

She grasped the table with her free hand, but Ruby placed her hand on her shoulder. "Scarlett, what are you doing?" she whispered. "What's inside your bag? Surely you do not provide Lowell with a gift. The time for gift-giving is over. What would you give him?"

Scarlett frowned. "I would give him a lesson that would make the gods smile. A gift, I hope, he will appreciate and remember for a long time."

Ruby reached for her sister and tried to grab her hand. "Scarlett, you must not. I don't know what's gotten into your fool head, but I beg of you, let our brother have his day, let us have ours."

Scarlett forced Ruby's hand away. "This is our day, dear sister, and we must rise to it. Watch and learn, but be careful where you place your hand."

The shock in Ruby's eyes reflected that she suspected what was hidden inside the handbag. "Scarlett," she appealed one final time, "don't do this."

"Listen to our sister," Rose whimpered, tears welling in her eyes. "Our destiny will follow if you don't change course."

The fear in Rose's eyes should have cautioned her behavior, but a notable deed had already been set through her own blood; she only needed to put her feet in motion. "Our fate is in our hands, and we must act," she remarked, taking a breath for courage, then stepped away from the table and approached the dais. King Rickard, Queen Cynara, and Prince Lowell barely took notice of her until she stopped in front of their high table and raised her hand.

"Your Royal Majesty, Queen Cynara, Prince Lowell of Velez, I would like to offer my gift as well. It would be impudent of me to forget myself and not celebrate your name day. I am King Rickard's first-born daughter. I am the Honorable Princess Scarlett and a half-sister to the prince by Her Royal Majesty Queen Regana. I have learned difficult lessons in my life. Permit me to share one with you."

Cynara appeared annoyed, but she watched with a keen, dark interest. King Rickard, his patience sorely tested, grew quick to anger. He struck his fist against the table and bellowed a warning.

"Who gave you counsel to approach? You will return to your seat."

Scarlett disregarded her father as he had always disregarded her and kept her focus on Lowell, who surprisingly seemed eager for his gift, but kept quiet, patiently waiting for the offering.

"I will never be queen, brother Lowell, so it serves you little to pretend we are not related."

"I know who you are, lowly sister. Don't bore me or the court with your history lesson. Get on with the show."

"Someday," Scarlett said, "you will be king, and in this role will face obstacles, perhaps courtiers will plot against you. Some agendas will be easy to thwart and others more deadly. You must be ready to face the trials and tribulations and act swiftly when they arrive. I give you this offering to remind you of the dangers."

Prince Lowell searched her expression. He leaned forward and placed his chin on his hand in consideration. "A sixth sense tells me, sister Scarlett, that with your history, with your poorer breeding, this gift will not please me as the others have. Still, I am ready."

"Don't do it," Rose screeched, rising to her feet.

Scarlett ignored her sister and stepped closer to her brother. She opened the bag, and in one swift pull, brought the king cobra wriggling forth. Lowell's eyes widened in interest. She held the muddy green animal tight at his head so it could not bite her—yet. She held its tail in her other hand so its length could not twist in protest.

"My spoiled younger brother, this serpent is a king. You may call him Cobra."

King Rickard rose upward and backed away from the table. He pointed at her while his queen remained in her chair. "You will remove that serpent from the hall at once. Should harm come to my son…"

Scarlett snorted and stepped closer to the table, so close she could see the fear and an undercurrent of warning within the king's pressing glare. She enjoyed seeing an emotion other than neglect in his eyes.

"Father, these are the most words I have heard from you since I was a young girl sitting in your lap. Since that time your guidance has proven false, so forgive me if I don't heed your advice now."

Ruby called from their table, her voice hysterically high. "Perhaps you should listen, Scarlett. We don't want anyone to get hurt, least of all ourselves."

Scarlett raised the cobra away from herself, her concentration on the snake. Unafraid, she knew what she must do. "Don't we, Ruby? Don't we want someone to get hurt?"

Scarlett wanted to listen to her sister, but magic more powerful than her spirit controlled her motion and compelled her to step forward. Struggling, she attempted to forestall her movement, but her footsteps were forced onward into battle. Somewhere inside her head, she could hear the witch, Queen Cynara, laughing.

Queen Cynara chided: "I warn you, Scarlett, if harm should come to my son, to His Royal Highness Prince Lowell, you shall die inside the belly of the snake you hold."

Scarlett peered at Lowell. She spoke, but the voice was not her own. Somehow, the plot had shifted. "This is a king cobra, Your Royal Highness. You must charm him, fight him, kill him, or die yourself. This is my gift to you, my brother. Happy Name Day."

Scarlett threw the cobra on the table among the dishes, and her voice lifted into a song she had never sung before.

> *Rise, rise, rise, Naja Colubra,*
> *Bend your neck toward the sky.*
> *Rise, rise, rise, Kyning,*

Lean this way lest we die.

The snake stiffened to alertness. Yet as Scarlett sang, it rose high on its slithering torso. Its neck flattened, its hood expanded, and it swayed back and forth. Lowell watched the snake carefully and kept his gaze on the cobra's eyes as if he knew he must. He cautiously reached for his new dagger, never losing eye contact with the serpent.

"This is an interesting obstacle you have forced on me, sister. It's true, I will be king someday, and kings need to kill. If I survive this creature, mayhap I will kill you."

King Rickard pushed his son aside and reached for the dagger, too, but his hand never grasped the blade. The commotion startled the snake and it struck, thrusting forward.

Rose screamed when the snake sank its fangs in her father's wrist. King Rickard yelped from the pain.

Lowell did not waste a minute. He grabbed his ruby-encrusted sheath, pulled the blade forth and drove the silver dagger through the serpent, slamming the animal against the table, crushing it among the trenchers, and soon holding the dead king cobra for the court to see. He raised it above his head, clutching it in his hands, staring at the prized animal, sneering. Then he pulled the blade from its flesh and threw the animal at Scarlett. The lifeless cobra lay at her feet while King Rickard, *her father*, stumbled backward and collapsed on his throne chair. She could only gawk at the animal in disbelief.

Prince Lowell leaned forward, clutching the dagger in his hand. Red serpent blood dripped from the metal. One hand broached the table while the other stabbed the ruby knife in her direction.

"What have you done?" Lowell screamed. "Are you happy with your lesson, daughter of a serpent, for you knew the dangers when you flung the snake on the table. You have killed our father. Murderer!"

Shocked, Scarlett stared at her father. Clearly in pain, he held his arm at his wrist.

Cynara's face went purple with rage. She rested both hands on the table and sat up, tall and straight of back. "Guards! Seize this woman and take her to the dungeons. And fetch the physician. Quickly."

Scarlett could see her father's demeanor changing, his blood likely a stinging fire, his breathing accelerated. She held the bag that had contained the cobra, but the folds were as empty as she felt inside.

"It's over," she breathed. The king cobra lay limp at her feet, her father was dying, and strangely she felt more compassion for the dead snake.

Scarlett's eyes filled with tears as confusion took hold. She didn't understand what had happened, nor did she understand the distressing emotion.

"I'm sorry, Father," she appealed. Two burly wardens grasped her arms and bound her hands behind her back, causing her to screech from the pain. She stumbled as they led her away.

King Rickard reached toward Scarlett with an injured, quivering hand, his expression a painful message she could not read. Already he struggled to breathe. She watched Lowell move toward their father with concern written on his face. He took the injured limb into his grip. She could hear Ruby wailing, and Rose crying. The people of Velez were silent. Some opened their mouths in shock; others looked away not wishing to see what they knew would come.

Cynara seized the throne. "Take her away. Get this filth out of my sight. Now!"

The last Scarlett saw was the queen kneeling before her husband, but King Rickard's perusal seemed to follow her as she was escorted from the great hall. She knew she'd never see her father again.

"Goodbye," she said, calling to him. "We will meet again in another life."

Chapter Three

PRINCESS SCARLETT

"What have I done?" Scarlett lamented as the wardens, Garrett Morris and Theodore Wilkins, removed her from the hall. Garrett held one arm above her left elbow and Theodore squeezed the other, their grip firm as they manhandled her from the great hall. She tried to understand her actions as her heart's blood thrummed in her ears. Fear registered in shocked waves, and she tried to move her feet in rhythm to her wardens' larger steps. Her shorter legs danced of their own volition, sometimes being swept along to match their longer strides as if she were a broom.

She couldn't escape from the nasty scene, too fresh to put out of her mind. The attack had happened so fast. She could almost feel the sharp sting of fangs as the reptile drove its venom deep beneath her father's flesh. Even so, King Rickard was never meant to be the victim.

Scarlett never intended to attack her father with the snake, but the hour grew late to correct her imperfect strategy.

She had only wanted to challenge Lowell and through this action force her father to notice his daughter in the most dramatic way possible.

Why had she thrown the animal on the table?

Where had the song come from?

When she had begun to sing, she thought the cobra would succumb to the pleasure of her song and steal away in another direction. Snakes only wanted to escape their fear, but this serpent rose upward and attacked in an unplanned direction. The venom was now spreading throughout her father's system to halt his breathing. What would her fate be when his breathing stopped? What would happen to Ruby and Rose, her beloved sisters, once she had met with Cynara's justice? Scarlett had no doubt what the judgment would be, and her stomach churned at the bite she must face. The bite she should already have faced.

Why hadn't she listened to Rose's warning?

And now Garrett and Theodore, whom she had once teased as a girl, held an angry and wounded air in their facial expressions. They handled her roughly and shoved her at times to keep up with their manly strides. *Where were they taking her?* Would they usher her to the deepest, darkest, and most vile dungeon in the castle? Perhaps throw her into a horrible hole she could never escape from or be heard from again? Knowing Cynara, she wouldn't like her coming fate.

Cynara doled out cruel punishments. The witch found pleasure in letting her citizens die hungry or thirsty, to suffer an agonizing death, screaming for a savior's helping hand that never arrived. The cobra's strike would mete a more honorable end, because in that bite, death came quickly. Maybe such an option could still find a way.

At the end of the corridor, Garrett pushed open a large wooden door. A violent wind whistled on the other side. Scarlett lowered her head in shame as he forced the door against the weather, pushing with all his strength. The three of them walked outside, bracing themselves against the elements as they made their way across the inner ward.

A strong and bitter wind mixed with a gust of rain bit at Scarlett's face and caused her eyes to tear. The brittle cold seemed to seep into her bones and she hunched her shoulders forward as she strained against the elements. When she tripped amid the cobblestones, the resultant pain stimulated her fragile emotions to tears. But she suppressed her feelings, ignored the liquid running from her eyes, and kept walking.

Garrett nudged her this way, Theodore forced her that way, and with each step she came closer to her grim fate. They walked for some time until Garrett reached the tower door and pulled it open.

She sighed when Theodore's grip slackened. "This way," he bellowed, ushering her inside the southern prison tower, a place that respected her royal position, which gave her some relief, but there were still stairs to climb. The turret passage bound them together in a tight circular quarter, and they would have to climb the stone steps separately.

Garrett released his grip on her arm before he took the first step upward, but then he turned a half-circle to face his lady prisoner. His sea-blue eyes imparted a dire chill before his voice bellowed a gruff baritone. "Now follow me up,

Princess Scarlett. Don't try anything. You know I would never want to hurt you."

Scarlett was trying to pull away from the hurtful pressure on her arm when Theodore roughly drove her toward the stairs. She struggled to find her footing. Her leather slipper caught in her dress and she stumbled, losing her balance. As she fell forward, the fabric tore. She scraped her cheek against the rugged stones. She wasn't sure what struck first, her knee or her head, but they both hurt.

"Why did you do that?" She wailed, slumped on the stairs. "Have you no mercy?"

"You don't deserve mercy after what you did," Theodore lectured.

Her forehead rested on a stone pillow and tears welled in her eyes. "I didn't mean to do it," she said, considering her grazed cheek and throbbing knee.

"That's a cock and bull story if I ever heard one. Lies from the mouth of the woman who held the serpent."

She broke in that moment and openly cried.

"I'm sorry, Princess Scarlett," Garrett fumed indignantly. He grasped her bound hands, supported her upper arms, and none too gently assisted her to her feet. "We did not mean to hurt you, did we, Theo?"

"But of course he meant to hurt me," Scarlett cried, gulping her sobs. "He pushed me."

Pain and worry creased her forehead as she squinted at the stone staircase; she had no choice but to climb. She would have dusted herself off if she could have. Instead, she appealed to both men in equal measure, silently accusing them of mistreatment.

"I am a princess," Scarlett stated, trying to calm her fragile nerves while taking shallow breaths. "I don't deserve this rough handling."

"Humph," Theodore huffed. "You deserve this and worse."

"This and worse?" Scarlett blurted, attempting to regain her composure. "What could be worse?"

"You're soon to find out," he grated, prodding her toward the stone stairs.

Scarlett didn't know what to say as she climbed. Each step upward challenged her throbbing knee, but although the injury produced a searing pain, the aching was less worrisome than the judgment to come. Inexplicably, a line of poetry came to mind:

A bleeding red sky, held hostage within a black night of horrors, had broken through the flesh. Soon she would feel the sharp sting.

"I have never seen the like," Garrett whispered. "When a daughter would act with reckless madness, and you, the daughter of a king."

He paused on the stairway and shifted his position to face her, glaring, scrutinizing her expression. The condemnation in his perusal judged her actions, and the resultant disappointment wrinkled the skin between his bushy brows. Scarlett considered his oppressive stance while searching for signs of compassion. He was a handsome man and his reddish-brown hair was curled from the moisture, and his beard gave that messy disarray character. She saw he was waiting for answers,

answers she could not provide. He appeared grave. The guilt caused Scarlett to turn away from him. The silence only made her burden more difficult to bear.

"I didn't know," she heard herself whisper. "I never foresaw the cobra would strike."

"That's the problem, Princess. Women of your nature don't consider the consequences of their behavior. You've caused unimaginable horror against your father and this kingdom, but you will have time to *think* now that you'll be locked in a tower cell."

Theodore Wilkins grew quieter still; he searched their perimeter as if contemplating who might be listening. "I fear for you, Princess Scarlett. This is an awful risk you have taken; one we can't save you from. God knows, your father would want us to try."

Scarlett was careful to keep her balance while considering what Theodore had said. His quiet concern, perhaps anxiety parallel to her own, and something else entirely unreadable, stilled her tears and gave her pause to state the obvious.

"Surely you understand, my father had no care for me."

But then Scarlett remembered that last glance her father had given her as she left the great hall. She wondered about the recollection.

"My father did not love me," she whimpered, her voice breaking while remembering their last eye contact.

Theodore peered at the staircase as if the devil might rise from beneath the stones. Garrett scanned the upper stairs and perused the lower area, too, and each man searched the space together before they bridged the gap and enclosed her between their solid strength. Garrett whispered in her ear.

"Princess, these stones cannot hold their tongues. Neither are we safe from the rats and vermin that might be hiding on the other side of the wall, so we must be cautious with our words. But I will not see you go to your death believing that a father did not care for his daughter."

"Sirs," Scarlett whispered, "I have killed my father."

"You have, but you have also released him from his prison to a better place," Theodore offered. "And we will speak of it no more."

But Scarlett couldn't be silent. "I don't understand. He's avoided me for years."

Garrett leaned in closer still. Scarlett felt his warm breath against her cheek. "He's kept you safe through his avoidance, but he can't protect you, or your sisters, any longer. Now, no more talk. We must take you to your tower cell."

They led her to the top landing. Scarlett trudged into a circular room, hardly recognizing when Garrett unbound her hands. She rubbed the raw skin while studying the room. A small bed with draperies of black gave her some comfort. A desk with a candle would be her friend. She walked to the window and regarded the lawn below. There would be no escape from this prison and she felt like a tiny bird trapped in a cage.

"What have I done?" Scarlett cried, swallowing. "Who will protect me now? Cynara will take my life. Who will watch over Ruby and Rose?"

Theodore responded. "We're sorry, Princess Scarlett, but death comes to us all, and you should know better than most that sometimes we must die before we can live. Otherworld help us, gods protect us all."

An ominous light seemed to radiate from the gray of his eyes, and Scarlett wondered about the scar beneath his right eye. In particular, how had the blemish formed? Did he know her secret? Because this secret she must carry to her grave, and the grave might still come first.

"Yeoman warders, should I perish from my sins, will you protect my sisters?"

Garrett shook his head with a grim foreboding. "I'm sorry, but your actions were foolhardy. Look out your window to the northern tower above the kitchens to learn what we already know, that saving the three of you will be next to impossible. From the moment you sipped your wine, I suspect the witch cursed your actions, but death called on your door when the serpent bit your father. Your sisters' future will stare at you from beyond."

Scarlett rushed to the window, her own mistakes forgotten as she sighted the northern tower. Ruby and Rose, two small but distinguishable figures, stared at her. She noticed the sheer terror chiseled into their facial expressions. Regardless of the distance between them, she felt their fear.

Ruby's demeanor exuded bleakness. Her youngest sister, Rose, appeared to have bruised and swollen lips, and her pale blue eyes were red from crying.

"Ruby! Rose!" she called to her sisters, gripping the window ledge of her prison cell, feeling helpless when Rose screamed.

"Aah!" Scarlett gasped, as each cry ripped through the night and stabbed her deep inside her chest. She squeezed her hands into fists, and her fingernails pierced through the flesh of her palms. She had initiated this horror, and now her two sisters were suffering for her actions.

"What have I done?" Scarlett wept, hanging her head. "Why didn't I listen to them when I had the chance?"

She had caused Ruby to weep and had affected Rose to scream. She alone had contorted their faces with terror and had placed this black fear in their hearts. Understanding their predicament made her breathing labored. She couldn't bear to witness her sisters' dire situation, so she lowered her head, her eyes searching the dust on the ground. Her fingers relaxed somewhat, sparing her palms, but she held tight to the windowsill, her nails digging a new trench in the casement.

Finally, Scarlett turned away from her sisters' plight, unable to behold what her actions had wrought. She hit the casement with her fist and screamed in frustration, her desperate tone rending from a place inside her soul.

Sorrow took her guilt to a new level within her mind, because she realized that none of their lives would be the same again. As she leaned against the ledge with her heart beating a sick staccato rhythm, and quick tears streaming down her face, she tried to control her emotions. She wiped at her eyes, took a deep breath, and twisted toward the northern tower, searching for her sisters across the distance. She grabbed the bars, waiting for them to come into view, but her sisters had left the window and the tower to the north seemed oddly quiet and empty.

Scarlett called their names again. "Ruby! Rose!"

Perhaps they might hear her calling and return to the window. She waited and counted the seconds as tears coursed down her cheeks. But no matter how long she watched, the window in the opposite tower remained empty.

Losing hope, she twisted around and pressed her back against the wall, soon sliding along the stone until she sat on the whitewashed floor. What would happen next? Garrett and Theodore had quietly left the room. She had not heard them leave.

Scarlett reached for the red velvet handbag, and her fingers, wet with her tears, moved across the fabric that had once belonged to her mother. Deep inside the folds, a secret pocket held a message that might yet bring hope. Perhaps Cynara did not yet realize Scarlett's true motive, although presently, Scarlett could not conceive a positive ending to her circumstances.

Scarlett pulled the handbag closer to her, carefully unsealed a hidden compartment beneath the fabric folds, and removed a paper scroll. Sighing, she unrolled the parchment and stretched the sheath wide to reveal a stylish script, written in her mother's practiced hand. She had read this note before and had pondered its message each time. She read the missive again, no longer questioning the hidden meaning.

Royal blood flows inside the princess's veins, poisonous matter blights the Cobra, and you are my eldest child. When the day dwells long and evil bids you black, bind the two together and accept the mark, the sting, and birth the destiny of your own Blood Royal. This sacrifice is the only way to guard your shield. The queen finds this message too late, but her royal seed can still endure.

In this I pray, HRM Regana

Scarlett rolled up the parchment, tucked the message inside the secret compartment and resealed the hidden panel. She closed the bag and placed the fabric close to her heart, as if the proximity would somehow keep the message safe. In spite of this, the day had turned long and evil had bid her black. She must accept she had failed to take the cobra's sting. It seemed the *Scarlett Mark* had failed.

Chapter Four

KING RICKARD

The wind settled into a light rain, a thick mist of a million tears that pooled in large puddles in the kingdom's courtyard. And inside a royal chamber, the king waited.

If King Rickard had had the freedom to select his own dying place, his death would have taken place far beyond this bedchamber and the wickedness rooting inside its space. If his legs were stronger, he'd walk beyond this misery to the calm of the garden, where Regana used to walk among a sea of roses. This floral bed would be the perfect place to die, though thorns and ravens would ravage him. The rain would wash away his tears, cleanse his sins, and baptize him whole into a new life. If only he could escape this chamber and go outside. He was ready to leave this life, more than ready for this laboring to end.

Time and circumstance had left him helpless. At this late hour, when he had reached his end, he couldn't help thinking about his sins, the hurt he had caused and the life he had lived. He could neither apologize nor atone for his wrongdoings, any more than he could change his life actions now. He didn't think about the consequences of his death to the Kingdom of Velez, his seed left behind, or what would happen to his people. On his deathbed, surrounded by a frame of carved red wood and floral forget-me-nots trimmed in gold, he worried about the afterlife, and the judgments he would face because of his crimes.

He tried to remember what his beloved had looked like, but her image blurred into a sea of sorrow. Regana, she had been his true queen. He could see this now, but when he was young, virile, and wanton with his affairs, he had not known the importance of commitment and the value of a woman who stood beside her king like a strong mast on a ship at sea. He had not known the simple grace of beholding the one you loved and the fulfilled desire of only coming into her port.

"Sorry, Regana," he moaned, panting like a dog into the madness of the night.

On their wedding night, he had come to her to consummate their marriage. He remembered her being frightened by his approach, but she had accepted him well. Likely that very eve he had planted a seed in her garden. If only he had known one little seed would grow into the daughter who would kill him.

"Aah," he moaned. His mind shifted from fear of his impending death to rage at Scarlett's mindless provocation. Although, he admired her courage, and had already forgiven her trespasses against him, but saving her life would be impossible. Should a dwelling place exist where peaceful waters flow, he would meet her again on that distant shore. He hoped Cynara would be more merciful to Ruby and Rose.

Regana had birthed two more daughters for him. Ruby was born on a bright morning with the sun shining like amethyst jewels through thick panes of glass, the babe falling into the waiting hands of a midwife. He had fallen into the arms of a courtly whore, and that warm bed was where the Lord Chamberlain had found him when he came to share the news of the child. The report brought disappointment. A king had responsibilities. A king required a son for the kingdom, and Queen Regana had birthed another girl. He had released his frustration by ramming his cock into the chit beneath him, and the woman had taken his sex in good form. Tears had fallen after the coupling, but he had not cared one bit. After all, rain fell during foul weather.

And then Rose had come into the world. He had waited at the door for her birth, certain that after the labor he would finally have his son. He had walked into his wife's bedchamber high with hope, and her smile had been disarming. In her arms had been a child wrapped in swaddling clothes. He could still see his wife's smile and hear the sound of the child's suckling noises.

"I've begotten you a daughter, and I have named her Rose. A precious Rose from my garden for my husband."

He should have appreciated all that his wife had labored to give him. Now, in the hour of his death, he wished he could return to that day and behold the babe, a precious flower with a swath of red hair. How he desired to hold her tiny fingers again, but he had failed her, too. It wasn't long after her birth that Cynara had become his mistress.

If he had loved his wife, he became a sexual victim to his mistress, a slave with a chain attached to his cock. She consumed him until he could pay court to no other woman but her. For a time, he believed love ruled their sun and stars, but love did not bruise a man's balls. She held his jewels in her hands like no other woman before her, and if he dared to let another profit in her place, she inflicted her punishment. He decided she was more a witch than a woman. If anyone could save him from this snake attack, Cynara could, but she would not come to his aid when another man could do her bidding, and that man was the son a king had always wanted. *Prince Lowell.*

"Oh yes," King Rickard mused aloud. He knew what this situation was really about.

When Cynara had birthed Lowell, King Rickard had been inside the room, not content to wait outside the door. The witch made certain that he watched her labor and that he held his son soon after the birth.

Hah! That's how she had trapped him. While the newborn cried his first breaths and stretched his naked limbs from the cold, she made her demands.

"I present you with a son. I have provided an heir to your throne, and one day this royal boy shall rule your kingdom. Your queen, your Regana, what has she given you? I shall tell you: three weak girls who will drop your throne at another man's feet. If you desire this gift I have placed in your hands, you must honor my sacrifice by making your son's birth legitimate. Meet me at the altar and place a crown on my head. Call me your queen and say goodbye to Regana. Send her to a nunnery or a far-off land, or to the dungeons for all I care. Do this, or I shall deny you of your *only* begotten son!"

King Rickard's wisdom had weakened in that moment.

He had held the future of Velez in the palm of his hands, a tiny crying babe he had long waited to arrive. But still, he had hesitated, questioning her honesty.

"Is this boy my son, Cynara?" he had asked. "He doesn't have my eyes."

She had laughed in good humor and had not seemed offended. "My lord, my king. He is your image—he is your son."

King Rickard would never know if this assertion was true, but as he lay on his bed dying, he hoped he had left a male heir behind, because his son's sacrificial cost had been great. On Lowell's first name day he had made a pact with a she-devil and cast his family aside, relegating them to a separate portion of the castle. He prayed a day might come when his son would see the error in his mother's ways, and hoped the boy would rule the kingdom with a steadfast and honest hand.

That day had come too soon. Surely the queen had planned it this way.

Oh, but then his thoughts returned to his present circumstances and the true cause for his pain. *Cynara.* She sat on a lounge chair at the side of the king's bed. King Rickard sensed her presence as his breath rattled in and out of his chest.

"I could end your suffering," she whispered.

If only she would, but King Rickard knew Cynara too well. She found enjoyment in suffering. "Take me," he tried to speak, "to the garden, to Regana..."

She snickered with ill humor, rose from the armchair and ambled to the bed. She grasped the huge wooden post and leaned into his death chamber. An unearthly power waged war against him. He sensed her cold fingers, like icicles of death, long before they rearranged his clothing. Her nearness stifled his breathing, and he shivered.

"You seemed so regal tonight, Rickard, in your royal blue. Such a pity your rotting corpse will lay waste to your handsome clothing. But not to worry, I have the power within my fingers to keep you looking well and young for a long time. I don't like the idea of maggots feeding on you. Not yet."

He wheezed. "Enough. Let me die, Cynara."

She stroked his face. She dared to come close and stare at his eyes. "I see how worry mars your forehead, but you should only have one regret, my lion. You should have chosen this woman before your first. 'Tis your own fault that worries crease your brow. You could have had four sons. Instead, you worry over the one daughter who sends you to your grave."

"Evil!" He spat. "Deliver me from this Netherworld. I know what you did."

She seemed to contemplate his statement before stretching beside him like a cat; her voice purring as her fingers trailed across his chest. She laid her hand across his throat and circled his Adam's apple with her index finger.

"Evil," she whispered, continuing her circles. "Such a strong word, and yet, what does evil mean? Some define villainy as a force that causes harm, and others liken the disagreeable taste to criminal justice. When you were younger, you enjoyed the power held within these fingers. Don't you remember? You liked the way I affected your manly desires, and I liked the taste of your skin on my lips. I could still make you want for sexual hunger, even now when you struggle to breathe, for old time's sake, my pet."

It was as if her hand held his breath. He felt the power above his throat. He was frightened. What would happen when she lifted her twisted fingers? "You have no heart. I am a man, not a pet."

"'Tis true," she said, shifting closer to his head. She nuzzled her lips against his ear and he felt a nether heat graze his lobe. A deadly kiss, the lingering whisper wandered to his mouth.

"Once upon a time I gave my heart to another man, and he thanked me by turning it to stone. You should blame Nicolai for my wicked ways. But I could save you still—a cobra is no match for my magic."

"I knew you were responsible for the bite."

She tittered again, seized his earlobe with her teeth and nibbled. Helpless, he could not stop her bite from spilling his blood.

The queen tittered with amusement. "Scarlett believes she is responsible for your demise. Between you and me, I find the situation amusing. But I do admire the girl's spirit. 'Tis sad a woman with such strength will die."

"Please, Cynara, punish me, but let my daughter live."

"I think not. A lioness must kill the cubs of her opposing pride, or the cubs will grow into lionesses with teeth and claws of their own. I must protect my son, and my throne. You see my difficulty, Rickard?"

"You bitch!" He grasped her throat and she responded to his slight by lifting her finger away from his Adam's apple.

He gasped for his next breath, relaxing his hold on her neck. The pathway between his mouth and his lungs became a living straw. He struggled, sucking oxygen through the thin airway. His heart raced, his head felt like it would burst and his ears rang in perilous alarm. He tasted blood at the base of his throat as he came closer to blackness. He tried to cry out. He wheezed; he sucked for life and fought to the end a hopeless battle.

"It's painful at first," she whispered, frowning, placing his hand alongside his frozen body, "but don't worry, sweet king, I won't see you suffer. Breathe deeply, Your Majesty, my sweet pet, and die."

Cynara lifted her fingers away from his throat, her index finger circling in the air as it rose above his chest. And then as his life slipped away along an invisible thread, the painful struggle to breathe began again. He so badly wanted to live, to take one more breath.

Breathe, he told himself, counting: One breath, two breaths, three… The desire to live was so strong that he struggled for a time. But as in all living complications, the labor became too much, and he let go. One single tear slipped from his right eye.

He floated above his human form for a time, but when he heard his name called, he moved toward the magical sound that led him to the tranquility of Regana's garden. He searched among the roses for his lady wife, but she could not be found. Laughter ricocheted in the corners of his mind, but even in death's garden, Cynara would not leave him alone.

QUEEN CYNARA

CYNARA WATCHED King Rickard resting peacefully for a long time. She lay beside his still form, searching for some sentiment, some emotion in a quiet sea that would cause her to react to his passing. Her heart was aggrieved, yet she had little response to the outcome—neither joy, nor sorrow. Even so, she did understand the regret to see this handsome man with his high cheekbones wearing a pinched and blue expression. She wasn't sure why one single tear escaped her eyes. That was odd. She wasn't the type of woman to succumb to emotion when saying goodbye. Saying goodbye simply closed a door and permitted oneself to move on to experience new possibilities. When it came to making decisions, sentiment had no place.

King Rickard had to die.

The man had not fit with her plans. Lowell must assume his rightful place, and she would help him sit on the throne, regardless of what she had to do to see him there. Cynara would call her son His Royal Majesty King Lowell on his name day. *King Lowell*, this title was the greatest and best gift of all the treasures he had received.

"Happy name day, my son. Long may you live—long may you rule."

The kingdom had seen King Rickard as a sovereign lord, and they had bowed to him as if he held the scepter of a god in his right hand, but she had known better. King Rickard had simply been a mortal man and, to her, a faithful pet. She supposed that's where her regret came from; she couldn't play with him any longer. She'd miss stroking his skin and punishing him when he was difficult. It was always fun to watch him sizzle when she shot him a current of light. She rarely moderated her plans, but perhaps she would grant him one last request and permit him to rest in the garden. After all, he had gained her the one gift she most cherished—a prince, her son.

"Oh dear, Rickard," she whispered, shaking her head. "I don't like seeing you like this."

She sighed, then lifted herself into a sitting position, still watching his frozen face, tapping her fingers against his royal blue surcoat. Perhaps she would turn him into a statue and place him in a prominent location in the royal garden, where the people could visit him. And with her magic dancing in his heart, he could watch as his court came to pay homage, but he would not be able to respond. The thought of him watching, but unable to make contact or break free of his stone shell, amused her. She chuckled.

What not test the limits of possibility. A touch of life couldn't hurt a queen.

"Sorry, Rickard, but I'm not ready for you to leave my life, and maybe I can still stroke your back after all."

Cynara closed her eyes, placed her hand above his chest and concentrated. Soon a warm electric current travelled from her fingers directly inside his heart.

"*Novo, recro, vivere!* Renew, restore, live!"

King Rickard vibrated at first and then convulsed on the bed. Cynara grinned with amusement when she felt his weakened heart beating beneath her palm, but she wouldn't burden him with the difficulty of breathing. Giving this man a voice again would not suit her plans, but she knew he could hear her now. She leaned close to his frozen emerald eyes and kissed him on the bridge of his nose.

"Sorry, Rickard, I know this spell comes as a surprise, but I wasn't ready to say goodbye to you. Regardless, I promise you'll have time to ponder your sins before I lay you to rest."

Cynara inched backwards, away from his corpse. It amused her to think that thanks to her magic, life still whispered inside a human shell, but it was time to report a king's death. Another king waited to rule.

Cynara straightened her skirts, composed her sadness, and walked to the outside chambers where she knew she'd find Thomas Pell, the dutiful and ever-worrying Lord Chamberlain. When she found him, she matched his grave expression.

"The king is dead. He is gone to his afterlife," she explained, sighing. "It was a dreadful passing, but he did not suffer overly long. We will peal the bells at the first light of dawn to announce to the kingdom their king has gone to join the gods in the Otherworld."

Thomas Pell wasn't as strong as she; tears pooled in his eyes, and she braced herself for the spillage. "I'm sorry, Your Majesty. This is a sadness. Such ill fate and unfortunate events."

"'Tis all right," she said, groaning. "I expected your fragile nature, but Thomas, we must soldier on. The king must be prepared for the viewing. He loved his royal blue, and he wouldn't want to be seen in vestiture less than perfect. A string of gold around his neck with matching sapphire stones if you please."

"Will His Royal Highness, Prince Lowell, visit his father?"

She thought about her son, viewing what he would think was his father's corpse. Her son had the stillness of his mother but somehow had adopted Rickard's fragile human nature. Sadly, her enchantments had not been passed on.

"He will see his father when the court and kingdom view his father. Until that hour, he has a duty to begin, and I don't want him burdened with sentiment. You will arrange for Lowell to take his oath."

Cynara contemplated the large wooden bed where King Rickard lay. "It is what His Royal Majesty, King Rickard, would have wanted for his only true born son."

Thomas Pell glanced at his feet. "And what about the princesses locked in the tower?"

While the cobra had not been part of her plans, Cynara had taken advantage of the situation. She knew Scarlett held no blame for the bite, but she must be punished for the situation all the same. She scrutinized Lord Thomas with a dark air that would not tolerate misunderstandings.

"Scarlett must die for her treason against the throne. The princesses, Ruby and Rose, must leave the kingdom or die with their sister. But don't worry yourself, Thomas. Once His Royal Highness is crowned, he will determine their fates."

She paused, sighing for effect. "A sad stillness lives in this room tonight. In the morning, after the bells toll, the servants should prepare their sovereign master for his final rest."

Chapter Five

PRINCESS SCARLETT

Bong. Somewhere beyond Scarlett's tower cell, a church bell tolled. Its metallic sound struck then rolled away into a silvery void, disrupting her nightmarish rest. She groaned and wiped the sleep from her eyes as the second swell overtook her. *Bong.*

Tired, she opened her eyes to a chamber suffused with gray and found herself searching in the direction of the sound. Pressing her hands to her aching temples, she ran her fingers through her hair, nearly jumping when the bell lamented again.

"Please stop," she moaned, awakening to the realization that the ringing announced a death. King Rickard had passed away.

She shifted the bed curtains aside, slipped from her sheets and stumbled toward the window, where she held the ledge for support. Searching the eastern horizon, she hoped the rising sun might promise more than a church bell hammering. The light, though beautiful, was far away, and she knew the prisms radiating in a perfect half-circle couldn't promise warmth or hope. Not yet.

She shivered when the bell pealed again. "The king is dead," Scarlett whispered, counting the strikes. *Bong*, the bell tolled, followed by a silent pause. *Bong*, the bell cried, shivering away to another gap. The fateful hammer struck again.

"Long live His Royal Majesty King Lowell," Scarlett murmured. He was the king now, and the thought of her half-brother taking the throne left a bitter taste in her mouth. She disowned the new morning, denying her guilt, denying the death of a king, and leaned against the window ledge holding her head in her hands.

"What will I do now?" She screamed at the rising sun.

The bell struck again, tolling her guilt. She counted the continual strikes, each one heavier than the last, her right index finger tapping the advancing numbers. Ten, eleven, twelve—*bong, bong, bong*—until the toll reached forty-seven.

"Forty-seven," she sighed, accepting the news and her part in it. "I didn't know you were of that age, Father, and now you're dead. My mother, your true queen, dead before you. I don't recall the bell tolling for Her Majesty, but surely it mourned all the same."

When the bell's pealing stilled to silence, Scarlett breathed a sigh of relief and returned to her prison bed. But a sudden cry from the inner ward alarmed her and she hurried to the window to witness the cacophony. Far beneath her prison, a woman shrouded in black knelt on the ground. She rocked back and forth, her hands on the earth, her figure consumed in emotion and grief. Sorrowful wails tore from the woman's lungs and vented into the morning air. Scarlett watched her hands slapping the ground, repeatedly striking the earth. She couldn't bear to watch it and turned away from the sight.

"I can't listen to this," Scarlett fretted, covering her ears with her hands, but she couldn't escape the wailing. The broken sobs penetrated her head, worse than the ringing of the bell. She crept to her bed, climbed atop the mattress, and pulled the tufted quilt close to her ears.

"Please stop," she called out, but the sobs continued nevertheless, consuming her with guilt.

What have I done—

Scarlett knew she had caused the bell to toll forty-seven times. *Forty-seven times!* She had also triggered this woman's grief, a grief so compelling the woman wailed for the entire kingdom to hear. What did the people of Velez, rising from their beds, think about what had happened? Were they silent with their emotions, choosing to bury their grief? Or did they mourn with the sound of tears but were too far away for Scarlett to hear?

Would the kingdom forgive her? And why did she care if they reflected on her absolution anyway?

Scarlett had known hours ago that the king would die. She lay on her bed, contemplating the other woman's sorrow. Why were her own emotions empty? She felt responsible, since she had carried the snake to the celebration, but she felt no need to cry. *Where were her tears?* Perhaps if she had enjoyed a closer relationship with her father, a reason might have presented to shed tears.

"It's your own fault, Father, that my emotion is lacking. You never gave me anything; no paternal support, no tender care, not so much as a rag doll. Not one item I would feel sad to lose; I don't even own a miniature of your image. You placed me beneath you and pretended I didn't exist…"

She felt as if someone she had once known, who had a significant name attached to their person, had perished. A royal man with the name "Father" was dead. She knew sadness should have consumed her due to the paternal attachment alone, but if such a bond had once existed, the familial link had been severed.

Nevertheless, she pondered Garrett and Theodore's statement, confided to her in the tower: that her father had cared enough for his daughter that he had tried to protect her, and now with his death, he could no longer be that shield. This news had earned her a night of insufferable dreams, worrying and wondering about the disclosure and the fate of her sisters. Throughout the night she had rolled on a bed better suited for a child than a grown woman. She couldn't remember the night terrors, but she had been mindful of Cynara's wickedness in the hours before dawn. And now that daylight had arrived and she was alert, her anxiety had not lessened. Her head pounded in time to the cries from below.

What would happen next? She'd committed a crime of treason. A steep price must be paid and she knew her time was short.

When the door opened, Scarlett was relieved the warden brought her breakfast. He could have escorted her to the scaffold, where an executioner would wreak havoc with an axe. She ate little as the image burned a hole in her mind. She forced herself to nibble at the bread and cheese, and sip at her ale, as the grieving in the courtyard mercifully fell silent.

In the hours that followed, she paced her prison cell, still wearing last night's kirtle and surcoat. She looked out the window often, searching for her sisters in the opposite tower, but no matter how often she stared at the distant space, Ruby and Rose did not appear. She remembered her last sighting. When she closed her eyes, they were in the tower beyond, with fear and confusion drawn on their expressions.

She had written the sorrow in their eyes. She alone was responsible for Rose's screams. Yes, if she focused, she could still hear them lingering in her head. Why hadn't she listened to Rose?

Scarlett no longer understood what her plan had been when she carried the cobra into the great hall, but with a certainty she knew she had failed.

The snake fiasco needed to happen, but not in the manner in which the incident had occurred. The situation was upside down and downside right. She couldn't change the outcome. She paced her prison cell, clutching her mother's purse with her message buried inside, knowing she had ruined this test. Once again, an enchantress had prevailed. Cynara and her son *held* the kingdom.

"Long live King Lowell."

Her breath left her in a huge sigh, and she knew without a doubt she would not disappear like her mother. Her hand went to her throat. The executioner's blade would come for her. She had failed in her quest—the mark inside her royal blood—and the promise of a new reign was lost.

The never-ending hours carried on into another sleepless night and another day of pacing. A day of looking out the window and searching for a familial face that couldn't be found. Garrett and Theodore brought Scarlett sustenance, and she wore the same crumpled gown, only having removed the surcoat to sleep. She held tight to her mother's purse, as if the bag could protect her, however foolish that might be.

Eventually, voices drifted to her window, and she observed the courtyard below, where a trail of mourners waited. When the trumpets blasted, Scarlett knew the time had come for the people to view their dead king for the last time.

King Rickard, by now cold and hard with rigor mortis, lay on a slab in the royal hall, where knights guarded his eternal rest. He would be dressed in his finest royal blue and laid on a bed of spun satin in a gold-plated casket. On his head a golden crown, adorned with rubies and his favorite sapphire stones. Wrapped around his shoulders and chest a shimmering gold necklet adorned with matching blue gemstones.

What would his people think as they filed past?

Would they believe they had lost a true and loving servant of the gods, sent to rule over them? Would they weep as they paid their final respects, or would they file by in silent repose? Would the woman who had mourned aloud in the courtyard wear her grief as visibly when she walked past? Would she create a scene there, too?

Scarlett didn't know how she would act if she could offer her final respects. She knew that only the responsibility of being a princess would compel her to witness her father's still form. The grandeur of his adornments would escape her notice, for jewels and gold did not a man make. Instead, she might marvel at his life and wonder what it was about him that the gods so loved this man that they had made him a king in the first place. For how could such a man serve a kingdom and not serve his own children, or protect his true wife?

"Balatron," Scarlett cussed, watching the mourners. The only respect a daughter would pay his due was silence.

The next morning, the sun threaded its way into her tower cell with a vibrancy that forced Scarlett awake. In the distance, she heard the lilting melody of a male choir singing. She did not have to rise from her bed to know what this mournful song imparted. The choir sang a haunting hymn, their voices lifting and falling in sad unison as soulfully as a harvest moon on a cold autumn night. She strained to hear the words. She closed her eyes and let the peace of Mary come to her.

> *Dies irae, dies illa,*
> *Solvet saeclum in favilla:*
> *Teste David cum Sybilla.*
> *Quantus tremor est futurus,*
> *Quando judex est venturus,*
> *Cuncta stricte discussurus!*

"Let the wisdom of the gods come to me and surround me," she whispered, hoping that a stronger force in this kingdom might save her. She meditated, praying to the God of War as the hymn bathed her with song. She barely heard the words of "Dies Irae," but she knew the song all the same.

King Rickard's funeral mass had begun. The final celebration of his life's journey. Soon the priests would place him inside the crypt. The chorus sang of a human will that in death would dissolve to ashes, or so these spiritual men believed.

> *The day of wrath,*
> *that day will dissolve the world in*
> *   ashes.*
> *As foretold by David and the Sibyl!*
> *How much tremor there will be,*
> *When the judge will come,*
> *investigating everything strictly!*

Scarlett didn't know the meaning of the hymn, but she understood King Rickard had reached his judgment day. If Valhalla existed, he was approaching the gates. Soon he would meet with their God Odin, and face his sins and be judged for them.

Scarlett folded her hands and prayed for her father:

"Grant King Rickard a peaceful and eternal rest. Bless this man, my Father, with a vision of the spiritual Otherworld that surpasses human will and understanding, where pain and suffering do not exist and life is everlasting. My God, Odin, have mercy on this man's soul, and teach him the lessons in death he never learned in life. Forgive this soul, his daughter, for her part in his death."

The choir members sang again, but this time the hymn was more chant than lyrical melody. Somber, Scarlett returned to the window and listened.

> *Take the last kiss, the last forever!*
> *Yet render thanks amidst your gloom:*

He, severed from his home and
kindred,
is passing onward to the tomb.[1]

The people of the Kingdom of Velez were kissing their dead king goodbye. Scarlett raised her hand and blew a kiss, permitting a mixed message of lost love and heartache to carry on the breeze toward the chapel. Then she turned away from this part of her life forever.

---

1. *The Stichera of the Last Kiss* by S. John Damascene.

Chapter Six

KING RICKARD

King Rickard couldn't recall a moment in his life when trials and tribulations had dropped him so low. He felt like a sculpture, a corpse buried in a frightening dream with no way of escaping the outcome of Cynara's evil. It was an impossible situation he had not anticipated. Hope slipped away into a rotten seed so horribly black, the dead cells couldn't support anything more than a stiff shell. He would lie or stand in a manner that suited the witch's fancy for an eternity, with frozen eyes watching the horror unfold. Minutes would stretch into hours, and hours into long empty days, while he waited for the years to pass.

On this day, he lay stretched out on a cold marble slab, listening to the chanting of holy men. He wished Cynara had let him die. He had considered many methods the witch could have used to hurt him. He never foresaw the evil woman turning him into a living statue. Black magic made such evil possible.

Cynara's spell had stimulated hurt and pain; he'd suffered

injuries by royal servants who had believed him dead. If he had been a whole man with air in his lungs, blood flowing through his veins and the strength to command, he would have chopped off their heads for their maltreatment. It was unthinkable, the indignities they had caused.

God's nails, he had been cut and bled. The piercing of his flesh had stung; the worst pain and unbearable suffering—to stifle his voice, to eliminate him from the kingdom—but the sharp knife had not ended his life. Neither had the loss of blood. The peasant women had scoured his flesh with lye and scalding hot water, raking and burning him. Sin and damnation, what stain did they think to scrape and wash away? His actions against others could not be so easily dismissed, and you couldn't rid death's stink, no matter how hard a servant scrubbed or how hot they made the water.

A maiden had been surprised when his skin colored a bright pink, but that didn't stop the bitch from spilling scalding-hot water on his flesh. He couldn't scream for the pain.

He could not smell the alcohol or the cinnamon-scented abramelin oil, but he liked the way it felt when one woman massaged the oil onto his skin. In his previous life, he would have risen up and demanded her cunny. In this new life, he listened to her preach about his less-than-perfect attributes while she worked his skin like other women kneaded their bread.

"You'll be losing this middle, King Rickard," she had whispered while massaging from his upper chest to his private quarters. "I've never touched a dead king before, but you're no different than other naked men. Fancy that. With all the attention paid in your bed, I'd have thought your jewels richer. My husband has a firmer shaft. It's a fancy the queen got a son from you."

She rambled on and on, and he couldn't tell her to shut her mouth or slap her hands away from his lower extremities. He wanted to kill her with his bare hands for the insults, but in this state, he couldn't command the guards to take her away.

"Although dull and lifeless, your eyes are still the most beautiful green, but I never liked the way you used this emerald sea to gain your pleasure. You should have had more manners. You might have controlled your temper, too. God sakes, you were a king."

"I'm still a king! God damn you, woman," he yelled—but his voice, his fitful anger, was only heard in his own head. How dare a woman of her rank talk to her sire in this way!

Gods help him; Gods grant him courage. King Rickard didn't know how to bear this new existence. In this funereal state, he was laid out in a golden box contemplating his own mass. Stiff as a statue and listening to the monks chanting, he was helpless but to endure whatever cruelty came next.

He, the king, would be buried alive in a tomb, waiting and wondering if death would ever arrive. God's bells, the witch Cynara could discard him on a bed of tree limbs and burn him alive. No one would know. If he broke free of this curse, the woman would pay for his suffering. Somehow, he'd see her head on a platter to feed to his pigs.

Cynara, that heathen, brazenfaced witch, held more evil inside herself than he had ever thought possible. She had stolen his breath from his lungs. The bloody whoresbane had robbed him of his manliness. He was paralyzed. Although the tiniest heartbeat fluttered inside his chest and he could hear beyond himself in a diminutive fashion, no one knew he was alive. No help could support his rescue; even a god was beyond his reach.

It brought him no comfort that he could hear the sounds around him in the church hall. Angels singing in all their glory brought him no closer to the Otherworld or the Netherworld, and if he could have laughed when the monks started to sing, "Dies Irae," he would have, with tears streaming down his face. A king would not shed his skin to ashes. Judgment Day had arrived, that was a surety; he faced the gates as bravely as he could.

As each person filed past to impart a last kiss goodbye, he gazed at a ceiling painted with angels. This dwelling place was the closest he would come to divine creatures, but he found no hope in the fresco with frozen eyes. He couldn't blink to suspend the drought. A fly could crawl up his nostril to lay its eggs and he would be helpless to prevent the indignity.

A golden crucifix lay on his belly, and his hands were placed on top. Some people who filed past commented on his appearance; he disregarded their statements. Others made the sign of the cross. Some planted a kiss on his hand or his cheek. Some touches were more fleeting than others. He imagined most people did not wish to kiss death.

One particular young girl stopped before him, stretched her small arms upward, and took his hand, holding it within her smaller one.

"Mama," she asked, "is the king dead?"

"Yes, child," the woman whispered. "But we must move along."

"No, Mama," she protested, standing her ground. "He doesn't look dead. Look, he's watching the angels."

King Richard couldn't see the mother or the child, but the young girl's voice gave him a measure of hope, as bleak as that hope might be. He tried to move his finger, so the young girl would know she spoke the truth, but his finger remained frozen.

"He's with the gods, Sibyl. His Majesty King Rickard is in the Otherworld. Now come, we must move on and give others their chance to say goodbye."

The girl stood her ground. She pulled on her mother's hand until her tiny fingers slipped free. King Rickard felt her climb onto his stone shelf where he lay, her fingers grabbing his neck and holding on tight until her ear rested near his chest. He heard others yelp in disbelief.

"Sibyl," the girl's mother scolded, grabbing the child and removing her from his shroud. "Have you forgotten your manners? We must respect the dead."

"I wanted to see if I could hear his heart. Mama, it's quiet."

King Rickard listened to the mother and child leave, but when the next person kissed his hand, hope left with their company.

Someone stopped and stood beside him but whoever it was did not touch him. "I wish you a peaceful and eternal rest, Father. Be with the angels."

It was his son, Prince Lowell. When Lowell spoke to him, King Rickard didn't know what to think. Surely Lowell didn't know his father heard his voice. Would his mother be so brazen as to reveal this indignity to her son?

Before he could consider the possibility further, a cold hand grasped his arm and leaned in to kiss his cheek. He knew Cynara held him.

"This is your last kiss, Your Majesty—the last stichera you shall ever receive. I leave you now to your blessed sleep."

It was a cruel twist of fate that Cynara brought his Dies Irae—his last judgment in this miserable world. It was laughable that a child, a flower yet to bloom in the desert, appeared to be his last hope.

What other form of treachery did Cynara have in store for him?

When the church became silent and the men, women, and children had left, someone approached him, perhaps an attendant or some other grim reaper, to collect him. Within the confines of his head, he screamed and screamed and screamed—

Chapter Seven

KING LOWELL

The drawing room smelled of a lingering musk that reminded Lowell of his father. He sat on his father's royal chair, a place where wild stags were embroidered on the seat cushions and silken tapestry extended from the ceiling. The scene of fat lords on their horses, chasing wild boar through a wooded glen, and their loyal dogs, racing, muzzles hungry for the kill. He thought the scene represented the struggle between man and animal, but the dogged skirmish over the swine and muzzles dripping with blood, reminded Lowell of what happened when life begat thorns.

It was a delicious horror that the flesh taken away from a pack of dogs soon benefited the high table, but the pig's heart, like a king's, beat no more. Lowell felt empathy for the kill—not because he cared about the pig, his deliberation altered from the plated pork to the people, who would feast their worries and subsequent demands on a new monarch.

He stretched his legs in front of him and leaned his elbows onto what a week ago had been his father's roll top desk. Now the treasure belonged to him. He placed both hands on the wooden veneer and slid his fingers across the surface. *Damn it!* Since his father's death, he couldn't stomach entering the room until today.

He swallowed his anxiety, placed a bronze key inside the lock and released the lever. A myriad of boxes filled with bric-a-brac and papers came into view. He stared at the assorted clutter, not caring much about the contents, but these items had belonged to his father, and he wanted to remember his father.

Lowell lifted a golden inkwell from its chariot, removed the lid, and swirled the indigo liquid round and round. He remembered his father's fingers, the king's fingers, and the simple act of a royal hand holding this delicate clay pot, before returning its majesty to its holder. He reached for his father's quill, slid his fingers along the peacock feather, and dipped the nub in the ink. Finding a piece of parchment, he wrote: HRM King Lowell.

He sighed as he rested the quill on its golden stand and replaced the lid on the ink pot. "I'm much too young to have big initials in front of my name," he said to the empty room.

He examined the wood grain of the desk and slid his index finger along its surface, lost in thought. A black smudge appeared where ink must have marked his fingers. He did not care about the dark blue stain left behind, as King Rickard's fingers had glided here, too. He saw a larger indentation on the left-hand side of the desk, and found its impression so deep and rounded, he imagined his father must have rested his foot on this spot again and again.

Lowell leaned against the soft cushioned chair and raised

his legs, placing his feet on the rounded spot, one on top of the other, and contemplated what his father must have considered while his royal feet wore the wood down. A king deliberated many questions, and while in this pose, he must have pondered many scenarios. Or maybe, in this pose, relaxed against the setting of a hunt, he had escaped to faraway places to dream about more complex issues.

Lowell sighed, then reflected on his weighted thumb. It held his father's ring, a large sapphire stone held fast by a circlet of gold. His mother had given him the ring once his father rested in the tomb. It was too big for his slender fingers, so he wore the gem on his thumb. He twisted the band round and round. He took the monster off and inspected the dark blue stone. Truthfully, he didn't care for the gem. He'd rather wear the silver band of a knight, than weigh himself down with the responsibility that one gold ring symbolized.

He twisted the ring off and threw it on the desk. He didn't care that the resounding thump added a new impression to the surface. Although he understood the ring represented his birthright, he was reluctant to celebrate his royal line. He wished he could say sard it all, because he was too young to have a kingdom of responsibility.

"Long live His Majesty King Lowell!" the crowd had shouted, when he had appeared at the barbican after taking his oath. He had smiled tightly, waving to his father's people, his head smarting from a heavy crown marking his forehead. He had grimaced from the pressure, and counted the minutes until he could leave the barbican and return inside.

He wasn't ready to hear those words spoken. He wasn't

prepared for the pressures of being a king. He had only been proclaimed a man. Shouldn't he have had the chance to mature in his wisdom, but especially in his fun? He wanted to gallop across the countryside on his new horse, Drakones. He wanted to find the most beautiful woman in the land and lose his virginity to this mistress. In fact, any woman would do, frankly. It had grown tiresome finding illusive women in his dreams, and embarrassing losing his seed to vapors.

Instead, here he sat with responsibility at his father's desk, confined to a life of servitude to the people of Velez. This royal job should rest in a wiser man's hands, and it would be many years until his wisdom matured. He blamed one woman for his sad state of affairs.

"Princess Scarlett," he said, slurring her name, "you're not royalty."

She was responsible for his feet resting on this desk, and this new stain that marred a desk and his life. The brainless chit, the daughter of a bitch. Maybe she wasn't fathered by a royal sire. What kind of princess would throw a serpent at a prince, let alone a king? She would suffer for her actions. She shouldn't expect mercy from the likes of a boy who had just become a king. Mercy belonged to the people who didn't mean to cause sin, or the wrongdoers who didn't take away his fun without just cause.

Scarlett would face a scathing justice for harming the one man Lowell had respected—his father. Perhaps he would make the hunt come alive: let the dogs have her, and feed her whole to them after.

Lowell heard the swish of his mother's skirts prior to her entering the drawing room. A fleeting thought occurred to him that his mum might have played a role in the death of King Rickard. More than most, Lowell understood that Cynara conjured steadfast wickedness in her affairs, but he shook away thoughts that his mother could be a murderess. She would never cause harm to her possessions. Lowell did not delude himself: to her, he was more of an object of desire than a son.

"Lowell. Remove your feet from your father's desk."

He stared at her for half a second, at her serious expression that brooked no argument, and then at his feet. He removed them from the desk and pushed forward, angry at once. "Must you always play the mother? A woman, even if that woman is my mother, does not tell the king what to do."

She stood beside him and toyed with his clothing, her fingers wandering across his surcoat as if plucking at imaginary threads. "You may be a king, but you shall submit to my guidance."

He pushed her fingers away and stood abruptly, sending his chair to the ground. He was not yet taller than her, but at least he could meet her eye to eye.

"You no longer command me. I am no longer the boy who will adhere to your demands. I am king by right of passing, and a king does not answer to his mother."

She retreated a step to consider his opinion. She assessed him quietly, weighing him as her gaze travelled up, then down, his length. The silence made him uncomfortable.

"I have created a monster. Still, regardless of your station, you must humor me with your ear because a man cannot be made in one name day and neither can a king. You have much to learn."

"I have a king's council to bend my ear, and you do not have the control you exerted over my father. I know what you did."

She smiled again, but this time her humor did not reach her eyes. "Do you challenge me, Lowell, days into your reign?"

He stepped toward her, raising his voice and his hands in appeal. "Stand down, Mum. A son stands before you, but by no fault of my own, I must stand before you as the king. I am more than your progeny, and I will not suffer slights from my people, thinking I sup at my mother's breast." His mother's brows rose and her face paled at the comment, but it was too late to salvage his offense. He cleared his throat. "I take council from the men trained to whisper in a king's ear. Only then will I earn respect from my people."

"I have much to say on this subject, but this is not the time for redress. I have come to request your presence in the privy chamber to meet with the council you plead to instruct you. We have much to discuss, including justice for your father's death. Princess Scarlett must die, and it is time for you to confront her punishment. You must sign the death warrant."

Needing time to think, Lowell reached for his chair and righted it. He sighed in frustration and then sat. Thinking about his half-sister's death was simple enough, but signing her death warrant made him shudder. As he pondered, however, he decided it would be no more difficult than the hunt for game. Gratefully, he would not be the man to swing the axe or the dog to bite the flesh; only his signature from the quill resting on his father's desk would be required. He had already held the feather and slid its nub across the parchment. It would be no different to slide the point across a more official document. Mercy? Mercy was best left at his father's tomb.

He regarded the tapestry again. "I will see this business completed, Mum, and soon."

Cynara must have noticed the ring on the desk. Lowell watched her grab it, ponder it, and then all too soon, place it firmly in his hand.

"You've cried out, King Lowell, to be your own man. Be a man, then, and see this justice done. Take council with men if that is what you must do, but make it quick or your people will think you're weak. I didn't raise my son to be weak."

"Leave me be. I know what I must do; I will see this business done."

After Cynara left him, King Lowell surveyed the tapestry and the hunt one more time. He understood more clearly why Princess Scarlett must die. The hunt presented the true nature of life, and his sister represented the blood weaved in the stitches. The red must be washed away. While she lived, she ushered in a hunt that stained the kingdom and threatened him. He would spare her the torture of an axe or dogs tearing at her flesh. He, King Lowell, would mete the crime with justice from her own damn serpent.

Chapter Eight

PRINCESS SCARLETT

Scarlett usually welcomed rain, but today the moisture mixed with perilous winds. She listened to the howling, the dampness seeping into her bones. Instead of breathing the sweet scent of dew, she choked on the mildew settling in the air. Wrapping a tufted quilt around her shoulders in a futile attempt to generate warmth, she shivered while sitting near the desk, her thumb stuck in a book of poetry.

She flipped the parchment pages to pass the hours, holding the edges of the coverlet. If only the rat-a-tat-tat would stop, perhaps then the sun would air-dry all that had spilled, but the rain could never wash away her crime.

Locked inside this prison tower, she had watched the sun rising and falling for at least a fortnight now with only her wardens and a holy man for company. She had resigned herself to the fact her death was imminent, and had asked Father Clement for a book to help her prepare for the ending of her life. He had presented her with two books, one of holy writings and the other of spiritual poems. She had cast aside the holy book, seeing no measure of forgiveness in scriptures. Instead, she held the book of poems, fascinated by the stained-glass appearance of the leather tome and the star medallion on its cover. However, no matter how much she read, words of inspiration did not ease her fears.

She supposed she read the verses out of boredom, for her thoughts were in a constant state of anxiety and worry. Focusing on words, let alone entire stanzas, was difficult when a woman had to come to grips with the ending of her life. Scarlett sighed, returned her attention to the yellowed pages, then opened the cover to the passage Father Clement had asked her to read.

> *The night has fallen black and still,*
> *but I will not be afraid,*
> *Mist settles over the land and the loch,*
> *and a sexton is digging my grave.*
> *Yea though I walk through*
> *the wind and the storm,*
> *where rain pelts over my eyes,*
> *A boat will arrive at my rocky shore,*
> *and I will prepare to ride.*
> *For the Lord is my master who'll carry*
> *my fate,*
> *my soul is bound to His sea,*
> *Whatever crimes I've committed here,*
> *A God's waves will wash them free.*
> *I'll run to the shore of His merciful*
> *word,*
> *and goodness shall flow to my feet,*

For though I've walked from the valley
of death,
the desert can't follow me.

Scarlett grasped the quilt while considering the passage, her fingers needling the wool. Sighing, she placed the book against her lap and reflected on the last phrase. "*For though I've walked from the valley of death, the desert can't follow me.*"

Scarlett believed that during a crucial moment of her life, her judgment had been impaired. When she held the cobra in her hands, she had felt empowered to act, but an unknown force had taken control of her abilities and she had delivered the snake in an unplanned manner. She hadn't known it then, but during decisive moments, she had walked in the valley of death. Now, she felt trapped in the desert.

Even so, after this life, what *god* would care for a soul, or forgive a soul, who had abandoned moral principles without thought of the consequences, costing a king his life? She brought the snake. She threw the snake. This death lay at her feet, no one else's. Devilish terrors and sword-like nightmares were a reasonable consequence. She didn't want to think about what her ending might entail, but couldn't help contemplating the penalty phase. Here in this room, a vise screwed with her consciousness, disabling her breathing. She was trapped like a moth above the Netherworld's flame, unable to retreat from the heat.

The thought of what must be faced made her physically ill. After eating meager meals, overwhelming anxiety caused her to vomit, or worse, made her sick to her stomach with all manner of twisted guts and wet bowels. She might escape the desert, but deliverance to the devil's Netherworld, to boil in flames for all eternity, was difficult to comprehend.

Was there a place other than the lowlands? Her hands trembled, unconsciously shifting to her neck. After death, she prayed a better life existed and a forever sleep would not paralyze her soul. Could mercy live there, too? Could she be forgiven?

Scarlett reopened the book and read the last stanza.

> *Lord, take my hand to Your foreign*
> *land,*
> *where the fruit is laden with gold.*
> *I'll descend from above in a blue*
> *current of love,*
> *where worries will have no hold.*
> *Still waters will wash and bless my*
> *soul,*
> *and I will lie down alongside,*
> *Goodness and mercy shall anoint my*
> *head;*
> *in my Lord's home, I have arrived.*

The last stanza was hard to grasp. She closed the book, permitting it to fall to her lap, feeling frozen and devoid of emotion.

Dies Irae. Wrath, judgment.

She faced a difficult journey through turbulent waters to reach this place, and she doubted such a home existed, but Father Clement had encouraged the reading for her fulfillment. *How does he know what waits for any man or woman in death?* She sighed, waiting for her punishment, wishing she had as much faith.

The door to her prison chamber opened, and Garrett Morris, her warden, stepped inside. She didn't utter a word, searching his sea-blue eyes, reflecting on his red brows, wrinkled and pulled together.

"What is it?" Scarlett asked, pondering his distress.

"I'm sorry, Princess," Garrett said, drawing his hand through unruly red hair. "I have solemn news. His Royal Majesty King Lowell has signed your death warrant. I am to take you to your place of death at once."

Scarlett choked on a scream; her hand rushed to her mouth. Garrett knelt before her on a single bended knee and reached for her hand. She was sure it quivered in his grasp. "I knew the Grim Reaper would come, so why is the news hard to take now that the angel of death has arrived?"

"I'm sorry," Garrett offered, squeezing her cold fingers. "I wish I could do or say something wise that could help you win this battle."

"*The night has fallen black and still, but I will not be afraid,*" she recited the poem. Meeting the warden's eyes, she asked, "Garrett Morris, why am I so afraid? How can I do this thing?"

"Comport yourself as if it were any other day. Rise to face what must be faced. Have courage, Princess. Hold your head high."

Scarlett tried to rise, but she slumped against the chair. The book of poetry fell to the floor. Her free hand visibly shook as she tried to grasp the arm of the chair.

"I can't," she cried out, refusing to look at him, "I can't do it."

"You must. Rise. Find courage for what lies ahead. Try not to think about what you must face. The facing is enough. Breathe, just breathe. Take my hand, and rise."

Scarlett scrutinized the open window. "If only I were a bird, I would fly far away to face that perilous breeze." She heard her voice and felt ashamed of the weakness in its tone.

"It's too late for ruminations."

She ignored him. "*Mist settles over the land and the loch and a sexton is digging my grave.* Garrett, my soul is lost and damned to the Netherworld. I've read this poem repeatedly, and though I'd like to take wisdom from the passage, a mortal man wrote this poem. How can I trust the author's prose? How can I be sure of judgments I must face? How can I know a God will save me?"

A new voice came into the room. "You can be sure, Princess, because this is His promise and your saving grace."

The tears began anew as soon as she saw the rounded form of Father Clement, her only rock in this world. "Thank you for your offering, but the world you speak of is simply too big to find." She hastily wiped the tears away and dug within herself to find strength to stand on her own two feet.

"Help me, Garrett." With his assistance, she stood. "My father will not watch over me after what I have done. I am wretched."

"Your godly Father, Princess. But before you take this walk, I am permitted to hear your last confession. Is there anything you want to declare?"

Scarlett contemplated admissions of guilt and almost

laughed through her sadness. "I have nothing to confess. You know of my sins."

"Then grasp your courage for the walk you must take, but first permit me to anoint your head and pray for your soul."

The religious man made the sign of the cross on her forehead with sweetened oil. She smelled cinnamon as his fingers drew down and across her forehead.

"Father Odin," he prayed, "take this child's hand in her time of need. Let peace be her comfort and angels her guide as she walks through the valley of death. Let her fear no evil, surround her with your holy light. Bless her, keep her, and restore her soul with mercy, leading her toward your kingdom. In Odin's name, I pray."

The warm touch sent a peaceful heat to her head, neck, and upper shoulders. Comfort suffused throughout her, but Scarlett couldn't rest in the spoken words. She glanced downward so Father Clement couldn't see her shame or her lack of hope. She didn't deserve his prayers.

When she raised her regard and saw Garrett's mixed expression and grave concern, one clear and sharp image awakened. The axe! This single vision filled her with such terror, no words could assuage the mental picture.

Father Clement, his expression grave, peered into her eyes. He offered her his hand. "I'm here to walk beside you until you can walk no more, and I promise you that when you can no longer feel my hand, the gods in the Otherworld will hold you instead."

"I understand."

"We must go, Princess Scarlett," Garrett spoke softly.

"The Otherworld is good, and it's waiting for you. A blue

current of love endures, a place where worries have no hold, and come what may, you will find this place."

Scarlett glanced at Garrett, whose expression had become earnest. She thought she might be sick, but a hidden strength in Father Clement's expression calmed her nerves. "Take me, then, and let this waiting be over. We shall see about the other side of the ocean."

They led the way out of the tower removing her from the chamber that had been her prison. She glanced back, knowing she would never see this place again. The rain beyond the window had slowed to a light mist. The book of poems lay askew on the flooring. Funny, but the tome had opened to the poem she had been reading moments before. *How unusual.* Scarlett turned away to focus on what must be faced.

Round and round she went on the stone stairs, each step downward taking her closer to her final punishment. Too soon, she stood on the landing. She paused beneath the archway and gulped a breath as Garrett opened a large wooden door that led to the outer courtyard. Passing underneath the doorway, she welcomed the mist on her face. She walked through the wind and the rain, breathing the musk. All too quickly she would fall silent, buried by wet mud in her grave.

Garrett beckoned her forward, and like a solemn soldier he reached for her arm and ushered her into the gray. "Come," he whispered. "We must move forward. One step at a time."

Scarlett shivered, drifting toward the approaching night,

trying to hide her weakness. At that point, Father Clement took her hand in his warmer grasp.

She trembled, recognizing her fear more than the cold. She could feel her heartbeat pulsing inside her chest as she placed each foot in front of the other. The sands of time ran through the hourglass and if a meter clicked in the sky, the time lessened with each passing second. Rain fell, collected on her face and mixed with her tears. Soon, the last wet grain would fall, and she would drown.

No ocean of blue for this princess. My ocean is blacker than the approaching night.

But then it occurred to her that she wasn't being taken to an execution site. The hill was in the other direction. "Where are you taking me, Garrett? This is not the path I expected to walk."

"To the hall."

"Why? Surely Queen Cynara would not permit blood to be shed in a regal place?"

"I don't understand the decision any better than you, but these are my orders. Please, we must hurry. They will be waiting."

"Who, who will be waiting? Surely not the royal family?"

Garrett studied her with an expression she could not read. He seemed concerned. "Key courtiers have been summoned to Camden Castle. I know not what awaits you, but Queen Cynara and King Lowell will be present."

Scarlett took a deep breath. They meant to watch her die.

When Garrett and Father Clement ushered her into the great hall, the people of the court were milling about the chamber. The women quieted as soon as they saw her, but the men continued their conversation in clipped tones, courting her every step. Scarlett paused to regard them. The lords scrutinized her with contempt in their eyes. Their ladies sniffed the air with disdain and retreated from her approach as if they might catch her disease, forcing her to look away. Lesser men held the guise of the curious, the type of street rats who didn't want to see the horror but enjoyed the spectacle all the same. They watched her as she shuffled past, taking in her expression, assessing her gait, and pondering her shabby clothing as she traversed the crowded center aisle. The impatient shifted their attention in the direction of the throne, where she needed to face her treason against the kingdom. She didn't care at this point, who witnessed her demise.

"Traitor!" someone yelled.

Look at me where I go. Watch my blood spill as I die. It's too late for me to care what anyone thinks or witnesses. We were all born to die.

But then she viewed the throne where her judge and jury waited, and all hope vanished. Garrett and Father Clement escorted her up the center aisle to where King Lowell, Queen Cynara, and a few advisors of the Kingdom of Velez waited. The king held a determined mien, and Scarlett had never witnessed a sterner facial expression. He was not the boy child she remembered. The queen seemed ready to strike her, but satisfaction and joy etched her expression too, as if she had planned this moment, regardless that the king had signed the death warrant.

Scarlett discerned her own breathing whooshing in and

out of her nose. Her heartbeat pulsing between her ears, pounding a deadly rhythm inside her head. The court quieted when she was finally within reach of the royals. She didn't bow or curtsy. Such courtesies seemed pointless. Instead, she inclined her head, glanced at the floor and waited for the penalty phase to begin.

"Princess Scarlett," King Lowell decreed with cutting purpose, "you have come here to die. I have signed your death warrant for the treason committed against this throne. I want you to know, I take no comfort in watching your death. But die you must."

Scarlett did not utter a word while assessing her brother. He seemed small and uncomfortable sitting on the large throne. A slight tremor wrinkled the skin around his right eye, and she sensed his anger. He attempted to control himself, but his hands balled into tight fists. Was this man-child about to throw a tantrum? Perhaps he would murder his half-sister with his own two hands.

"Have you anything to say for yourself? Do you ask for mercy? Will you plead for your wretched life?"

"I ask only that my sisters, Ruby and Rose, do not suffer for the crime I alone committed. I will not beg for what cannot be gained, but if my half-brother is inclined to mercy, I request that my punishment be swift."

He smirked then and turned to share a sickening half-smile with the queen mother, who openly shared in his amusement. Then his attention returned to where she cowered like a dog.

"I can promise your ending will be quick," he chortled. "We will not waste this court's time, or mine, on your wretched life. Executioner, bring the viper."

Scarlett shifted uneasily. The onlookers retreated a step to make way for a heavyset man who strode forward carrying a serpent. He didn't seem the type to hold a snake, and Scarlett imagined his hands might be more comfortable with sharper instruments.

She recognized the animal for both the threat and the potential victory it offered, and she understood the coming sentence to be faced. She released Father Clement's hold, her hand flying to her lips. She faced her brother, understanding the sentence of *an eye for an eye* and thrust herself against Garrett, feigning a faint to create distance between herself and the holy man so he could not hold her hand. When the warden caught her in his arms, as she had hoped he would, she tried to hide her expectation of a second chance at life.

King Lowell smiled in satisfaction. He seemed to delight in her dramatized show of fear. He stood, removing himself from his throne chair as if rising would make him taller, as if standing with his legs braced apart would make him more of a man.

"You not only killed the king, my father, but you took away my freedom." He pointed at himself. He spit as he talked. "I accept my duty, but I cannot accept how I gained this throne."

Scarlett cringed when he thrust his index finger at her and descended one single stair. "I want you to pay. I want you to taste the venom you drove into our father's veins. I want you to die, gasping for air, like he did."

She supposed her brother wanted her to think about what it might feel like to struggle. The joke was on him. She had known adversity her entire life. At first she thought he might continue his descent down the few stairs and kill her with his boyish hands, but the king took his seat after the lecture. The king didn't get his hands dirty. He had an executioner to do his bidding.

"I will watch your dying breath, and my face will be the last you see on this earth."

Scarlett raised her head to scrutinize her brother, measuring his anger. The game had begun. But still, she had to be careful. She dared not look too deeply into his eyes, for his mother would glean her secret.

"I am ready, Your Royal High Ass." She slurred the words, hissing like the snake that had come for her. "Bite me." A shocked hush filled the hall at her audacity.

If Lowell could have left his throne to strike her, she could see he would have. It must have taken self-control the boy didn't have to remain on his seat. Instead, he yelled at the executioner. "Enough, bring the cobra!"

Father Clement whispered beside her, praying. He reached for her hand, but Scarlett didn't accept his kind regard. She could not. Garrett moved aside to make room for the executioner who would enact the king's ruling. She glanced at the burly man stalking toward her, seeing he was uncomfortable carrying the serpent. Taking the snake would be like stealing from a baby, for while the man was large, he was clearly terrified of the bounty he held.

"You know not what you do," she said, stepping toward him. "Here, let me help you."

Scarlett seized the cobra from the executioner's hands. She was surprised how easy it had been to take the serpent. "I cannot believe my luck," she cried in disbelief, holding the scaly skin, "to hold this animal in my hands."

Turning toward her half-brother, she snickered, glimpsing Lowell rising from his chair in shock, and rushing behind his throne. "Perhaps you think I will throw it at you, again?"

"Guards, to attention," Queen Cynara commanded.

"Your Majesty," Scarlett exclaimed, keeping her focus on the frightened animal, "you have nothing to fear."

She plunged the cobra's head against her neck, screeching when the fangs met their mark, puncturing her flesh. Venom coursed through her artery. She felt it. At this fleshy spot, death would come fast. With the fangs skewered at her throat, she staggered on her feet, staring at her nemesis, as she had meant to the first time.

Pain caused tears to well and fall from her eyes, but she saw the dawning realization in Cynara's expression. The queen suspected her triumph but still hoped death would come. Scarlett released the snake, dropping it to the floor. Those closer to her screamed and shifted away as the snake slithered free.

Amused by their fright, she struggled to keep her balance, swaying, praying that her mother's secret tucked inside the purse beneath her crumpled dress proved true, for otherwise she was bound for an early grave.

Somewhere beyond this miserable kingdom, she could sense someone watching over her; an instinct foretold that in order to live, she must die. As she slumped to her knees, with her breath whistling in and out of her mouth in quick gasps and her heartbeat skipping, missing beats, she smirked a smile that must have appeared odd to those watching.

"I don't understand," King Lowell retorted. "Why did she do that?"

She didn't peruse the boy king; she observed his mother instead. At that moment, Cynara's brow lifted in suspicion.

"What game do you play?"

The queen seemed to notice the change, seemed to understand that as Scarlett's life force weakened, a deftness dawned inside of her. She sensed Cynara felt the mark. The seed was like a heavy weight pressing against her royal chest.

Scarlett beheld His Royal Majesty King Lowell, who peered at her from behind his throne. She fought to maintain her concentration as the venom coursed through her veins, making her stronger, but the work made her weak, too. She lost her smile and crumpled to the floor, her lifeblood altering like a caterpillar would transform into a butterfly. Father Clement took hold of her hand, reciting his prayers, while she called to her brother for what still could be the last time.

"Tell me when my heart stops." Scarlett laughed like a maniac, her breathing shallow and weak. "For then my punishment will be over and my debt to you paid."

Chapter Nine

LORD NICOLAI GRAYDON

When the sun slipped beneath a blood-orange horizon, two hungry ravens descended from a twilight sky. Their ebony wings stretched wide, gliding toward an animal's bloody carcass on the ground. A black panther waited for their company.

Nicolai heard their cawing long before he saw their shadows, drifting gracefully with the wind, gliding closer to the forest floor. He watched the mated pair with grim satisfaction from where he crouched near a tree, his feline coat almost hidden in the thick weeds. The birds made one final rotation in the sky and then swooped toward the woodland. They regarded him with a sly awareness before approaching the dead deer he'd left.

The male raven stepped toward the carcass and poked inside the gut. The bird gripped a rib with footed claws, ripping a purplish strip of flesh, then offering the morsel to his mate. The female received the gift and swallowed the offering in one bite, then climbed inside the hide to join her raven lover at their grim table. Nicolai listened to them, their beaks clicking as each bird picked at beetles and squished them flat inside their mouths, or licked up white larvae as if the worms tasted sweet. They were anything but sweet; the stench filled the air regardless of the distance.

Nicolai sat upright in his panther form, comfortable with the dark, watching. He couldn't remember what life felt like to live as a normal man. Years ago when he had been mortal, scavengers poking at their meal would have caused him to wretch, but now as he watched the ravens dine, he mused about his sad state of affairs. He had carved the deer's flesh with long sharp claws and feasted on the metallic taste of warm blood. He felt no remorse for his actions as the hunt committed no crime. Men were made to hunt. What rendered his life unusual was the way he hunted. He was the cursed black panther stalking his prey, either early in the day or late at night, with his nose on a quest and his ears alert to sound; his footed paw a silent tread, one step closer to the unwary.

He did not hesitate when he found his victim. He enjoyed the leap that led him to a life and death struggle, always imagining that the throat gripped in his jaws belonged to his enemy, Cynara. The kill was never rushed. Life shouldn't be rushed. He enjoyed the fear that overcame his victim. Likewise, he felt no remorse when he brought the animal to the ground. He often watched as the life force in the eyes drifted away, while red blood trickled, seeped, and soaked into the ground.

He wished Cynara had killed him in this way, for then he would not have known endless suffering, and the human soul might have remembered the man—Lord Nicolai Graydon.

Who was that man? He shook his head, despairing. He didn't know anymore.

Nicolai had suffocated for years within this black velvet sheath, and the cruel instinct of the panther, more so than his loneliness, had left him cold and calculating. He was the darkness that prevailed on the weak. He supposed in some respects, this life held no more stealth than the existence he had lived a long time ago, when his victims were women. Once a fair face and a sweet bosom had encouraged various liaisons. Once the scent of virginal honey had come close to providing material salvation. Alexandra—a timid blue bird— whose soul had lifted to the sky too soon.

"Hmm," Nicolai purred. He had lived this other life a long time ago, but if he closed his eyes and thought hard, he could still visualize women dancing at the ball. Fair maidens with silken dresses that floated across the floor as their feminine figures moved in rhythm to the music, dancing with a willful grace in an attempt to ensnare a husband. Carnal and carefree women, too, the fonts of nourishment with their sugary breasts, who encouraged improper advances with their seductive and sexual dramas. He had stalked women before they knew they were being followed. He had reached their sides while they were unaware, taking their soft hands, matching their steps, easing their fragile bodies backward, and then bringing them so close to his lips, he could hear their throaty breathing.

Why? Why had he acted in such a churlish manner?

He had learned too late that a lord should not entertain certain women near his lips—and a handful of vixens—a man should never dare to kiss.

An evil woman had cursed Nicolai and forced him against his nature to chase much darker pursuits. He should have avoided Cynara, for she had infected him with her black poison, and in the process, had unmanned him. Now, with each kill, her hands were at the heart of the terror. Every throat he held, Cynara had forced him to watch the lifeblood slip away. Presently, a table set on the forest floor held a white-tailed deer that bled rancid odor, and two hungry ravens were his only amusement and company.

Beneath the weeping arms of a sessile oak, Nicolai watched the midnight scavengers. He felt like a thoughtless man-cat, a decrepit soul forced into this constrictive space, held hostage in this black panther sheath. His life force was decaying. A tortured mind had malformed into diseased black; he was crazy.

Nicolai envied the ravens. They were smarter than him by far. The pair fed each other and showed obvious affection and commitment. When their appetites for venison declined, they preened each other. The male groomed the female's head where she could not reach herself. She closed her eyes in contentment as he went about his love affair. There were no words for the affectionate act. The tender scene always left Nicolai barren, and wanting for the warmth and fondness he could never touch. So he brought the two creatures to this banquet, again and again, dying inside a little more with each preen of a black feather. And now that a cursed man craved real affection, real affection was denied.

He would never share a meal, never offer comfort to a woman. No love token or affection, sexual or otherwise to his mate. Ever! Nicolai Graydon—doomed to walk the nether land of earth with the urge to kill, again and again. Yet, he wasn't alone. He shared the darkness and all that he was with a pair that understood the definition and ate from the shadows with satisfaction.

But on this night, as two ravens turned their attention on him and gathered close, the love he could not embrace became too much. He screamed his cat cry at the black lovers, pushing his head forward, jealous and angry all at once. They didn't flinch, nor did they fly away. The ravens were accustomed to his company and felt safe in his presence. He cried again, revealing his fangs and berating them with his eyes, and then turned to the forest and charged into the woods, his voice a cry in the night.

"I am the darkness that preys on the weak," Nicolai screamed as he ran toward his manor, leaving the kill and the birds behind. "I am the evil seed that lesser souls seek. I am the watcher that crouches beneath the tree. I am the black panther who will never be free."

Nicolai bounded forward through the dense bush, running until his lungs heaved for breath. He reasoned that while he could run a great distance, he could never escape the curse that bathed his soul in darkness, so he settled into a walk. He noticed the liquid leaking from his eyes as he leaped over a fallen log, but the water trickling was not his miserable tears. Panthers did not feel weakness. The wind encouraged the weeping. Still, he felt the emotion constricting his chest and wished for a way to overcome the bondage. But time had dictated that Nicolai could not hope for a positive ending to this plight.

Not even his butler had offered hope. The lightning strike had left Bensen with permanent disabilities, and other servants—the cook, the gardener, the maid, his personal valet—had escaped his employment years ago. Cynara had stimulated a mass departure, all in one great wave. He was alone to provide for himself. Even so, he didn't require much, and he didn't care that Drum Manor had slowly altered into an old ghost house. The walls stood tall and strong, even though the inside rooms reeked of dust, mold, and clutter. The lord felt equally haunted; though he didn't care for wealth or pompous attitudes anymore. Selfish need had brought him to this Netherworld in the first place.

Nicolai changed from his panther form to resume his naked stance as a man and walked on weakened legs to the manor. The chilly air, combined with a whistling wind, caused shivers to tingle his spine now that the covering of fur and forest was gone. He should have advanced to his mansion to seek warmth, but instead, he proceeded to the cliff edge where he sat on a large boulder beside the ocean. His hair flying wildly while staring at a raging black sea, then gazing lower still, sighting an ocean tidal wave as the water surged over monstrous gray and shadowed rocks.

He leaned into the spray, closed his eyes, and breathed in the sea air. He considered stepping over the edge and ending this madness on the rocks below, thereby releasing him from misery—although with his misfortune, he would probably transform into the cat and land safely, but wet and cut on his feet. Damn it all, a rash ending never earned hope. It was time to put this night of suffering to rest, find his messy bed, and sleep. He left the boulder and plodded toward his manor house, his head bowed against the cold.

Chapter Ten

PRINCESS SCARLETT

Scarlett struggled to breathe. Gasping for air, she thought her battle was over when she slipped into unconsciousness; her lungs heaving, fighting to gain a much-needed inhalation of air. She succumbed to nightmarish dreams where time held no meaning and whispered voices waged war in her head. *Was that her mother's face, or Cynara's enraged voice?* Maybe Lowell stood near her bed. She rolled back and forth, trying to respond to their voices, lashing out when someone—Lowell?—came too close, then she succumbed once more to sleep and darkness.

When Scarlett finally opened her eyes, her breathing had returned to normal. Her eyelids felt so heavy that she could only hold them open for brief moments before sleep forced her into a fantasy world again. Once fully alert, she forced her eyes to remain open, recognizing a new truth. She was alive, held hostage inside the tower, and deliverance from death likely came with a startling change, and she felt certain an inner transformation had occurred.

She removed her arms from the blankets and stretched them out for her perusal, flexing her fingers and then squeezing them into tight fists. In the gray darkness she contemplated the changes. Strength coursed through her veins, energy flowed like a river through her bloodstream, her instinct appeared keener, and her personality held an aggressive tack. The night no longer held wickedness now that her eyesight appraised the distance perfectly. In fact, she could see farther into the darkest corners of the night. The ground beneath the tower pulsated with life. If a rat scampered across the inner ward, somehow, she knew these abilities would aid in catching the rodent.

Scarlett swung her legs out of bed and stood. Despite the change, a weakness overcame her, causing her head to spin and her breath to quicken at the exercise. She drew the quilt around her shoulders and on wobbly legs, stumbled to the window to inspect the night shadows. She clutched the window ledge for support, searching for her sisters, Ruby and Rose, who didn't materialize at the window of the opposite tower.

Hearing a sound, Scarlett peered downward at the inner ward, and noticed a woman shrouded in a black cloak, hiding in the shadows. Who was this woman? And why did her line of vision shift upward?

Chapter Eleven

QUEEN CYNARA

A draft swept inside Lowell's bedchamber, but Cynara didn't feel the cold. The anger fueling her inner furnace kept her warm and pacing in front of her son, as she considered the drama that had occurred inside the hall.

How had Princess Scarlett pulled off this mischief? No one survived a snakebite, yet Scarlett was alive and breathing. Cynara had failed to bury the girl in the ground and she didn't like to fail.

"How could this happen?" Lowell growled, grinding his teeth while scrubbing his face vigorously with a wet cloth to remove all traces of Scarlett's poison. "The bloody dog is alive! Damn it, how has she risen? What changes do I see in her eyes? And what sort of caustic spittle did she spew at my eyes? My half-sister is a monster walking the earth. She was supposed to be in a box by now, rotting."

Cynara stopped her pacing to study her son. He stood in front of a golden reflecting glass, suffering. It had been his grand stratagem to use the snake—*an eye for an eye*—and her poor calculation as Queen Mother to let the boy make this decision, so he could identify as a king. *A king?* The king had learned his first lesson.

"You should have chosen a more public display of execution," she barked. "I don't understand her survival any more than you, but it's too late for regrets. I'm more troubled that because of your foolishness, the girl has gained some sort of power."

"Don't be unkind, Mum. I could not have known the outcome."

Cynara scrutinized her son. Where was his black heart hiding? "You have learned your first lesson in terms of ruling our kingdom; regardless of the privy council, who assisted in your royal decree, your best advisor is your mother."

He slumped into an armchair beside his bed, still holding the cloth in his hand. "If you think you're so wise, why didn't you warn me?"

Cynara paced beside his bed, her forehead wrinkled with concern. She paused in her stride to regard her son and his red eyes. "I didn't know her intention with that serpent any more than I know how she survived the bite, nor do I understand the transformation or what it means. But I will discover a solution. Death can still come to this traitor. I'll find a proper grim reaper to wield the scythe, since somehow she is immune to my power."

Lowell harrumphed, returning the cloth to his eyes. "A solution to end her miserable life may not be possible, and if I can't have her dead, I want her removed from the kingdom— her sisters, too. Mayhap fate can still be cruel. Send all three of them away. I care not where; any dungeon will do."

Cynara stepped toward her son. "I promise you, we will take proper care of King Rickard's offspring, but if we send them away, the destination must offer a positive ending."

She pondered this difficulty with her finger on her lips. *Where can I send Scarlett to meet with the end design—death?* What were her options for killing this traitor? Because sending her away to live some other life was not a satisfying conclusion.

When a foul idea sprouted, she stopped pacing. A memory, long buried in the recesses of her mind, resurrected a solution.

"I don't know why I didn't think of this sooner," Cynara tittered with amusement, placing her hands on her hips.

"Don't keep me in suspense," Lowell said, glancing at her. "You must have a grand strategy in mind to smile at me like that."

Cynara approached her son. "I know where we can send this vexing seed who refuses to wither and die—Drum Manor. And the setting will be perfect. A fit ending for two troublesome individuals I want out of my life. Perhaps one bite will lead to another and two fates will confront death."

"Sounds perfect," Lowell glared, eager. "When will we send the dog away?"

"Immediately. The sooner the blight is gone, the better."

Cynara sat on the armchair next to her son, relaxing, soon sliding her fingers through his black hair. "It's best the people of Velez believe the princess has perished. You should sign a proclamation that the traitor passed during the night."

"I wish I had a head to place on a stake," Lowell whispered. "Far better than a royal decree."

"Your wish can be granted. I'm sure we can find a subject to take the princess's place on the pike. It would deliver a strong message."

"No. An innocent will not suffer for the crimes of my sister."

"A pity," Cynara commented. "Fear is a good weapon to keep your people mindful of their actions. But rest, my son, while I take up your work and rid the kingdom of this traitor."

Chapter Twelve

PRINCESS SCARLETT

The wind whispered, a tawny owl hooted, and moonlight lit the evening sky, illuminating courtyard shadows where two guardsmen escorted Scarlett through the inner ward. Ill at ease, she tried to ignore the curtain wall towering high above her, but disregarding the stronghold had never been possible. Even as a young girl, she'd been afraid of the structure. Tall and imposing during the daylight hours, it menaced even more at night when the shadows elongated the walls. The uneasiness didn't dwell in her head alone. One couldn't look at the castle without feeling the wickedness that consumed its space, and though she held new strength and abilities, abilities that couldn't yet be comprehended, she felt small and insignificant walking beside the curtain wall.

Her desire had been to abandon the castle a long time ago, or at least the unkind creatures who oppressed the common people, but now that two men escorted her from the place she'd always called home, she was afraid to leave. It had been the only stronghold Scarlett had known, and she, a princess, had never felt protected within its walls.

It interested her to know not only why the royal family was ushering her toward an unforeseen danger, but also why they couldn't take care of their problem princess on their own.

When they reached the carriage, she grasped the iron handle and stepped onto the wooden footrest, then lowered her head and pulled herself inside the boxy prison. The space was stifling. A death trap. Yet surprisingly, even though the night was as dark as pitch, her sight was picture-perfect. She managed to accept that the simple conveyance was barren of comfort, and the wood-engrained bench would make her journey uncomfortable. Sighing, she reclined to a seat, and observed her jailers standing near the box carriage, two dark shapes speaking in discreet tones.

Garrett, the taller of the two, appeared stern and almost grave as he conveyed what must be strict orders. Theodore grasped the handle and frowned, glancing downward, seeming to take notice of the ground. He kicked at the cobbles, seeming distressed by their conversation. Perhaps he was reluctant to accept his duty, but she perceived he would.

Her anxiety levels rose while waiting for the guards to conclude their war of words. Feeling weak, she had been forced to consume pottage earlier. The taste of sour onions lodged at the back of her throat and her stomach gurgled with unease. *No, I won't be sick.*

She tried to dispel her worries, but the waiting caused her anxiety levels to rise. She scanned the interior's tight width and its coffin length. The plain wood ceiling, and beyond that a small window with black bars for slats, held there to remind her and others that escape was impossible. When the door shut and the key twisted inside the lock, there would be no way out. The realization nauseated her. Confinement inside this horror caused her stomach to churn, more so than the terror she was headed toward.

But you're alive. Does it matter where they send you?

She reached for the talisman at her side, her mother's purse, and pulled it closer to her heart. Unconsciously, she grasped the straps and massaged the length while pondering her future.

Hearing a sound, she glanced at the doorway. Father Clement made his presence known. He bent his head downward, and then climbed inside the conveyance and sat on the opposite seat.

"I'm surprised to see you, Father."

"Take this," he offered, handing her a woolen blanket.

"Still you care for me. Thank you," she said, placing the bundle on her lap.

"A shepherd always takes care of his flock." He reached toward her and placed the book of poetry into her hand as well.

"I didn't expect this. I'm grateful for your kindness."

He gazed at her with concern, appearing so serious, Scarlett didn't know what to say while waiting for him to speak.

"I wish I had more to offer. The blanket will help keep you warm and the book will give you peace. I know it belonged to your mother and she would have wanted you to have these inspirational poems."

"I don't know what to say."

He leaned closer. When Scarlett's hands quivered, he squeezed them. "The gods are watching you."

"You've said that before."

"I know you don't believe it, but the gods have brought you safe thus far. I have faith they will guide you further."

Her mother's note had brought her safe thus far, but she kept this secret to herself. "I didn't say I wasn't grateful."

He patted her hand. "I will pray for your salvation. I won't forget you."

Scarlett trembled, slipped her hand away from his grasp, and laid it on her too fast beating heart. "Thank you for the blanket. I will accept the book, as you have been kind to me. The phrases paint a pleasant depiction of what the Otherworld might be, but as far as I'm concerned, they are only words."

He took her hand back. "Sometimes phrases are the content of salvation, of wisdom, but only when humans are ready to receive the message."

Father Clement sighed, patted her hand, and entreated a silent message Scarlett would never know because their paths might never cross again. It appeared as if he wanted to say more. He muttered unintelligible words and studied the wooden slats on the floor.

"Enough of meaningless assurances that don't support the princess's situation," Garrett grumbled, standing outside the door. "It's time for the carriage to depart. Theodore has taken his seat on the driver's box."

"It would serve you well to have more faith and less doubt," Father Clement said, while making the sign of the cross on her forehead. "God go with you, Princess, and keep you safe from harm. I will pray for you."

"Goodbye, Father."

When he stood, the carriage rocked under his weight. He left her then and was soon hidden from her sight, but she knew he was waiting for her departure and would watch the prison carriage as it departed from this miserable place.

Garrett examined the space around him, as if to see who might be watching, then leaned into the conveyance, stepping on the rise to get closer.

"I won't be traveling with you, so this might be the last time I see you. Yet, I have a feeling we will meet again. I am not a religious man, nor do I believe that the gods will come to our rescue, but you have bested a fiend and can surmount more still. I could lose my life for saying this, but you are your mother's shield and your father's sword. No matter what difficulties lie ahead, don't forget this truth."

Scarlett didn't respond to the assertion prior to Garrett closing the door. Instead, she listened to the wooden bar scraping against the iron, confining her inside the box. Alone, two men had given her much to think about. She placed the book inside her mother's purse. She rested her hand on top of the fabric bulge as she prepared to journey toward the unknown.

Theodore reined the horses and the carriage jostled forward, rocking slightly, soon departing from Camden Castle. As the carriage passed underneath the portcullis, Scarlett stood on feet that threatened to give way. She tried to match the rhythm of the swaying carriage as the wooden structure bounced over the cobbles. She extended her arms forward and reached toward the iron bars, swaying. When the wheels ground over the drawbridge, she caught hold of the metal bars and pulled herself the final distance, peering between their blackened lengths to the outer ward.

After leaving the outer gate, she searched the space beyond a darkened field and soon sighted a tower situated along the north stronghold wall. She remembered her last horror-filled sighting of her sisters in the tower above the kitchens. The image decried her feelings of guilt and helplessness as the carriage removed her from the stronghold, progressing farther away from the castle. She gripped the cold, black iron, closed her eyes, weakening to silent tears, hoping Garrett's foresight proved true; for then, three sisters might be reunited, perhaps even within these fortress walls. Wherever her sisters were imprisoned, she hoped they'd be safe until her return, if she could revisit this life.

And what of Garrett's statement? How could a shield and a sword save her parents? Both of her parents were dead. She could not shield a mother who had been lost for years any more than she could protect a father who lay dead inside a vault. Whatever could Garrett have meant by his assertion?

She sighed, releasing a pent-up breath. Forcing her attention to the inside of the carriage, she released the bars and slid to the corner seat. She wiped her eyes, unwrapped the blanket that Father Clement had provided, and wrapped the wool around her shoulders. This vehicle had probably driven victims to their death, and the secure box might yet bring a princess to her demise, too. She huddled into the corner and pulled the blanket closer still. This blanket, a book, the red dress she wore, and a bag whose inner secrets had saved her life were her only possessions.

She was surprised that Cynara had not robbed her of the precious memento, an heirloom she held close to her heart. The memories buried inside the fabric still offered comfort and peace.

Closing her eyes, she tried to relax, finding comfort in the rocking motion of the carriage. Eventually she slept as the wheels jostled over an earthen path, leaving her first trial behind.

Chapter Thirteen

LORD NICOLAI GRAYDON

Nicolai was reaching for the knob of the manor door when he heard the ambling sound of a horse and carriage in the distance. He paused, released the handle and left the stoop. Turning toward the laneway, he stepped off the stone landing and considered the pathway through the forest. It had not been used in years.

"No, it cannot be," he whispered into the wind. "Who would come this way?"

The grind of wheels and the clip-clop sound of hooves had not been heard since that horrible night years ago, but there could be no mistake. A horse nickered in the night, and wheels creaked, grinding into the rutted ground. Willing himself to investigate, he transformed into the form of the black panther and surged forward.

He ran toward the conveyance, keeping to the forest edge, following a path grown thick with weeds. Soon, a large black shape emerged in the distance. He leapt to a tree, settled on a branch, and stretched forward to see what stranger loomed.

Horses' hooves lumbered across the earth, beating in the night as two large mares sauntered forward. A large box followed behind, assuming the rectangular shape of a wagon. A stocky driver sat on the box seat holding thick ebony reins, unaware of the danger above.

When the wagon came nearer, one horse squealed a warning and stopped abruptly, strutting backward in fear. Oblivious to the cat above, the driver struck the reins against the animals' backs and forced them onward. Nicolai could have attacked the man and bit his throat, but he was too curious as to why this traveler had come to Drum Manor.

Once the conveyance passed him by, he leapt to the ground and kept himself hidden in the shadows, trailing behind. He followed the wagon as it struggled up the difficult pathway to his manor house. The box carriage was not empty; he had clearly seen someone inside. A man? *A woman?* Who could it be? He prowled to the side of his house, peered around the corner, and waited for them to stop.

Nicolai watched the driver secure the gear and place the reins on the seat, soon climbing to the ground. The stranger removed his gloves, tossed them on the seat, and examined the surroundings. He shook his head at what he saw.

"Grrrr," Nicolai growled, watching the intruder proceed to the rear of the wagon and pull the door open.

A small foot dressed in leather stepped to the riser. Tiny and dainty, the appendage could only belong to a woman. But no, that couldn't be. Could it?

He sucked in a breath, his chest expanding with air and his gut knotting with excitement as a woman came into view. She seemed to stare in his direction.

Can she see me? he wondered, studying her pale creamy flesh, a tempting moonbeam stuck beneath the black sky. *But that's impossible.*

She grasped the driver's hand and descended to the ground.

He heard her pulse beating strong at her neck. Thump-thump, thump-thump—he crept forward toward the thrum. He wanted to leap at her neck and bite.

Why have you come? Who sent you?

He howled like an animal caught in a trap and contemplated the difficulty her presence brought to his life. He watched her tremble, smelled her fear, and listened to an unsteady heartbeat, prior to bounding like the wild cat he had become, returning to the forest.

Gods help him, a woman had arrived at Drum Manor. What would happen now that his territory had been encroached upon?

Nicolai worried, thinking about the prospects. He needed distance to consider what to do, so he escaped to the forest, leaping from the ground to a branch and back again to the ground with one thought compelling him: she was a beautiful creature. He had not only noticed the pale face with golden-brown eyes, but also the long dark hair curling to her slender waist. Nicolai knew a beauty when he saw one, but this curse had garnered darker instincts, and the cat inside challenged him to welcome the next meal.

Gods help me. The black curse buried inside my heart desires the next kill. Whoever this woman is, she must leave.

Chapter Fourteen

PRINCESS SCARLETT

Scarlett had begun to feel a sense of safety within the prison wagon, but standing outside on the open ground, she trembled. The shivers may have arisen from tailwinds that blew cold, moist air in from the ocean, but Scarlett knew her fear grew more from the unknown perils that hid behind the massive doors of the manor. She tried to rein in her awareness of danger and took two steps toward the entrance, but fear clutched at her throat and she paused to study the structure.

Once upon a time the stone edifice with its stately columns and triple-gabled facade must have waxed impressive, but the home she studied now revealed obvious signs of neglect. Green vines clung haphazardly to the sandstone, and broken panes of glass suggested that the inner chambers most likely offered no more than an asylum for forest creatures. A threat didn't seem to be lurking near the house or the overgrown shrubs, and standing this close, she couldn't discern so much as the feeble shrill of a bird or the tiny squeak of a mouse, either inside or outside the manor. A woman never knew where a thorn might be waiting to catch her by surprise, but the manor appeared abandoned. Not a single light flickered on its landing and the inside appeared equally barren and still.

She shivered, knowing for a certainty that an unspecified menace lived inside that manor house. She sensed it. Felt it.

Why have you sent me here, Cynara? What type of danger could possibly exist inside this woebegone manor?

If Theodore noticed her discomfort, he ignored it. Instead of looking at him, Scarlett pulled the blanket tighter around her shoulders and searched beyond the manor. She breathed the damp decay of the forest and felt the salt spray as the moisture suffused her face. She tried to ignore the sixth sense that warned that something wicked was watching and waiting for her her arrival.

She pivoted toward Theodore. "Why did you bring me here? Do you expect me to walk inside that desolate mausoleum? It appears to be a home for ghosts more than men."

"I had no say in this destination," he stated simply. "When the queen instructs her minions to do a chore, the overseers scramble to attention. Going against her wishes is unwise."

"Ahh, I see, so that's what you would have me believe— that you support the queen instead of the princess who has been wronged. Theodore, what is hiding inside that manor?"

"I have no idea."

Scarlett considered the building, listening, waiting for threats to rise, but soon a presence was felt outside. The hair on the back of her neck rose and anxiety danced in her stomach like an angry swarm of bees. She knew someone was watching her where she stood.

"Who's there?" she asked, studying the far corner of the manor to see who had caught her unaware, and that is when fear clutched at her breast causing her to tremble.

A large panther strode into her view from the farthest corner of the manor. Black velvet hair expanded from a sleek and trim build. Its torso hunched upward, filling more with warning than the threat of physical force.

It howled—snarling in the night, and she recognized the threat for the cunning menace it could be and was grateful when the animal ran into the forest. She didn't want to go inside the manor, but with a large cat on the prowl, the house seemed the safest option.

"Come, Theodore," she said, putting her right foot forward while scrutinizing the area for the panther. "We had best get ourselves indoors before the creature returns. A pity our choices are a cat in the night or whatever lies in wait inside this old house."

He didn't move. "I was instructed to leave you at the door. Now that I have kept my bargain with the queen and delivered you, I am to return to the castle at once."

"Truly?" Scarlett growled, becoming angry. "Don't you care about my circumstances? How dare you unload me in a strange place, in the dead of night as if I were baggage, dropping me into unknown dangers and then leaving me to fend for myself."

"I have my orders. I will follow them."

"You would leave me to face an unknown enemy, alone? What kind of a man are you?"

He kicked the dirt with his boot, focusing on the wagon. "I fear the queen more than what hides inside this hovel. If she demands my return, then I return."

Angering, Scarlett bridged the gap between them and grabbed his arm. "I require your escort inside this manor. I will not face this strange place alone," she said, trying to stem her quaking voice. "Please, I beg of you, assist me, Theodore."

"I cannot take my orders from a woman such as you," he protested, twisting away from her grip. Scarlett grabbed him again and wrenched him around to face her angry expression.

"How dare you speak to me like that," Scarlett bellowed, squeezing his arm. "You make me sound as if I'm as evil as Cynara. I'll have you know, my father's death was embodied with black magic."

He shook his head, clearly not believing her account. "I recall your behavior on that night, and that's all I need to understand."

Scarlett didn't know that her eyesight changed as she assessed the warden's stubborn manner. She wanted to slap the man across the face to encourage his cooperation. He took a step away from her and a strange expression came over his face. He regarded her as if he'd seen...

"What is it?" Scarlett asked. "Why are you gaping at me like that?"

"Your eyes," he murmured, "have grown a yellow stripe through the center iris."

Scarlett mocked him, not believing what he had witnessed. "You have a ripe imagination. But do lead me toward that door before I pierce you with my night vision, or some other nasty gift."

"All right," he grumbled, relenting, but Scarlett supposed that by morning he would be gone, and she could not prevent his resolve.

"Thank you," she whispered, as a reluctant Theodore took hold of her arm. His hand barely touched her elbow as he escorted her to the large set of double doors.

"You're welcome. But regardless of my assistance, I suspect my escort won't aid your situation."

"I don't doubt it." Scarlett fretted, but she was grateful for his presence and the warmth emanating from him.

She trembled, feeling the cold as they crossed a rocky pathway grown thick with weeds, soon navigating hedges that had to be pushed aside. A branch scratched her arm, but she barely felt the minor cut. She pressed closer to Theodore. When he leaned away, his fear of her was apparent, but Scarlett took what she required and forced him closer. Together, they stumbled up two steps of crumbling stairway to a landing.

Scarlett focused on a matching pair of lion knockers, still afraid of what lingered inside. *Welcome to the beast*, she thought.

"Let's see if anyone's home," Theodore said, then grabbed a brass pull and struck the knocker against the wood-grained door.

Scarlett heard a hollow echo inside. "Perhaps the mansion is deserted?"

"I doubt it. The queen wouldn't be so careless. Someone knows their prisoner has arrived."

"If that's true, why doesn't anyone answer the door?"

Scarlett shivered with cold despite the blanket on her

shoulders. After waiting a lengthy period of time, she lost patience, reached for the doorknob and pressed the metal housing. Opening the door proved difficult. She threw her weight against the grain and pushed with both hands until the door gave way with a loud screech. She glanced at Theodore momentarily, and then peered at the entryway inside the manor.

It was dark. Not one single light from a tallow candle greeted them. The country house was as dark as a tomb and smelled of mold and mildew. It appeared as if no one had walked this corridor in years.

"After you," he whispered, leaning away.

She shook her head in disgust. "Are you eager to see your responsibility for my well-being at an end, Theodore? Who do you think I've become? I'm not some monster that would see you undone. Nor am I the woman you think me to be. What is waiting for me inside this crumbling house? Do you know?"

He didn't respond right away and avoided looking at her eyes. Instead, he walked ahead of her and crossed over the threshold, grabbing her arm and wrenching her forward. He closed the door with a louder screech, corralling them inside.

"I have no idea what justice waits for you," he grumbled, scanning the area. "But knowing Cynara, you'll receive a fitting retribution."

Scarlett brushed his arm away from her as if he were a gnat. "That's a mean observation. I'd never voice such an unkind sentiment to you, however much I want to."

Angry, she hugged the blanket around herself, shivering, wishing he would leave but needing him to stay.

"Sometimes the truth is hard to accept. Our actions even more so."

"You're an utter fool and an unkind man, Theodore."

Standing in the entranceway of the manor house, Scarlett didn't want to talk to this insipid fool any longer. Instead, she observed the night shadows living inside this hovel. The only light, a streak of moonlight beaming through a half-circle of glass in the upper door. On either side of the entryway were opposing doors to darkened rooms and just past their opening, one by each threshold, stood two marble statues. On the left, a freakish girl held her arms open in welcome. On the right, a lackluster lad offered an open book as if the parchment imparted an important message.

"Princess…"

"Hush," Scarlett whispered, stepping past the girl and peering into what appeared to be a drawing room. "I don't want to hear another word from you. Be quiet while I see what's inside this place."

She stepped inside the chamber, considering the shadows stretching across a worn fabric sofa littered with objects. Cobwebs, filthy with dust and oil, hung from the candelabra. Scarlett would have believed that no one lived here if not for the footprints in the layers of dirt and dust on the floor. From their appearance, they were not all human. Did the black cat linger inside the manor, too?

Theodore said not a word as she ventured to the opposite side of the entryway to peer inside the library. The room was equally dusty and disused, and the far wall held a cabinet that stored leather-bound books, but some had spilled to the flooring as if a rat had swept them aside with its meanderings.

Despite the disorder, Scarlett couldn't help herself; she entered the room, cautiously treading across the planked flooring. Books were strewn everywhere, some with their pages spread open. Others lay in forlorn piles, ready to topple.

A half-dozen scissor chairs, upholstered with leather, were situated in various places. Scarlett moved past one that lay on its side as she advanced toward an intricately carved, large mahogany desk that sat at the far end of the room. Parchment, ink, quills, and more books littered the wooden top, and a fine layer of soot and dust spoiled its surface. A solid armchair rested behind the desk, and a wingback stood beside it with nary a speck of dust on its surface. Someone had used this chair.

She glanced at Theodore, who stood in the entrance hall watching her, taking in their surroundings. "Where are we, Theodore? Where have you brought me? This is not a prison. This is an abandoned house more fit for ghosts than men."

Scarlett had barely uttered the words when she heard someone stirring, moving across the flooring upstairs. She looked at the ceiling and imagined the step of a larger foot, and then a sliding, grinding motion, as if someone was dragging their foot across the flooring. The stab of a cane followed. She turned to Theodore and stated the obvious. "We are not alone."

"I don't hear anything. The house is giving rise to your imagination."

Scarlett retreated from the library, walking past Theodore and returning to the entry hall, leaving the mystery and its sounds behind. She grasped the wall, and leaned into the entranceway, sighting a staircase.

Step, slide, step, drag, and stab. Scarlett shivered, trying to be as quiet as the rats that lived inside this manor, hearing the sounds again. *Step…*

"Hello?" Scarlett called out hesitantly. "Is someone there?"

She heard a cackle, a rambling banter buried deep in a man's throat as someone took a step down the stairs. Theodore came up beside her and Scarlett leaned against him, not knowing what else to do. She searched his wary gray eyes, then considered the staircase, waiting for whoever lived in this rabble to receive them. Step, thump, creak, and stab went the sounds on the wood.

The mutterings began. "Who calls at this hour? 'Tis not the master, who I know is lighter on his feet. Who calls, I say, waking me from the dead of sleep? I will have their heads."

The man came closer. Step, thump, creak, and stab resounded on the stairs. Scarlett's heart beat faster. She stepped away from her warden and returned to the front door. She grasped the door handle, ready to flee, but Theodore grabbed her shoulders and ushered her back toward her fate, holding her close.

"You will not run," he mumbled, his tone decisive. "If you escape, 'tis I who will pay the price, and it's better you engage this fee, than me."

"You're a brute of a man, Theodore," Scarlett berated him, watching for their host, and soon sighting the bent stature of an elderly man on the upper landing. He wore a white sleep shirt and leaned heavily on a cane. He scrutinized each of them at length, carrying a lit taper on a tallow plate. The glow within the flame captured deep wrinkles etched within his forehead and a wide sneer forced his lips into a slim smile. He peered at them from the stairway. Scarlett stepped backward, brushing against Theodore's chest, with no desire to cross this old man. Surely, she should not fear one who moved so slowly, but sometimes slow-moving beings were all the more dangerous.

"What stranger arrives at our door? Who visits this manor, at this hour, uninvited?" he cackled again. "A lady, and her companion?"

A sinister chortle rolled away from his voice and a sour odor wafted to where Scarlett and Theodore stood. The man bent forward and stabbed his cane against the wood, descending toward them. "I thought I had seen the last of surprises, but a woman inside the manor, this is an interesting development."

Theodore cleared his voice and spoke before Scarlett could think to reply. "I have brought a traitor, a prisoner, to the master of this home. Queen Cynara decrees that the lord of Drum Manor take suitable care of this woman."

The elderly man stopped his shuffling in the middle of the stairs and struck the wood with his cane in a loud thump. His laughter stopped. Anger lit his expression.

"Queen Cynara, you say," he drawled, licking his lips as if to taste the sound of her title. "The chit has risen to higher ceilings? Hah! I remember this power-hungry vixen and her strange name. Regardless, the master has strict rules, and the first you best learn is never to utter the mistress's name in the manor. Unwise, most unwise."

Theodore urged Scarlett aside and stepped forward as if to force his insolent authority on the old man. "She is the queen, and the man who does not permit her name to be spoken aloud should fear the penalty of such a traitorous move."

Scarlett heard a door open at the rear of the house. She searched beyond the two men, just past the staircase toward a wooden threshold door, that eased aside so silently, she almost missed the sweep. Someone had entered the manor house.

Scarlett swallowed her fear, glimpsing a black shape penetrating the shadows. Someone moved along the hallway, and she listened to the soft footsteps padding closer. A tall man with broad, strong shoulders emerged from the gloom. Muscles rippled underneath the skin of his lean arms and legs as he slowly closed the space between them. He was dressed simply in a white lawn shirt that fell over black breeches, and she noted his chilling beauty. A stormy blue sea of fury consumed her attention and she was frightened by his disturbing gaze, set in a cascade of wild black hair that spilled around his shoulders.

Who is this man? A spellbinding current roused her awareness, causing convulsive shivers; she stumbled backward, her breath caught in her throat, and she found herself too afraid to inhale, exhale, or escape his ugly regard. He soon stood so close that she heard his aggressive huff. Long slim fingers swept a length of black hair away from his eyes. His hands moved to his hips. She didn't dare breathe, or move, or speak. She felt helpless, her vision trapped like a moth to the flame, held in the half-light of his soul. His eyes bore into her.

Theodore stepped forward, but the handsome stranger raised his hand for him to stop.

"Queen of the damned," he whispered in a deep, throaty

growl. "You'll do well to listen to my butler's warnings and never mention her name again."

The master's words might have been spoken for Theodore, but his firm expression remained on Scarlett. "I don't know who you are or why you've chosen to travel to this place. Neither do I care. You are trespassing. Leave my manor house, and take this woman with you."

The old man harrumphed. "I wouldn't be so hasty, Master."

"She must leave." he asserted, his right hand pulsing in and out of a fist. "I will accept no other alternative."

Scarlett quailed under this man's angry, cruel eyes. The blue in his eyes darkened, seeming to reflect the blacker shade of his soul, a regard she saw hiding within their depths and further reflected in the bite of his voice. She braced herself for violence, giving only a fleeting glance to Theodore's concerned expression.

"I have my orders—I must do as the queen commands." Theodore's voice faltered, wavered. "My life, sir, should I not deliver results. Her Majesty insisted I bring this woman to the lord of Drum Manor."

The butler snickered as if the situation presented amusement. "Your life visits another man's doorstep. You had best listen to your own heartbeat as the fearful warning emits a wiser thrum."

Scarlett breathed in her courage and let some of her fear escape in a deep sigh. "You may let this fool's puppet leave, but until this challenge is met, I will never know my freedom." She was embarrassed by the weak sound of her voice, now that she had the courage to speak.

The lord of Drum Manor stepped closer to her, a brooding expression on his face while breathing her essence. He glanced at her arm and Scarlett looked at her arm, too, noticing a scratch. It was minor, but drying blood had trickled from the wound.

He sniffed. "You must leave. It's not safe for you here."

Scarlett inched forward, trying to overcome her fear, praying for inner strength. She sensed her rising heartbeat, her figure swaying to dance in a kingly courtship, her pupils forming an oval yellow shape. This keener vision searched the tortured depths of his eyes, scanning his soul, recognizing a truth that mirrored her own sorrow. A need appeared to be wanting deep within him. Yet the man did not retreat; his brows merely rose in question and Scarlett broke their connection.

"I cannot leave," she cried out, her eyes downcast. After a moment, she explored his serious visage again and appealed to him further. "Can't you see, for better or worse—I am condemned to stay."

She could see that anger waged war inside his heart when his brows knit together in obvious frustration. She dared not breathe. "Who are you?" he demanded. "What wickedness has this evil woman sent to me?"

Theodore responded. "This woman has done the work of the devil."

"Silence," the lord shouted. "I will hear her name and her story from her own lips."

Scarlett braced herself, appealing to him with her palms held upward. "You may know me as Princess Scarlett. I am the eldest daughter of King Rickard and the true Queen

Regana. Recently, unfortunate circumstances caused my father's untimely death. His queen, having no use for his offspring, wanted me gone. Wanted me dead."

Theodore harrumphed. "She murdered her father. This woman is here to be punished for her crime against the kingdom."

"I bear some responsibility," Scarlett replied, biting her lip, "but I assure you, I did not murder my father."

The master didn't respond to Theodore; his attention focused solely on Scarlett. "I don't care what sins you've committed. We all commit our crimes. If you stay here, I won't be able to protect you, and you could perish. I don't make these statements for my own amusements. I am telling you the truth."

Scarlett sighed and raked her hands through her reddish-brown hair in frustration. She wanted to scream. She wanted to tear the earth apart in her agony, but all that was left to her was to appeal to this man.

"Do not try to frighten me, for I might also live. Do you hear me, sir?" Scarlett said, whimpering. She threw her arms wide, daring his scrutiny. "I might also live."

A naked pause permeated the dank air. Scarlett didn't know what more she could say in her defense. If only he would smile, he would be beautiful. He studied her intimately, perusing her facial features. What did he hope to find? A woman's sorrow would fall deeper into darkness with each discovery. The old man, the butler, finally broke the uncomfortable silence.

"'Tis true." He descended the final steps to the entryway, a sly smile painted on his old face. "The woman might also live. An interesting position we find ourselves in, Master Nicolai, and one a wise man, such as yourself, should ponder."

Clearly frustrated, the lord of the manor glanced away, and then met her expression again. "Lady Scarlett—Princess, if this is your title—I know this man brought you here, but he can easily be taken care of and you will be free to leave. Free to go about your life. I assure you, no harm will come to you, but only if you leave this manor."

"But where would I go? It's the dead of night, my lord, and I have faced a harrowing journey. I wish circumstances were different. I do see your displeasure at my arrival, however, even if I had the freedom to leave, where would I go? Where do you propose my journey take me? I've only known Camden Castle and now this, this befouled place. Queen Cynara has placed my life in your hands, and for better or worse, I feel safer with you, a stranger to me, than that witch."

"You know not what you ask for."

She peeked at him, tears filling her eyes. "I am weary from my travels. My soul weeps from the journey I have been forced to endure. Send this nasty buffoon on his way and show me to my final resting place. Death is an ending, sir, and the afterlife does not scare me anymore."

Chapter Fifteen

LORD NICOLAI GRAYDON

No man who called himself a man could stand before a woman's raw emotion and not sympathize with the reason for her distress. Beholding the princess's distraught expression wrenched at his heartstrings. The anguish glistened in her eyes like a lake of pent-up tears whose dam threatened to release, to secrete emotion along the cheeks of her attractive face. Nicolai didn't want to see her cry. The contrast to his own grief was too difficult to bear as he understood how life begat sorrow, and how grief could ravage the human soul. As days changed to months and months to years, one's distressing circumstances could weaken even the strongest heart.

Oh yes, he understood much more than the tears leaking from her eyes.

He had known the same hopelessness, loneliness and weariness, a wasteland was buried within the darkest reaches of his miserable, cursed soul. As the princess had said, for better or worse, he had no choice but to accept this woman as his guest.

"Princess Scarlett," he said, his tone tender, "I'm not without compassion. You may stay the night. Permit me to introduce my butler. Bensen will show you to your bedchamber."

She nodded at him, lowering her head. "Thank you, my lord."

"As you wish, Master Nicolai," Bensen said, smiling. "This way, Princess Scarlett, daughter of a king."

PRINCESS SCARLETT

SCARLETT TRAIPSED across dirt-packed floorboards at the butler's urging, not only because she was obliged to follow him, but also for the reason that life circumstances sometimes forced oneself to accept transitions to grim places, places in which disturbing people, like this lord, lived, too. While passing the lord of the manor, she contemplated his dour expression. The uneasiness and unspoken worries caused her head to ache. A nervous tension threatened to spill her to the ground while wondering where the aged butler was ushering her to within this wretched manor.

She sensed the lord watching her as she walked past him. His stare burned into her person as he scrutinized her with unspoken concern and perhaps curiosity as well. He didn't have the courtesy to wish her a good night. Instead, he offered further instructions to his butler.

"Meet me in the library after you have seen to your duty. I will retire there now."

"What about myself?" Theodore asked.

"The hour grows late," the lord grumbled, "and my patience has been sorely tested. You'll find a stable behind the house. Although the stalls have not housed a horse in years, you and your mares will find the quarters comfortable. Go there now and leave me in peace."

Nicolai gave her one final glance as Theodore escaped the house, and then the lord of the manor pivoted on his naked feet and strode toward the library. Scarlett wouldn't think of this darkly handsome man. She had other worries to consider, and right now the need for a bed overruled other concerns. Exhaustion compelled her to shadow the butler's footpath toward the grand staircase.

Holding the lit taper, she matched the butler's elderly pace as he struggled to climb the stairs, while fighting her own exhaustion. With the apparent weakness in the man's legs, each step upward became a long, drawn-out affair. She became curious of her surroundings, and in particular the three portraits lining the walls above the right handrail. The golden frames glowed with richness, and the handsome individuals, wearing distinctive clothing and worn expressions, were captured with precise brushstrokes.

A stern gentleman dressed in black with broad shoulders, appeared irritated. Scarlett could see the anger in the way his brows knit together. The next portrait captured the images of two children, a boy and a girl. Each lacked a sense of joy with their thin lips shut tight in sadness, as if their toys or candy had been taken away. Finally, a woman with a slight smile wore a flowing dress of brilliant sapphire blue. She appeared to stare at Scarlett in longing from her chaise lounge. Her portrait was the most compelling. The artist had captured the light within her bluish-gray eyes with such precise brush strokes that the image seemed to stare at her with a steadfast mien, regardless of where Scarlett stood on the stair.

When Bensen glanced at her, he caught her staring at the portraits. He paused on the stair-tread. "The painting you find captivating is the image of Countess Leonie. The portrait should have been placed beneath the earl, which would have been more appropriate, but the lady, more a dog in heat than a countess, rose to the greed of grandness and luxury. Much to the earl's despair, she came close to bankrupting his beloved heritage home. Look at him, his image above the bottom step, his portrait beneath his children. I'm sure in death he is still aggrieved for his taste in women. But she was a beauty, wouldn't you agree? It's said the painter thought so, too."

Scarlett didn't respond while climbing a stair, following the strange butler.

"The painting in the middle shows their children. Sadly, the earl and the countess's match was not a love affair, and the countess produced only one daughter and a son. The boy is Nicolai. A handsome lad, even then."

Scarlett paused to study the image of the boy for the longest time; she only glanced at his sister dressed in white, who seemed lost in the portrait beside her brother. Bensen stopped his struggle long enough to let her study Nicolai's boyish image. A young man with his dimpled chin, he had been handsome with his dark hair curling at the nape of his neck. He wore such a serious expression, much like his father whose portrait rested beneath the children's.

Scarlett's curiosity helped her to find her voice. "Is Nicolai the lord of the house now?"

"Oh yes, he certainly is, but although he became the fifth Earl of Drum Manor at the death of his father, the title has brought him little joy. You may refer to him as His Lordship, Nicolai Graydon."

"Lord Nicolai," she whispered, tasting the sound of his name on her lips. "When did he become so grave?"

Bensen harrumphed. "A long time ago, Princess, when he attempted to save his family home in the only way a man understands. The sins of the father were passed on to his son. The affair ended gravely, I'm afraid."

Scarlett contemplated this revelation as they approached a large ivory door. The butler reached for a golden knob. He motioned for her to pass by him and enter the room.

Barely inside the bedchamber, Scarlett gaped at its beauty. Despite the smell and obvious disuse, the room was lavish. "I'm astonished you would permit a stranger to retire in such an elaborate bedchamber. The room is grand."

Bensen's attention fixated somewhere beyond the chamber. "But of course, after all, you are a princess, and as such, you are entitled to luxury."

"It's strange to hear you speak it all the same, knowing the reason that I'm here," Scarlett said with a yawn. "Bensen, who did this bedchamber belong to?"

"You have the former countess to thank for your comfort. She owned every extravagance. This room has not suffered neglect like the rest of the manor, as the door has not been opened in years, thus not permitting much to get inside to disturb the furnishings. It's much the same as—that night, long ago."

Scarlett contemplated the butler's wrinkled old face and noted the discomfort creasing his brow. She saw that his mind was drifting elsewhere as his demeanor quieted to a painful lethargy. She supposed he was as weary as she felt. Scarlett glanced away when he caught her staring.

"After I leave you, you must bolt the door," he stated, "if you have a care for your life."

Scarlett assessed his serious expression. *What did this warning mean?* He stepped backward, closed the door, and left her standing beyond the entranceway, alone to contemplate exactly what bolting the door implied. She didn't disregard the advice. She reached for the latch and slid the bolt home.

She couldn't say his warning surprised her. She knew unseen dangers lurked inside this ghastly manor. She could sense them, smell them; parts of her vibrated with the awareness. She didn't want to breathe the stench in, but she would, if only to save her life again. Sighing, she pondered the chamber.

Scarlett considered the ceiling and let out one big sigh. The flame she held quivered from her breath and illuminated a lady's bedchamber that breathed as much beauty as the silence mourned despair. She didn't know what she had expected when arriving at this house, but staying in a room as opulent as this one, regardless of the dust, had not been one of her considerations.

She leaned against the whitewashed door, permitting its

solid strength to hold her weight while contemplating the opulent furniture, or what must have been exquisite at one time and would be still if someone had not permitted the beauty to spoil.

A pungent odor filled her nostrils, an odor similar to the rest of the house. The room could use an airing out to rid the air of the mold and mildewed stench, but as Scarlett moved away from the door, stepping toward a large canopied bed, it occurred to her a servant's hand had not cleaned or dusted this room in a long time. She walked farther across the space to a beautiful dressing table, cream-colored and edged with golden leaf. She saw her reflection in a trifold mirror with ornate gilded edges that glistened in the wavering candlelight. Scarlett reflected that she appeared beautiful as she stared at her image in the mercuric glass.

Few articles lay on the surface of the dressing table. Scarlett fingered a porcelain vase whose floral bouquet had once been vibrant and alive, but now hung sad and forgotten in death. Yellow roses had withered to faded ivory stems. Some yellow blooms had once stretched their petals beautifully in a circular swath but now appeared so brittle, Scarlett knew if she dared to touch their edges they would crumble. Whatever occasion their blossoms were meant to promise had likely been broken, too. Blue delphiniums combined with white baby's breath were equally withered, and tiny bits of blue and white lay on the ivory surface like confetti, neglected, forgotten, and dead.

It ended gravely, Scarlett remembered the butler saying. Clearly, as evidenced by this room and the rest of the house, misfortune had caused this ruin. She smelled death at every turn.

Scarlett picked up a woman's silver brush, complete with blonde hair still twisted between the bristles. She noticed an ivory jug and basin with washing cloths laid out beside them as if they still waited for the lady of the manor to use their linen softness in her toilette. Scarlett replaced the brush. Who might this woman have been? Surely not the Countess Leonie, whose hair had been painted a rich chocolate brown.

Tired, Scarlett sighed, pivoting to reflect on the dour bed. The headboard matched the golden mirror of the dressing table. For a certainty, this had been Countess Leonie's bedchamber, but another woman had shared this space, too. Perhaps the mystery woman had left the brush. But why? What had happened to her that she would leave her personal belongings behind? How interesting that this was the chamber where she would sleep.

On edge, she sighed, took a tiny puff of air into her lungs then walked to the closest side of the massive bed. Covered with dust, the coverlet was the palest sky blue. She touched the fabric and grime coated her fingertips. She leaned against the mattress, feeling its support, and noted that the cushioned layers might offer some comfort. In its newness, the several layers of mattress would have made a queen comfortable.

Scarlett shifted away from the bed while wiping the dust on her hands to the woolen blanket still covering her shoulders, but some happenings could not be wiped away as easily. The bedding required a thorough laundering. She winced, gritting her teeth, since she would have to sleep inside these wasted sheets. She shook her head in despair.

No longer was the coverlet suitable for royalty, but she wasn't a princess of royal blood any longer, only a prisoner disguised as a guest. She'd have to climb in this decaying bed to yield to her rest. She wanted to sleep, but she dared not close her eyes.

The room smelled of mold and mildew and ages that had passed. This space had not been used in a long time, left to neglect, to die like the flowers—much like the rest of the manor.

She walked to an end table beside the bed and placed the candle atop its ivory surface. The candlelight danced on the tapestries and shimmered in threads of gold. Ladies with their beaus at garden parties seemed to watch her where she stood. 'Twas a work of art.

A timepiece on the wall still held the hour and minutes of 7:36 p.m., with its weight still and silent. Time had stopped turning in this manor house. Why?

Why should she reflect on the meaning of a manor's history when she had her own fate to consider? She held the key to her own prison. She could run if she wanted to, unlatch and slide the bolt, open the door and flee. But where could she escape to? If she had a place to run, how would she get there? On foot, she would never survive.

"Why did you send me here, Cynara?" she mused aloud. "What is your plan and who is this lord? He wants me gone but I cannot leave. He might be alive, but death lives inside his eyes. If I touch him, he'll break like the flowers on the dressing table. Death infuses this house. I sense it. Feel it. I'm suffocating within this space— I will die here."

The absence of sound or noise exuded the mansion's long-suffering for a moment, but when she heard telltale signs of someone's approach, she nearly jumped.

Step, thump, creak, and stab.

The clatter, which she now knew was the thump of a cane and the drag of the butler's damaged leg, moved toward her room. He soon knocked on the door. After his warning, should she unbolt the door? Curiosity moved her to take a risk. Wrapping the blanket tighter around her shoulders, she opened the door a pinch and peeked out. The butler stood awkwardly, balancing a covered silver tray on his left hand.

"I thought you might be hungry," he whispered. "We don't have much, but what we have we will share. You must pardon my skills. A gentle lady has not shared this manor since—well, since that night, a long time ago."

Scarlett opened the door wider, her curiosity overcoming reason. "That night?" Scarlett inquired.

"'Tis nothing but a sad story of misfortune. I must go to bed. I will take my leave and wish you a good night."

"Thank you," Scarlett whispered, accepting the tray.

"Remember to bolt the door. Sleep well, if you can."

Her fingers shook while closing the door. He seemed to notice her fear and reached to her with his aged and gnarled fingers before thinking better of the gesture and stepping away. "Good night, Princess Scarlett. Sleep well."

"Thank you for your kindness."

Scarlett closed the door, placed the tray next to the burning candle on the side table, and then returned to the door to lock it. She let out a sigh, walked to the bed, and pulled the coverlet off. She shook off the grime as best as she could, sneezing when the dust floated in the air, then replaced the cover haphazardly. Fortunately, the pillows were tucked under the bedding, and although she knew they would smell, at least they were not covered in filth. She puffed them up and arranged them neatly, and then placed the woolen blanket in the side table drawer. Climbing into the bed, she grabbed the covered tray and removed the lid. Under the dome, carefully plated, lay bread, cheese, and three strips of dried venison.

Why? Why would they feed me?

Her stomach rumbled, and she did not think to further question the generosity. She grasped a square of white cheddar and placed the morsel inside her mouth. The taste of goat cheese brought a welcome relief to her hunger. A goblet of white wine rested on the tray as well, and although it had been diluted with water, she gratefully sipped the drink while nibbling the cheese, not permitting the tiny tidbits escaping her lips to go to waste. When she finished, she placed the empty plate under the silver dome and left the bed to remove her red surcoat.

Scarlett folded the overcoat and placed it with her mother's purse in the side table drawer, wearing her thin and worn linen kirtle. She wrinkled her nose as unpleasant odors greeted her nostrils again, but now that her hunger was satisfied, fatigue overcame suspicion and she returned to the bed. She slipped between the sheets and buried herself within the folds. For fear of fire, she blew out the candle, losing the light. She stared about the darkened room, imagining what the night shadows might bring. She squeezed her eyes shut tight, imagining the mental image of an ivory rose, slumped in death. She took a shuttering breath, twisted deeper in the bedding, and pulled the covers over her head.

Frightened, she lay inside a cocoon of bedsheets, listening for movements inside the manor, listening to her breathing, but fatigue soon overcame conscious thought and she succumbed to a restless sleep.

Chapter Sixteen

LORD NICOLAI GRAYDON

Candlelight flickered on the library walls, casting shadows on the bookcases, derelict possessions, and a silent man whose memories were lost within the library's rotten space. Nicolai sat on his chair, leaning against a grimy writing bureau with his head held in his hands, his elbows resting on the desk's surface, and his face contorted with frustration. He loosened one hand from his aching temple and reached forward to finger filthy books and scattered parchment papers, whose words were so marred with dust and dirt, the passages no longer held meaning. Finally, he grabbed a quill and studied the ruddy edges held between his fingers. Regrettably, the feather held so much burn, it no longer had any semblance of a peacock's tail.

"Dear lord," he worried aloud. "How has your life come to this?"

Sighing, he leaned against the chair rest and stretched his aching back. He slid his naked feet underneath the desk and stretched them, too, while examining the quill held in his right hand. As if the quill were the fault for his disrepute, he sucked in a breath, grimaced, and threw the barb across the library.

"Nicolai Graydon," he muttered into the empty space, "you miserable sod, you were almost a great man. Almost."

Nicolai knew he had succumbed to his own ego. Nevertheless, he had also come close to building his stature as a grand gentleman. His hopes and dreams were dashed away with one wave of a witch's hand. Now he sat with his ass cheeks buried in shat and his hands stuck in a quagmire of filth he could not wipe away.

"I have no one to blame but myself," he whispered, recognizing his own truth.

Since the first transformation, he had permitted his own downfall and subsequent neglect to take its toll on his life. He reflected on the layers of dust soiling his once beautiful library, from a mud-caked floor to a ceiling that had changed from a pasty white to a tarnished buttercream. Books were strewn about the room with their yellowing pages and broken bindings. And spider webs, whose threads had long ago turned black, hung from the ceiling candelabra.

"Sixteen years have passed since my life was stolen," Nicolai reflected, "and each year the filth increases, layer upon dirty layer."

He might as well have climbed inside a coffin and committed the box to an early grave since his life was already buried in a hole, gasping for its next breath with no hope of survival.

Nicolai had become a man who permitted his mind to linger in depravity. But now a guest had arrived at his doorstep, reminding him of a time lost, a time when his life had been worth living. Her arrival brought discomfort, since he couldn't see a positive view of his future. Nicolai Graydon, an older man now, sitting on an old oaken chair with his fingers tapping on the armrest. *How had his life come to this?*

He had not forgotten the woman who had buried him in this filthy ash. *The whoresbane of his existence,* Cynara would appreciate the changes her witchcraft had wrought. A once luxurious home, now gloomy with spider webs stretching across the ceiling, their web layers as intricate as the branches of despair threading throughout his mind. He stood so deep in the quagmire that black creatures, such as spiders and ravens, were commonplace. He didn't know if he could escape this inky black night. From a self-created hole in his mind, the sun was merely a blip on the horizon, and he was too weary to search for the light.

Cynara had brought him to this place. As if this torture was not enough, she had sent him more grief in the form of a woman. God damn the mistress to the Netherworld for all eternity for the pain she inflicted. The evil enchantress knew damn well what would happen should he hunger for this woman, and Cynara had sent Princess Scarlett for this ugly reason alone.

"Master Nicolai," Bensen entreated from the hallway. "Our guest has been laid to rest in the lady's bedchamber."

Nicolai growled, circling his fingers through the dust on his desk. "Our guest? The lady's bedchamber, you say. I have not considered that place since Alexandra vanished in a halo of light. And now a sweet temptation waits for me in a worm-infested bed? What am I to do now, Bensen?"

Nicolai regarded his butler's wistful expression, seeing a myriad of emotions creasing his old face. Not responding right away, Bensen sighed, then placed his bony hands on a cane to support his weight. The man had accepted the thunder streaks covering his left arm, imprinting a lightning pattern that stretched from his neck to his fingertips, marring his skin with a lasting tattoo.

Although Nicolai wasn't to blame for the scarring, he regretted his culpability in the wrongdoing.

"Hmm," Bensen hedged, pondering the question. "A difficult situation presents a puzzle."

Nicolai watched Bensen's stronger leg step forward. He pulled the other crippled weight behind him. Without his cane as a crutch, he would not be able to walk, but although he struggled, a hidden motivation kept him moving.

"A puzzle," Nicolai replied, scowling, "and what am I supposed to do with this puzzle when the picture loses its shape and is torn into bloody pieces?"

Bensen grimaced, his eyebrows raised while hobbling closer. "Master Nicolai, I have no idea what actions should be taken, but I find her arrival to this house an interesting development. You should reflect on the possibilities."

Nicolai shook his head. "You know what I'm capable of, Bensen. The only way to keep her safe is to keep this panther locked in a cage. I don't intend to be confined inside my own home. I once had need of a woman, any rich woman to solve my financial needs. But now as I consider the charms of this princess, the only desire that comes to mind is the hunger for food. She has to leave the manor house immediately."

Bensen finally reached a chair near Nicolai. He collapsed

against it, sighing painfully. Climbing up and down the stairs was not easy on the old man.

"There are two problems with her leaving."

Nicolai sat up straighter, taller. He fixed his butler with a keen stare. "What problems? If I send this woman away, do you think Cynara can threaten the panther already marked with a black curse? I am what I am, and with the exception of the queen, no mortal person can fix me. I do not fear this problem."

Bensen raised his eyebrows in enquiry. "After years of punishing yourself, do you know everything? Perhaps your wisdom speaks the truth and no further trials shall test you, but you must consider that this gentle-born lady could be the option to gain your freedom. Master Nicolai, she could be the possibility we have both been waiting for."

Nicolai harrumphed and pulled his fingers through his black hair before looking directly at Bensen's silvery-blue eyes.

"An option? You believe this princess, this woman named Scarlett, could be the girl to save me from this curse?" Nicolai shook his head, laughing apprehensively. "You speak as if she's a liberator, perhaps a redeeming savior, too. It's doubtful that anyone could save me from this misery, and I don't think Cynara, the woman who would do me harm, would send a boon for my salvation."

Bensen cackled, then openly laughed, his breath causing the dust to flutter about the room. Perhaps his smile transformed to an angry leer because of the man's own inner turmoil and frustration. Whatever the reason for his rising anger, he banged his cane noisily against the floor, and the loud smack garnered Nicolai's attention.

"But why would a wicked witch send such a vixen now, Nicolai, all these years later? There must be a reason."

"It's obvious. She wants me to kill her."

"Yes, of course, but think about the implications. Why does the Queen of Curses desire this virgin mare to trot along a new trail?"

"I don't know. What man could comprehend the madness that is Cynara? I do question why she couldn't take care of the princess herself. Surely she has the power to do so."

"Mayhap she believes the spell weaved on you still controls a bit held between your teeth. Perhaps this situation is no more than a bridle that will drive her sordid problem to greener pastures. A critical issue must be faced here, one that we must ponder. If this wicked woman wants our guest delivered to the Netherworld, then the princess is more valuable to us alive than dead."

"I would never intentionally hurt the princess, Bensen. But you saw her; she's a gorgeous creature. The temptation concerns me."

"Don't think about the appeal, Nicolai. Think instead on the sudden visit. Do you believe this woman could break the curse? If you can overcome the power of the curse, you might be able to end the enchantment."

Nicolai placed his head in his hands. "I'm beyond such hope. I stopped searching for such a likelihood a long time ago, and I can't bear to think about the possibilities, for the disappointment would be too difficult to face."

"At least you'd know that you tried?"

Nicolai took a deep breath and faced Bensen. "I don't believe any scheme can break this curse. It's been too long, too many years have passed. I don't want to talk about it any longer. You know what happens when my excitement grows. The princess will become prey to my hunger-starved eyes, and I will rip out her throat. I'll eat my fill of black pleasure and plunge my soul deeper inside this black curse. I don't see a way out."

"If the mark be the means, Nicolai, then so be the carnage. I can't help but ponder the possibilities, and there's only one way to glean what might be possible, which means the princess must be our 'guest'. I've always believed we would find a way to escape this madness, and if sex encourages your hunger, love might be the pleasure to break the spell. At least play the game, Nicolai," Bensen said, pleading. "If you don't move your pawn, there's no way to catch the queen."

"That's ridiculous." Nicolai slapped his hand against the desk and dust scattered in the air. "This hex can't be broken. I don't want to play these games. It hurts too much to lose. Allow me to accept my fate gracefully, and get this woman out of my house so I can live in peace."

Bensen banged his cane against the floor a second time. Nicolai winced at the sound, then watched a weary butler stand. "If you're not prepared to gamble with the opportunity, then we are doomed to the Netherworld, my friend, but until the fire licks at our souls, I will take the risk. I had no control over the lightning that marked my skin, but this, this opportunity is delicious. You must take your chances, Nicolai, in order to discover what might be possible. And I for one would chase this young woman, doing all that is necessary, if it means breaking the curse."

"Taste," Nicolai mused, pondering the girl upstairs in his

previous bride-to-be's bed. "Taste is the problem. I can smell her sweetness and well imagine the strawberry tart I desire to drive my teeth into. You think I don't want for affection? I watch the ravens preen and wish with all my being a kind hand might deliver a solution for this curse. But each morning when the sun rises, I find myself buried within a cocoon of filthy sheets red with blood, and I realize the only love I'll ever yearn for is the coppery taste that comes from dripping meat. There will never be an end to this curse. Never!"

Bensen stepped shakily forward. He appeared angry. He stepped the few feet to Nicolai, braced himself, then brought his cane above his head and swung hard, striking Nicolai against his right hand. A resounding thwack echoed throughout the library.

"Damn you, Bensen!" Nicolai yelled, rising from the desk abruptly, his chair falling loud and hard in the sudden rush. His pupils changed to coppery-yellow ovals, disturbed and angry, his head flattening with the possibility of changing into his panther form. He crouched and bent his neck forward, but somehow, he remained a man.

"Why did you do that?" he yelled, holding his aching hand, rubbing his throbbing fingers. "Why did you strike me?"

The old butler was not afraid. He had the audacity to step closer to his master, larger than life, tapping the cane against his thigh with a self-assured mien that angered him.

"You refused to listen to my guidance, disregarding what I was trying to say, and I needed to make a point."

"A point?" Nicolai gaped. "You high-handed fool, it seems

like you would strike me a second time. How dare you! I should beat you for your cocky attitude. But I need you; I can't survive without your good company."

"Can you survive not considering my advice? I have never led you down the wrong path. Does your hand hurt, Master?"

"You damn well know it does."

Satisfied, Bensen nodded, his lips pressed into a slim smirk that came nowhere near a smile.

"Good. Nicolai, it's about damned time you felt something, anything, even your own pain. Change is on this house. I can sense the supernatural stirring in the air, but if you are content to permit this filth to fester around you, then so be it. I for one will not go down without a fight, and this fight has been long in the coming."

"Lead on," Nicolai harrumphed. "I'm sure you already have a strategy in mind."

"Let me tell you," he snickered, "a woman rests in the lady's bedchamber, the room that should have been used for your new wife. Life is how we look at the clouds and dream, but if you refuse to recognize an opportunity resting near to your nose, you'll never know a moment's peace. Nicolai, a woman might yet scratch your cursed back."

Bensen turned away from him and ambled across the library, leaving the way he had come. Nicolai stepped toward him while considering the possibilities his butler had mentioned. "Where are you going, Bensen?"

"To bed, Master Nicolai. You had best be taking your rest, too. There is much to be done, much to consider. A rested mind will help you understand much more in the morning.

But you might want to stop by a lady's bedchamber and peer inside at the possibilities."

Nicolai placed his hands on his hips. His fingers still hurt. "You're crazy, old man."

Bensen pulled his leg across the flooring, stabbed with his cane, and slid his weak leg forward. When he reached the entranceway, he leaned against the molding and stared at Nicolai with a determined expression.

"And get rid of the guard. Send him to his queen or share him with your ravens. Just make sure he leaves the manor."

It wasn't lost on Nicolai that the butler was now instructing the lord, and he was damn passionate about his position, too. Perhaps he should listen to the wise, old codger.

"Hmm. I thought to torture him, perhaps steal his horse and wagon or force him to do chores, which sadly have been lacking of late, but you know best. I'll return him to Cynara in the morning. Perhaps I shall send the witch a lock of my black hair as a gift."

"Good night, Master Nicolai."

"Bensen?"

"What?" he growled.

"Thank you," Nicolai said. "Thank you, my trusted and loyal friend."

Chapter Seventeen

LORD NICOLAI GRAYDON

Nicolai sat at his desk contemplating the conversation that had taken place with his butler, and for the first time in sixteen years, he looked past the filth. *Was it possible?* Could the arrival of a gentle-born lady alter his circumstances? Bensen's insight regarding the princess's arrival, and the potential implications that could alter his future, gave him much to ponder.

Nevertheless, as far as Nicolai was concerned, Bensen's theory blew hot air. A cure to the black curse seemed unlikely, regardless of the feminine circumstances, and he didn't welcome exploring the possibilities if ending the curse couldn't be achieved. Even so, his butler's confident tone and the forcefulness of his convictions, piqued Nicolai's curiosity.

Can it be done? Could he rid himself of this ill-fortune? Could the curse be destroyed? If the current circumstances inside his household posed a favorable solution to end this enchantment, he had to consider all options.

The night had stretched past the midnight hour, and he longed for his bed. He rose from his desk with a yawn.

Exhaustion drove him toward the entrance hall and the stairs leading to his bedchamber. He climbed each tread with a dark-haired woman firmly rooted in his thoughts. When he reached the top riser, he paused to glance at a closed ivory door. A woman lay in the bed beyond the wooden frame. The scent of her lifeblood filled his nostrils, and he wished he could turn the handle and step inside the bedchamber, but the door would be bolted. Bensen had likely advised the act for her own safety. He sighed, grabbed the handle of a more masculine wood-grained door, and entered his own bedchamber.

Nicolai took off his shirt while walking toward a side table beside a large four-poster bed, then tossed the old linen on a chair. He removed his black breeches and discarded them in the same place. He climbed underneath a quilt decorated with a strap-work pattern of golden acanthus leaves and tried to relax into sleep, but his mind buzzed with possibilities and he tossed and turned, unable to find his rest.

Too close, Princess Scarlett rested nearby.

He lay on his back with his eyes closed, but he could sense her, smell her in the bedchamber beside his. Could almost hear the beat of her heart. He turned onto his side, only to visualize her face in his dreams. Frustrated with himself, he gave up on sleep and climbed out of bed to sit in a chair, where he sat, tapping his fingers on the armrest, staring at the secret place in the wall that would lead him to her. Finally, after running his fingers through his hair, he stood and walked toward the floor-to-ceiling mirror.

Standing before the secret entrance, Nicolai stared at his sorry reflection. A man without hope gazed back at him, appearing older and graver, as if his mirror image knew this midnight adventure would amount to disappointment. However, Bensen had planted a seed. In the hope his prospects might grow, Nicolai forced himself to contemplate options he had not considered before, or at least to examine the true motive behind why this woman had been delivered to his home in the first place.

Nicolai studied the upper corners where the reflecting glass gave way. Would the hinges release for him? A long time had passed since the latches had swung free. Held at the top center and bottom of a golden-edged mirror, metal grated on metal as he struggled to release one and then the other latch. The mirror was attached to a massive frame, so once the springs were free, it took some strength for him to pull the door open. He paused to catch his breath while peering at a dark, dank hallway.

He was keen to find the lady's bedchamber and the woman who rested there. So great was his interest, he stepped inside the cramped space, a dimension not much wider than his shoulders, and shuffled along the narrow corridor. Damn crazy idea, he told himself, sliding forward. However, side-stepping along the space empowered him, if for no other reason than the movement garnered a new adventure. He felt the wall crevices with his hands and swept away old webs. He imagined the possibilities, however slim, and what he would do if he were ever free, and as he crept along the secret hallway, he dared to hope. What if Bensen was right?

Princess Scarlett

Deep in a dream, Scarlett heard the scratching. A wicked rat, with a long twitching nose, rose on two dirty feet. It's tiny paws rustled here and there, discerning the wall's surface. Not finding so much as a small crumb, the rodent continued its pursuit along the hallway. Of course, the animal tried to be secretive as his tiny paws took him first this way and then that. Just a rat in the wall, Scarlett mused within her dreams, not at all surprised. Leave me alone, she begged, willing herself to sleep. The rat could not hurt her as long as it scurried inside the wall.

The shadow cloaked within Scarlett awakened. A keen sense stirred within her belly, verifying hunger. With each flick of a tongue, a serpent could smell a rat. It liked the rat and knew precisely where to find the tasty morsel. Uncoiling from a soft wrapper, the cobra princess moved within the sheets and soon slid from the bed to the dusty floor, crawling toward the mirror.

Lord Nicolai Graydon

It didn't take long to reach the end of the corridor. Nicolai soon stood at the backside of the reflecting glass that matched the silver mercury in his bedchamber. Each mirror had its vices, and he searched for that special place where seeing into the chamber would be optimal, but dust streaked the surface and needed to be cleaned away to make his viewing possible. Nicolai wiped at the surface, stifling a cough and wrinkling his nose as he worked away the dirty layers. When the area was clean enough that he could see through the glass, he gasped. He stepped backward, surprised, when a hand met his inspection.

The princess stood directly on the other side. His curiosity was piqued, and he stepped forward to find her again, but she lifted her hand and he saw her golden-brown eyes, lit with a long yellow stripe through the center of her pupils.

"Who are you? What are you?" Nicolai asked, whispering. Her strange eyes peered at him. Perhaps Cynara had cursed this woman, too, but why? What did her strange eyes imply? He could tell that Scarlett knew someone was standing on the opposite side of the reflecting glass.

She shifted closer, perhaps searching for the lord who hid on the other side of the barrier. Her hand slid up and down the glass, as if searching for a way to join him inside the passageway. Unafraid, he crept closer and placed his right hand close to her curious fingers. Mere inches kept their touch apart. He stood so close to her scrutiny; he witnessed the odd color of her eyes. He noted their shape while studying her petite nose and full mouth.

Her tongue dotted out and licked her lips. He was hidden in the darkness, but the action intrigued him.

What curse had Cynara placed on this princess to draw her so near to his hiding spot? Did this woman mean to finish him off for good? Could this be the real reason Cynara had sent Scarlett here, to end his suffering by ending his life? He knew he must be right. His first instinct had been to remove this woman from his manor, but now he was stuck seeing this cursed game through to its conclusion.

He withdrew from the mirror, but her observation followed his retreat. *How strange.*

Yellow slits within golden-brown orbs seemed to find him in the dark, but he knew that seeing him through this secretive barrier was impossible.

"What type of curse is this, Cynara? What further black plague have you sent me?"

Chapter Eighteen

PRINCESS SCARLETT

Snuggled inside the coverlet, Scarlett stretched her arms above her head and flexed her fingers, opening her eyes to a new morning. She took a deep breath, feeling good, though dark memories lingered from the night before. She wished she could remember what had occurred in her dreams, but her dreams were gone, forgotten. She glanced at the windows at the foot of the bed, where thin streaks of sunlight strained to penetrate the closed draperies.

Scarlett rubbed her eyes, and then climbed out of bed. Yawning, she walked lazily toward the light.

When she reached the draperies, she nudged them open, creating a tiny gap in the folds, and peered outside at a bright new day. When her eyes adjusted to the light, she surveyed an ocean view where thousands of tiny diamonds sparkled across a blue sea. White-capped waves gently rolled toward the shoreline. Last night, she hadn't known what to expect in the morning, but a landscape as serene and beautiful as this one had not been her anticipation.

She turned away from the draperies. The world outside glowed with beauty, but her situation inside this room had not changed. Flowers lay dead and forgotten in their vase, and dust and mold still offended her nostrils. Stagnant, the air barely flowed. What had happened here?

She pulled the draperies open fully to let in the light. Dust fluttered from the top railing, and she sneezed as the particles floated above her nose. Two windows shared the same wall, so she repeated the action on the opposite side, surprised to learn that the second space did not hold a window at all, but a doorway to a balcony. She fussed with the latch until it jostled free, all but stumbling over the ledge in her eagerness to get outside.

The balcony was full of leaves and broken branches from years of disuse, but Scarlett didn't care about the mess. She walked toward the stone railing and grasped a thick balustrade in her hands. Leaning toward the water, she breathed the salty sea air. The warm sunlight felt so good on her face that she didn't see or hear her host until he stifled a cough.

"The building's old and crumbling. Be careful where you lean."

Scarlett gasped then pivoted to face the bearer of the voice, but she remained against the railing. His lordship sat in a lounge chair wrapped in a woolen blanket.

"Seems solid enough to me," Scarlett responded. "But perhaps all is not as it appears."

While waiting for Nicolai to reply, she focused on his eyes, eyes that mirrored the color of the sea. The sunlight illuminated his fatigue, and she observed dark circles penetrating the hollows beneath his eyes. Despite his weariness, Scarlett determined the man possessed a handsome if not formidable air.

"'Tis funny," he whispered, coming to his feet. "Just yesterday, I enjoyed this view without encumbrance. One day later—one evening—the view has changed. If my eyes do not deceive me, a woman shares the balcony."

A nervous giggle trickled from Scarlett's lips like a silly schoolgirl's weakness, but the sound lacked any taste for good humor and she didn't know why she did it. "I suppose it's as awkward for you as it is uncomfortable for me. I've clearly invaded your territory."

"If only you knew," he grumbled, tolerating her presence.

"Lord Nicolai, only a moment ago I admired the ocean, but now I worry you'll toss me over the railing and out to sea, to be swept away like one of these lonely leaves. But I'm hardly worth the effort. I probably wouldn't die."

He grimaced. "Is that why the queen sent you here, because you wouldn't die?"

"Precisely," Scarlett replied, crossing her fingers in the hope he would believe her lie. She had to craft her idea carefully, as her survival would be easier if the lord of Drum Manor believed she couldn't die. But Scarlett knew better—everyone could die.

"I survived her brutality. I arrived on your doorstep because she had no further power over me. Living came to be as much of a surprise to her as it was to me."

"Hmm," he muttered, mulling over her words, "so that's the truth of the matter. If I choose to believe what you say, Queen Cynara would have me take your life because she failed in her deceitful plans."

"So it appears, since I am standing before you. But how would you harm me, Lord Nicolai? Are you a lady killer?"

He chuckled as if she had indulged him with a joke. He glanced away, coloring, perhaps contemplating a place unseen, gazing at the ocean. "Once, ladies may have perceived me as a lady killer, but now…"

Sadness and measured anger darkened his expression.

"What are you thinking? You look as if you could seriously harm me. But you don't want to, do you?"

Lord Nicolai stepped a pace closer to Scarlett and soon leaned against the railing, too. He searched her eyes and touched the side of her face with his fingers, stroking downward with the tip of his thumb. Then he removed his hand as if the touch of her flesh burned his fingers. "I saw you last night. This is the second time I've witnessed what you are, but I will not be frightened in my own home."

The comment took Scarlett by surprise. She touched her skin where he'd stroked her. "What are you talking about?"

"I am talking about the changes I saw—in your eyes."

Scarlett stepped away. "My eyes? When did you see my eyes?"

"When you arrived at my door, your brown eyes with flecks of gold appeared normal. But after you retired, after you went to bed…"

"I bolted the door," Scarlett forced out. "How did you see my eyes or anything else?"

"Secrets hide inside this house that only I am aware of, and I was curious."

"What did you see? How did you see? I don't remember much after…"

He stepped away, raising his hand as if to ward off her evil. Scarlett retraced her steps to the doorway. *What had she become?*

His voice wouldn't let her alone. "There's a secret passageway."

"What? A passageway? But what about my eyes?" Scarlett begged of him. "What did you see?"

"You seem frightened," Nicolai said, seeming surprised at her confusion. "You don't know. You don't remember, do you?"

Scarlett raised her hands in exasperation. "I don't remember much after eating last night. I went to sleep. I had an awful rest. Nothing comes to mind after my head touched the pillow. Except, maybe a creature scurried in the hallway. I may have sensed a rat. Was the rat in the hallway you, my lord, trying to sneak inside my room?"

"I assure you, Princess, I don't have to sneak about in my own home. I go where I want. I thought to peer at you from afar, but you were waiting with your disturbing eyes, which changed to yellow slits, hidden within your golden-brown retinas. I think you mean to harm me. That's the real reason Cynara sent a cursed princess, isn't it? To tempt my appetite to dine on your poison."

Scarlett examined Nicolai's angry expression. He had spat Queen Cynara's name from his lips. Obviously, he despised the woman. The evil witch had a hold on this man. Whatever the state of his affairs, Scarlett was determined to learn the unspoken truth hiding between them.

But he was right. She could also be a threat to the lord of Drum Manor. Surviving the snakebite had given her new powers. It scared her to think she moved about her room at night with no memory of her actions. But she refused to believe she'd cause harm to another human being, *unless provoked.*

"Yellow slits, you say," she said, mulling over the information. "Lord Nicolai, were you drinking last night?"

"Don't. I know what I saw."

"It's clear what you think you saw, but this transformation is news to me."

"Woman, do you expect me to believe the fantasy you attempt to deny?"

Scarlett was afraid, but she chanced a step toward his angry expression. She was sure the devil danced somewhere in the stormy blue depths of his eyes, but she needed to face her fears and assert her situation.

"I expect you to understand that I came here under duress, and that my entry into your home was not of my choosing. I expect you to recognize that we share a common problem."

"Tell me, Princess," Nicolai said as if he didn't believe her, "what is our common problem?"

"Queen Cynara!" Scarlett all but yelled, her forehead furrowed with frustration. "A common enemy."

"Hmm."

"I knew it," Scarlett blurted, her hands rising in appeal. "It is the truth. Queen Cynara threatens me as much as she threatens you. I assure you, Lord Nicolai, I am not a threat to you."

"I don't know what to believe, but we shall soon see which truth proves honest."

He didn't trust her at all. He wore his suspicion like a shield of armor on his chiseled face.

"We certainly shall see," she stated forcefully. "Now, if you'll excuse me, I shall return to my bedchamber."

"As you will," he said blandly, extending his left hand toward the doorway. "You must be hungry. Bensen awaits your presence in the larder. If I know the man, he's begun preparation of the morning meal. And Princess Scarlett—you might want to wear a kirtle that covers more than your threadbare under tunic."

Scarlett blushed a deep shade of pink while attempting to conceal her chest with her hands.

"Take pity on a poor creature," Scarlett beseeched, her voice about to break. "I may hold the title of a princess, but I own little of consequence."

Nicolai sighed, more annoyed than sorry. "Fortunately for you, you'll find a trunk full of lady's garments at the foot of your bed. The previous owner has little use for these belongings now. They are years old and out of fashion, but you may have them."

"I thank you," Scarlett whispered, her arms crossed tight to her chest. Holding her head high, she retreated from his presence and returned to her bedchamber. Once she passed over the threshold, she eased the door shut, closed the curtains, and contemplated the conversation they had shared. She also considered other pressing needs.

The time had come to dress and to learn what the previous lady had left behind. A large traveling coffer, decorated with burgundy leather and ornamental brass, rested at the foot of her bed. Scarlett leaned forward and drew her fingers along the hundreds of rivets lining the upper edge. Someone with affluence had owned this beauty, and she was anxious to see what fabrics hid inside. She grabbed the brass plate and pulled the lid upward.

When beautiful kirtles and surcoats met her sight, she sighed in wonder at the treasure trove.

Four kirtles greeted her fingertips: two of soft white linen, one of royal blue, and one of pale blue; all four had intricate embroidered edges. She pulled out the royal blue kirtle. Unfolding it, she brought the fabric to her chest and permitted the linen to fall along her slender form.

"So beautiful," Scarlett whispered, laying the fabric on the bed. In her entire life, she had never owned such an undergarment. Accustomed more to hemp than fine linen, she reached inside the trunk and searched underneath the layers for the surcoats that lay beneath the kirtles.

Scarlett counted six beautiful gowns, three on each side of the trunk. The woman who had owned these creations must have favored the color blue, for at her fingertips lay a pale blue silk, a royal-blue velvet inlaid with brocade, and a dark midnight blue with intricate gold thread. Beneath a creamy yellow taffeta hid more serviceable gowns of forest green and winter white.

Scarlett pulled the front covering of the trunk downward to reveal two bottom drawers. She knelt and pulled the first drawer open, finding head coverings and four white linen chemises with matching white linen braes.

"Oh my," Scarlett sighed, when she lifted hose and stockings, which matched the color of the gowns in the drawers. She reached for a pale blue silk and drew the soft fibers across her face. She, a princess, had never owned goods as luxurious as these. She glanced at her feet and noted the holes in her own woolen stockings. Soon she would throw them to the wind.

A tiny bag, a purse with the image of two lovers woven into rich brocade, caught her attention next. She grabbed the purse, flipped the fabric fold upward, and reached inside. She felt a jewel of some sort wrapped in a napkin. A gold necklace met her astonished gaze. Its golden band held a mix of tiny seed pearls and numerous white and dark blue sapphires, which would flatter many a woman's neck.

"Could this gem be mine, too?" Scarlett marveled, gazing at the rich jewels clutched in her hand. She soon fastened the necklace around her neck and then proceeded with her discovery.

Scarlett reached inside the purse again and found an elaborate brooch and a dark sapphire ring. Her fingers were bare. She returned the brooch to the purse and set the ring on her finger.

"I can't believe it," she whispered in awe, "what a dark beauty you are."

Scarlett left the prize on her finger while she searched the bottom drawer. Within its layer she found a dark blue, almost black, hooded cape and several pairs of shoes. Some were silk, but most were made of a serviceable leather. Scarlett reached for a dark blue satin pair, sat on the floor, and pulled them on her feet. She was surprised, the shoes actually fit.

"All mine?" Scarlett whispered into the empty space. "Truly? Can this be so?"

Lord Nicolai Graydon

Nicolai watched Scarlett from behind the floor-length mirror, surprised that this time Scarlett did not return his stare. She knelt on the floor in front of the trunk, her attention enraptured by clothing and gems. She reminded him of a little girl, fascinated by her wealthy booty, lost in her fantasy world. He liked the situation much better this way. He could study her feminine figure at his leisure and without interruption.

Jewels were a pretty fascination to a woman, but in his man's sea of trouble, gemstones didn't hold the same meaning as they had in the past. Alexandra had owned few golden pieces, but what she had brought to their betrothal with her dowry dawned impressive. Nicolai couldn't see Scarlett wearing the pale blues that Alexandra had once loved. The red dress Scarlett had worn on the first night of their meeting suited her olive complexion much better than a pale blue frock. Thankfully, two bolder hues were inside the trunk, and if he was good at sizing the fit, the gowns would mold nicely to her tiny dimensions.

Especially that pert little bottom.

Scarlett stood and pulled the coarse tunic over her head, tossing the old garment to the floor. A moth-bitten chemise and thin ripped braes soon followed in quick succession.

"Holy nether land," Nicolai whispered when creamy skin met his discerning eye. Regardless of the poverty or wealth that adorned a woman's figure in poorer or richer textures, all female figures were built the same once their clothes were removed. Nicolai studied the line of her neck, traced the spine of her back, his attention wandering to the rounded curves of her bare bottom. A dangerous view, he realized. He sucked in a breath.

Nicolai hadn't seen a naked woman in so long, his shaft reared up and stood tall. He could feel the blood rushing through his veins, causing a tenuous ache to throb within his breeches, but such urgencies must be denied on pain of death —Scarlett's death. Still, he watched as she reached for a delicate chemise and panty brae, providing him a tasteful sight of a round and plump breast.

Nicolai scrutinized her with longing, his manhood pulsing, awakening to desire. Scarlett slipped the white chemise over her head and stepped into her braes, soon tying the delicate fabric at the side of her slender waist. A new hunger took control and a changeling transformation began. Soon, a black panther watched a woman pulling a kirtle over her head, followed by a royal blue surcoat.

And the cat was hungry.

Scarlett paused in her dressing as if she knew she was not alone. She glanced at the floor-length mirror, behind which Nicolai crouched. The gown slipped from her hands and fell to the floor. She crossed the space between the trunk and the mirror and stared at her reflection in the glass. At first, Nicolai thought she was admiring her changed image, but as she stepped closer to the mirror, she looked intimately at the molecular surface and touched it with her fingers.

"I know you're in the hidden passageway," she whispered,

"and it's impolite to stare at a lady while she's dressing. I will have you gone, Lord Graydon. Now."

Nicolai touched the mirror with his paw, panting, and felt a mounting hunger gnawing in his belly. She stood before him, beautiful in royal blue, but viewing her nakedness before had caused a sexual tension that had ignited his panther's raw hunger. He listened to her heartbeat. He opened his mouth, feeling the sharp fangs with his tongue while he breathed her scent in the air. Even with the barrier, he smelled the blood flowing beneath her skin.

Nicolai stood on his forelegs and searched her brown eyes with his panther's coppery-yellow ones. Ah, but she would taste delicious. Fortunately for Scarlett, the panther could not open the passageway, which made her safe for now.

He dropped to the ground, shifted on his paws, and pranced along the musty hallway, leaving the secret passageway through the opposite mirrored door. He couldn't close the opening in his present form, but if he stayed, he knew what he'd try to do. He'd jump at the glass, hoping it would break, then take his greedy feed. He knew for sure this situation would not end well. He would kill the beautiful Scarlett Princess and plunge his soul into the Netherworld.

Chapter Nineteen

BENSEN

Standing in front of a large brick fireplace in the larder, Bensen reached for an iron poker and stoked the logs beneath the kettle in the hearth, listening to the wood hiss and pop while waiting for the water to boil. He could use a strong black tea with a shot of aqua vitae to give the brew a kick, but liquid spirits and other provisions were in short supply. The grain hutch barely held enough flour to make another loaf of bread, and the cold larder was barren of fowl. He was sick and tired of the extensive work that had to be done to maintain the simplest of necessities in the manor. His circumstances needed to change.

Years ago, when Bensen began his service at the household of Drum Manor, he never imagined that serving Lord Nicolai would entail assuming roles that other servants once filled, but he made the best of the situation with discipline and dignity. Yet, dignity didn't feed a man, and all the master provided these days was a roof over his head, careless conversation, and a few choice kills. More material goods came by way of begging, borrowing, and more often than not, stealing. And with a bum leg, foraging grew more difficult as time passed. Walking to Culley's Cove, the nearby town, was a forced effort.

He suspected the villagers took pity on a poor man and left their foodstuffs on their windowsills for his greedy hands to plunder. They would give up their bread, but wouldn't talk to the butler who had once worked alongside them. Women shuffled to the other side of the road to avoid conversation; and those same lower-class dogs pointed, stared, and whispered in muted tones as if to imply the butler of Drum Manor carried some sort of plague. But the only disease he possessed was the feather-like scarring that marred his right arm, and he knew they were afraid of his natural tattoo as well.

Men acted differently. Shopkeepers, sailors, and fine upstanding folk regarded Bensen as if he had committed a crime. They heckled and mocked him. He wasn't a criminal, nor was he insane because he chose to serve his master. But he couldn't blame the villagers for being afraid of what Lord Nicolai had become. Men and women equally understood the threat—a great many had witnessed the transformation, an evil change they were wise to ignore. Who wanted to challenge a large black panther? Better to keep one's distance.

Bensen knew Nicolai didn't threaten his well-being, nor did he threaten the welfare of men and women from the Cove. However, the time had come for action. Come what may, he would be loyal to his master and look forward to the day when this damnable curse might be broken. Perhaps then the staff could return to their duties, and he could retire.

Although whatever happened, he would see this nasty business ended, once and for all.

He placed the poker in the iron rack, grabbed a protective mitt, and pulled the steaming kettle off the hook. He turned in surprise when the manor's female guest, and the hope he had been waiting for, trudged into the room.

"Good morning," she whispered.

"A good morning to you," Bensen replied, placing the kettle on the tabletop. He rubbed the ache in his thigh. "What do we have here? A lady no less—dressed in fine blue."

She glanced at the floorboards, seemingly indifferent to his comment, but her slight smile said she welcomed the compliment. "Lord Nicolai said I could have the belongings in the trunk. And I'm grateful, because I didn't arrive with much."

"Those old things," Bensen muttered, grabbing a teapot from the wall larder. "After all these years, I'm surprised the fabric lasted without growing holes. You've seen the master this morning?"

"Yes." Scarlett tapped her toe on the slate floor. "On the balcony, earlier."

"Ah yes," Benson said, filling the teapot with an assortment of dried leaves. "The master enjoys watching the sunrise from the balcony."

"He said you would have breakfast waiting, but I'm surprised I'd be given clothing, grand clothing no less, and also a meal to break my fast. I'm supposed to meet a cruel fate."

Bensen merely smirked at the comment while filling the teapot with boiling water. "'Tis true that fate can be a cruel monster and grant an abysmal fortune, regardless of where the wind blows. But you are our guest, my dear, and as our guest, we will take care of you. No more talk of cruelties. The water in the pot is hot and fit for a cup of tea. The bread is fresh from its earthenware pot, and herbed eggs await your palate in the skillet. Shall I dish them up for you?"

Scarlett looked at him quizzically. "You may."

"Have a seat at the table," Bensen said, preparing a plate, "The larder does not hold the luxury of the dining room, but you'll find it warm, comfortable, and clean. The master once took his meals at the banqueting table in the dining room, but much like the rest of the house, the room has slid into disrepair."

Bensen watched her scrutinizing the room, assessing the space before she grabbed a wooden chair and sat, sliding the chair close to the table's surface. He knew where her thoughts lay. "You're wondering why this room survived to offer a different story than the others?"

"It did occur to me the home is in a state of decline," Scarlett commented, tapping her finger on the tabletop. "And given its present condition, I am surprised that man or beast could live within its walls."

"Yes, well, we humans do what we must to survive when a period of our life spells trouble," Bensen snickered, placing a plate before Scarlett. He added two cups, the china pot, and his own plate at the opposite end of the table. Sitting, he stabbed a forkful of eggs. "Sometimes, when life begets thorns, all a man can do is take a break and attempt to find humor in the situation."

"How did this misfortune come to be? I'm not sure I should even ask the question."

"Oh, it's a bewitching story. A horribly twisted plot, a sad tale that is perhaps better shared from the lips of Lord Graydon."

She searched his expression with a sense of knowing. "Queen Cynara had something to do with the destruction of this manor, didn't she?"

"Aye," Bensen said, matter of factly. "She did."

Princess Scarlett studied her plate, scooped up a large forkful of eggs, then began eating. She chewed thoughtfully for a time. "And Queen Cynara, did she harm the servants of this manor, too? I mean no disrespect to your food skills, the eggs are delicious, but it is odd to not find a cook or scullions in the larder."

"Oh yes," Bensen replied, rolling up his sleeves, revealing his Lichtenberg scarring. "Queen Cynara enacted her revenge on this place and all who once lived here."

Scarlett stopped eating. Bensen watched her eyebrows furrow before her expression met his with measured concern. She dropped her fork and reached across the table. "Did she act out her revenge on you? Is she responsible for the scarring on your arm?"

Bensen pulled his shirtsleeve higher, further revealing the raised scars. The welts had never healed or lessened in their ugly purplish coloring. He hated the witch for this painful reminder. If he could ever repay her heartlessness, he would find a way to provide justice for the atrocity done to him.

"Aye, Queen Cynara is responsible for my skin tattoo."

"But how? How did she cause such an injury? It looks like…"

"It looks like what it is," Bensen replied. "A lightning strike."

"You poor man. I had no idea her powers were so strong. It frightens me to learn she could command the elements in such a way. Witnessing your scars, I imagine Queen Cynara must have behaved especially cruel toward Lord Nicolai."

"Years ago," Bensen elaborated, "she wasn't a queen. When Nicolai met the woman, he believed she was a common wench hoping for a playful pairing with a lord, but Cynara was not satisfied with a pleasant rendezvous. She desired more than the master could give, and the lord of Drum Manor couldn't choose a simple woman who was beneath his stature when the wealth of a lady waited."

He watched Scarlett sip her tea before responding. "There's nothing worse than a woman scorned, and Cynara would not take lightly to being treated like a wanton wench. It would have gone better for your master if he had found more pleasure in her company, for then less harm would have befallen my royal family, and your arm. But I digress. What happened to Lord Nicolai?"

"The master," Bensen paused, remembering, "suffered a terrible fate. And his soon-to-be lady wife, Alexandra, breathed her final breath. The pair would have married had Cynara not intruded on their betrothal."

Scarlett gauged him with concern. "Cynara murdered someone inside this manor house? I'm sorry to say, I'm not surprised. I'm afraid to ask what further crimes Cynara undertook, but I must know. You're delaying the truth. What happened to Nicolai?"

Bensen rolled his sleeve down and searched her eager expression. He hoped to press his wants and needs on the princess. He knew he required her full attention and involvement—somehow. But in order to get this woman to become a puppet in his drama, he must bait his hook carefully to make certain she gobbled the lure.

"She invoked a black punishment. A scourge that not only threatened Lord Nicolai, but also men, women and children, who served in this household, which sent everyone running for their lives. I need your help to break this curse. Princess, you might be the answer to my silent pleas."

"The answer?" Scarlett questioned. "How could I be the solution to your problems? I am merely a woman with fragile needs of my own. I can't change the scarring on your arm any more than I can set this house to right. I had best consider my own fate before I involve myself in the misfortune of a man I hardly know."

"But Princess Scarlett," Bensen appealed, "surely you realize that fate has bound two lives together for a compelling reason. If you don't assist me with the discovery, perhaps the curse will find you, too."

Scarlett reached for her fork, slid it around her plate, and then took another mouthful of egg. Clearly, she was not happy. "I don't like the sound of your request; it sounds like a threat. Nor do I understand the danger. Why me?"

"Indeed, why you? I could ask this all-important question myself. Why me? Oh, poor me. But to be honest, I can't explain why Cynara placed you in the middle of this madness.

Though I do believe you might be able to assist the master for a compelling reason."

"You request my help, but you're keeping a secret from me," Scarlett emphasized, staring at her plate like an insolent child, playing with her food. "What reason could compel me to do whatever it is you think needs to be done?"

"Princess," Bensen drawled. "Master Nicolai is a man, albeit a difficult man, but he has handsome capacities worth considering. Doesn't every woman want to save a man? And you're a woman with tempting gifts. You could be the one to…"

"I know, break the curse. I suppose no other option exists but to assist you in this venture, because if I refuse to help, the black curse you speak of could swallow me, too. I understand why Cynara sent me here. The black curse must be powerful enough to end my life."

"Indeed it is," Bensen assured her. "This is the reason the queen sent you here in the first place—to have you gobbled up by the curse."

"Perhaps your plan needs to be pursued." Scarlett heaved a sigh. "But if I am to consider your request, you must tell me more. All that you know."

Bensen grinned, grateful he'd caught her in his lure. He had not felt hopeful in a long time, but he wouldn't fool himself—for now, hope grew from a tiny seedling, a seed that could be swept away with the wind, perhaps consumed by a prevailing storm. And although she had requested to know the truth, he couldn't reveal all the sordid details. Princess Scarlett could not know his deepest secret.

His breakfast complete, Bensen placed his fork on his

plate. "Certain elements of this plan I have been assembling for a long time, but I've been waiting for an opportunity to test the methodical limits of the curse, so I was excited when you arrived at the manor."

"Yes, well, you are an evasive man, Bensen. You are not telling me much at all."

Bensen smirked, contemplating his accomplice. "I will tell you everything you need to know, Princess Scarlett. Everything."

Chapter Twenty

SISTER MARY MARGARET

Mary knelt beside a modest bed with her hands clasped in prayer, her attention fixed on a patchwork quilt that had been stitched using her own two hands. She didn't mind this simplistic life, nor did she worry over sacred vows that shielded her from past terrors. A vow of poverty and obedience seemed a small sacrifice to keep herself and her children safe from harm.

Still, no matter how much time passed, Mary missed her previous life. While it might appear vain, she yearned for the possessions and servants a royal life begot, yet, she could accept this change and the material losses, too, if her sacrifices saved her adult children, but they would always live in desperate straits while the evil queen lived.

She rolled a wooden rosary of carved roses between her fingers, preparing to recite her prayers. She didn't believe that divine thought would alter her situation, after all, prayers hadn't responded to her difficulties during the ensuing years;

nevertheless, she bowed her head and humbly addressed the gods:

> *I pray for a day of reckoning, a time when the gods might send an army to drive out the wickedness. I pray for my children, gifts of creation, flowers who wait to be saved from wrongdoings (Scarlett, Ruby, Rose, and…). I pray my children will rise above this nether-storm, and I call on the gods to deliver them from the evil, to bring about a new day, a day when the light burns the bedevilment of a woman, so her black reign will come to an end.*

> Amen

Sister Mary stood, and shook off the dust that had settled on her pale blue surcoat, then advanced toward a small wooden door. Opening it, she passed through the threshold, moved into the stairwell, and descended the stone treads and proceeded to the chapel. Once there, she greeted Father Clement, who stood by the altar. Though she attempted to hide her worries, he noticed her discontent.

"What's wrong, Sister Mary Margaret?"

Mary sighed, holding her arms at her waist while fingering her rosary. She glanced at the stone flooring covered with a simple rug.

"Another day begins without hope of positive change. Years have passed, and still—she holds the throne—and worse than before. The situation only grows worse, not better. The kingdom requires change. I require change. I'm sick of waiting. I yearn to hear the sound of my own name."

Father Clement approached her. "Sister Mary, it's best we not concern ourselves with the problems of the kingdom. Accept the situation. You know what happens when a woman becomes a nun. When you took your vows, you renounced your former self, including your former name."

Mary raised her hands in appeal, palms upward. "I may have renounced my former life, but I never gave up on the kingdom, or who should rule it. Father, I yearn to hear my real name spoken aloud again. I yearn for..."

He shook his head. "Sister, you must accept your lot in life. Forget the past. Leave the political decisions to men better equipped to handle a sword. Remembering your former self will only serve to offer further pain," he asserted gently. "Mary, forget all that you were and give praise for what you have become. I have never known a gentler or kinder spirit, and the work you do for the kingdom brings hope to repressed souls. What would these poor people do without you?"

Mary sighed. He didn't understand her position, but how could a religious man who had never owned more than a cross understand her losses. Forget her life? *Never!* Her church work was important, she knew that, but helping others did not assist her own family.

"If only the work could assist the revival of my soul. My family. Father, when will this nightmare end?"

"The night only seems to linger. Light wends its way from the east each morning. We should remember, hope rises with the dawn."

"I wish I held to your faith. I hope someday I might witness the return of my own, for hope seems bleak with one child removed from the kingdom, two locked away, and my last child lost to me."

Father Clement quieted, then placed his index finger on his lips while gazing at a small hole built into a column of stones, almost hidden from their view inside the chapel.

"Mary," he whispered, drawing nearer to her and speaking so softly his words were almost inaudible, "we must not speak of the children. This secret is too great to be revealed. Your life, and the lives of your offspring, especially the existence of your fourth child, would be forfeit if the queen learned the truth. Don't lose faith that the gods have a plan, though we can't always see their genius at work."

"Father, this world can't survive on religious convictions that don't hold merit. The gods have not responded to the crimes against the royal family. I pray, earnestly I do, but the gods never answer."

"Give it time, Mary."

"How much time? My hair is turning gray, that's how many years have passed. I'm tired of waiting."

"I see you're upset. Why don't you tend the royal garden? I know the sight of flowers pleases you."

"You're changing the subject," Mary said, sighing. "You're a good man, and I appreciate your support, but your words are no more than a lecture. A sermon that doesn't earn enlightenment."

"It's not like you to be so forceful. Consider the garden. A time of solitude might help you to see reason."

"Of course, you're right," she said, giving in to his counsel. "I must be grateful and have more faith. I'll be more mindful of my prayers; I'll tend the garden."

"Sister Mary—"

"Yes?"

He leaned nearer. "Please remember, the queen's rooms reside above us, and although she seldom entertains the spirit, she could spy on chapel activities if she chose to. Guard your words, be careful what you say inside this room. We are not safe from Lucifer's work, though we reside in holy chambers."

Mary knew they didn't have to fear Daemonis, but she saw no point in stating this fact. "I'm sorry, Father. Of course you're right. I'll be more cautious."

She gathered her bag of garden tools and proceeded toward the doorway that led to the east curtain wall. She glanced at the spiritual man who had safeguarded her from harm. He was her only counsel, her only protection, too, and she wished she held to his faith. Though, perhaps it was time to seek assistance from someone with less scruples.

"Father Clement?"

"Sister?"

"I don't want you to think I'm ungrateful; I do appreciate your guidance."

"Of course. I understand."

Sister Mary left the chapel, but even though she had retreated from their conversation, she couldn't escape the worries as she passed through an arched doorway that led to the barbican. She grimaced in frustration while standing outside at the top of the curtain wall. Even studying the royal garden below her didn't earn relief. Sighing, she proceeded down a flight of stone stairs, her nun's habit trailing behind, soon walking across a gritty walkway.

"Beautiful." She breathed fresh air, listening to a thrush singing. "It's always a pleasure to work in your presence."

The sun had barely risen. The dew glistened on petals of morning glory boxed in low and rectangular cypress hedges. Mary closed her eyes and smelled the earthy essence encouraged by a night of rain, imagining a time not so long ago when she'd come to this spot and sit among the flowers, gazing at noonday sun in a blue sky.

No longer could she relax in the garden, for now her job was tending the flowers, but at least with the gardener's role, she could still visit this place, which was as sacred to her as the chapel was to Father Clement. She reached for a garden fork buried in her bag and progressed toward the farthest hedge. Dropping to her knees, she worked the soil and pulled the weeds that attempted to choke the flowers. She moved slowly along the hedge, tilling through a purple and blue sea of morning glory studded with islands of white daisies. She paused in her work to admire ornamental trees standing guard at each corner, and a centrally located reflecting pool. She not only peered into it to stem her fears, but also to divine her future. After a time, she forgot her work and crawled to the water. She sat on the stone edge, rubbing her lower back.

She contemplated the other side of the garden, where a new marble sculpture of His Royal Majesty King Rickard had been erected to guard the barbican. The sculptor had fashioned the royal statue with a precise and skillful hand. The image possessed the true likeness of the former king.

Mary rose and walked toward the sculpture with her garden fork held in her hand. Standing beneath the figure, she studied a crown of gold and dark curly hair, framing a firm masculine face and full ruddy lips. She dropped her fork, leaned in for a closer perusal and touched her own lips, studying him intimately, remembering their first kiss.

King Rickard, her former husband, rested on a solid square platform. Regardless of the warnings, Mary couldn't help herself. She stepped upward, climbed onto the rock platform, and molded her right palm to his cold left cheek, drawn to his once emerald eyes. *His beautiful eyes...*

"Why?" she asked him, though she knew carved stone could not respond. "Why was I never enough for you? Look where your lust has brought you. Look where your neglect has taken our children. If you had real eyes, you'd see what your actions have gained your family. We could have shared a lifetime of happiness, but no— you had to share your bed with an evil woman. And now, the hour grows late for commiserations. I loved you..."

Mary sighed, removed her hand in resignation and stepped to the ground. "But this is silly. You're only a statue standing guard over the barbican and my garden, a chunk of mortar watching the flowers grow."

She studied the flowers surrounding the platform. She leaned forward, knelt on the ground, retrieved her tool, and removed the weeds attempting to creep across the king's feet.

"It's too late for misgivings," Mary whispered, squashing memories and keeping her attention averted from a face and a past she couldn't change. "I don't know why I torture myself with yesteryear's regrets."

⊷◦⊶♚⊷◦⊶

King Rickard

King Rickard couldn't believe the sight that met his steadfast gaze when he realized who tended the royal garden. At first, he thought the woman cultivating the flowers was a humble nun, but when she came closer, close enough to touch his face, there was no mistaking his former wife, Regana.

Many years had passed since Rickard had beheld his true queen. During this period, he had believed that Queen Cynara had caused Regana's departure. He had not known if she was dead or alive. Now he was surprised to learn she had hidden in plain sight of the kingdom, wearing the garb of a nun. The act was as courageous as it was foolish. He hoped Cynara never learned her true identity, for he knew what would happen should Regana's secret be discovered.

Even so, regardless of her risk, he was filled with joy simply to feel her touch again. After she removed her hand from his face, Rickard missed the warmth. He didn't blame her for her reproach, and he wished he could tell his former wife that his marriage and children were not the only tragedies to result from his sins. He'd paid a high price for unfavorable decisions, too. Though his former wife would never learn this truth.

He gazed at the base of his feet and watched Regana pulling the weeds with her bare hands, thinking it odd that no gloves covered her long, slender fingers. Dirt would mar her nails, and perhaps soil her curious new clothing, the garb of a nun.

He liked the pale blue surcoat that matched the color of

the sky, but he didn't care for the white veil with a bandeau swathing her forehead and chin; the entire costume hid her chocolate hair from his sight. Still, even with her figure covered with cloth from head to toe, her brown eyes radiated a regal loveliness, and being in her company, even in this pitiful regard, brought him comfort. A yearning stirred inside his nearly dead heart. Rickard admitted, he loved this woman still, and he wished he could tell her he was sorry.

If his lips could whisper sounds, he'd reveal this truth to her, but his voice had been silenced. A former king must stand in wait and yearn for the day when his eldest daughter, his sword, might break the spell that wove a horrible curse. But how would Scarlett learn of her father's demise when she believed her father was dead?

Queen Cynara was a clever bitch. The real hand of Lucifer doomed him to stand on this barbican, watching the ages pass, staring out at eternity.

Chapter Twenty-One

PRINCESS SCARLETT

After the conversation with the butler, Scarlett faced a challenge, and she couldn't consider Bensen's plan within the confines of the manor. The air was suffocating, stale, and she wearied of the ghastly vapors. The seaside seemed like a safer place to contemplate her future, and the reassuring warmth of fresh air and sunshine could only be found outside.

She ambled toward the front entry, thinking to temporarily escape her plight. When she arrived at the double doors, she gripped the handle, pressed the housing to release the latch, then opened the door, soon passing through its frame like on the previous night. But this morning, she eagerly stepped into bright light.

Standing on the front landing, Scarlett raised her hand to her forehead, and shielded her eyes from the glare while observing her surroundings. The sun's rays seemed to lessen the troubling prospect of her circumstances, though the light didn't minimize the anxiety thrumming within her mind, especially with Bensen's suggested stratagem. A mistruth hid within his story. She sensed an element of risk, cleverly woven within his request. Not knowing the man, she didn't know if she could assist in enacting his devious plan. She bit at her lip in concern, mulling over his words while welcoming the warmth that colored her skin and softened her fears.

Just get Nicolai through the doorway, I'll take care of the rest...

She sighed while surveying overgrown laurel hedges that consumed most of the front facing of the house, then smiled slimly as she noticed a pleasant floral patch where a handful of white blossoms with pink streaks stemmed. She stepped off the landing to get a closer look, then nestled their delicate petals inside her palm. So fragile. If she wasn't careful, she'd crush their beauty.

Dismissing the flowers, she glanced skyward at the house and reflected on three triangular peaks, noting the cracking veneer and general deterioration of the structure. Even so, where the gray stone had appeared monstrous with looming shadows on the previous night, now the manor emerged tired, sad, and age worn. Threats didn't loom—real danger presented itself through the black curse placed on Nicolai.

Had Bensen told her the truth? A mind-altering brain injury? And could she overcome his ugliness should the man revert to anger?

Scarlett didn't know if she could follow through with the plan to lead the lord on a merry chase. She pivoted and searched the forest edge where tiny birds bantered. She should brave the woodland and rush across the meadowland toward the unknown, escaping into the bush.

But where would I go? Which path would I take?

The thought of hiking an unknown pathway frightened her, and she knew she couldn't trade one worry for another. Perhaps it was better to confront the current situation and lead Lord Nicolai into the great hall.

She couldn't see the prison wagon in the general vicinity, which likely meant that Theodore Wilkins had left her to face her dark fate alone. If she survived the coming night, she would remember the queenly side he had chosen.

A light wind blew in from the ocean, and the salt-laden scent wafted on the breeze toward her. She couldn't help a new curiosity; the blue current called to her soul. She stepped away from the old ruin and progressed toward the water's edge, soon traversing a well-trodden trail that led to the sea. Once she stood on the bluff, she watched the waves rolling across a rocky shoreline. Her troubles seemed to melt away. Finding a large boulder nestled beneath an old and gnarled oak tree, she sat and admired the seascape, stretching across froth-laden water.

LORD NICOLAI GRAYDON

STANDING NEAR THE PRINCESS, Nicolai watched Scarlett where she lounged for an indefinite period of time. He didn't want to intrude on her private thoughts, for she seemed peaceful resting near the ocean. But intrude on her life he would.

Bensen had insisted that their quest to test the curse

should begin by inviting Princess Scarlett to dine with him. Whether he liked the scheme or not, he would press forward with the possibilities, understanding that a successful resolution benefited his freedom. *Failure?* He couldn't consider the potential losses, not yet. Hunger and regret already roiled in his belly while scrutinizing her beauty.

Nicolai, he noted grimly, his appetite ravening, courted his next meal.

He shook his head, trying to dismiss the rising scourge. Gathering his thoughts, he worked hard to suppress the dark desires. Such attempts were difficult with the Scarlett Princess lounging before his sight, a sweet lure next to his sea. He still believed she should leave Drum Manor, for her own safety.

He knew dining together would only bring more trouble, and he didn't want further strife marring his life. Yet, he was helpless to be a puppet in his own drama, watching the play unfold. He knew real misfortune could arrive, taking him deeper into debt, and the fear of what he might do filled him with misery.

He had never witnessed a prize as beautiful as this woman, who stared at the sea, her long auburn hair wafting in the breeze. He didn't want to crush her peaceful stance. He had been waiting for a sight such as this for far too many seasons.

What if the test failed?

He took one step forward and she noticed his movement, for she glanced in his direction. She gasped at the sight of him. Situated so peacefully before, now she appeared frightened.

"I'm sorry," Nicolai called out, "I didn't mean to startle you."

She raised her hand as if to shield her eyes from the sun. "You didn't frighten me." She lied. "You've surprised me is all, Lord Nicolai."

He walked the last few steps and soon stood beside the princess. He avoided her eye contact and matched her regard out to sea. "This land facing on the cliff edge is a favorite spot of mine. I come to this lookout often to study the sea."

She sucked in a breath. "Do you ever sight anything worthwhile?"

He turned to her, risking the glance, then returned his attention to the water. "Beyond the squawk of crying gulls, I've seen a ship a time or two, but the vessels always pass me by."

"How sad."

Nicolai glanced at her, ignoring the comment. "I don't want to intrude on your view. I only came to invite you to dine with me this evening."

He watched the fear mount in her eyes. She sucked in a wavering breath for courage and noticeably swallowed, but her sight never left his.

"I would be honored, Lord Nicolai."

He wondered at the silent pause after her response, thinking it odd. What game was his old butler playing?

"At the seven o'clock hour then, in the dining hall."

She rose from the rock. "How should I dress?"

"It matters not. You would be beautiful in any garment you chose to wear."

And nothing at all, he remembered.

"That's kind of you to say," she murmured. Her gaze shifted to a ring on her finger. He watched her massage it, twisting the gold back and forth.

"Found in the trunk?"

She removed the ring. "Yes," she mused, holding it before him. "But it's not mine, and I shouldn't have taken it."

He accepted the ring and rolled it between his thumb and index finger. "A grand jewel," he stated, considering the blue stone. "Seems a waste to have the ring hidden within an old trunk. It should circle someone's finger. Keep it," he urged, returning it to her.

"Are you certain? Surely the stone is precious and valuable to your family?"

"You're mistaken, Princess. The ring never belonged to my household estate, so it's not right that I keep it. The original owner would be delighted that a woman of equal measure and stature enjoyed her treasure."

She smiled slimly, then returned the band to her finger. Her apparent joy delighted him.

"She must have loved the color blue."

"If you would permit my honesty, I didn't know much about my fiancée's likes or dislikes, but I do suspect there is some truth to your observation. Perhaps our conversation should return to its original purpose. Dinner? Would you join me?"

"Would it be better to dine in the kitchen? The dining room is in…"

"A state of decline," Nicolai finished, sighing. "Poor Bensen, he's attempting to set the room into a more presentable condition. It's difficult with his bum leg."

"Indeed," she whispered, her eyes squinting, studying the sea.

"I'll leave you to enjoy the view, but don't linger outside too long. The wind is picking up; a storm could be threatening."

Unable to read her thoughts, he watched her forehead furrow with concern, seeing she bit at her full red lips. He was surprised when her interest returned to him.

"Thank you for the warning, Lord Nicolai. I will heed it."

It took strong willpower to leave Princess Scarlett alone with her thoughts, but she was safer by far with her solitude, reclining on the edge of a cliff, than with a man who would cause her harm. As Nicolai returned to the manor house, he wished with all his being their circumstances could be different.

Chapter Twenty-Two

LORD NICOLAI GRAYDON

Evening shadows were gathering when Nicolai transformed into the familiar shape of a black panther. Comfortable in his velvet skin, he traipsed beneath a canopy of tree branches, moving closer to a watery break near the cliff's edge. Thick muscles rippled and flexed in his legs as each paw stretched forward.

When he reached the old oak, he ran up the trunk and leapt to a silvery perch. Reclining into a sitting position, he sniffed the air while the wind ruffled his fur. He watched the sun slip beneath the sea. Soon the night would thicken, and he'd face the consequences of the curse—again.

When life begot thorns, Nicolai's favorite place to ponder his circumstances had always been this large, gnarled oak. The tree had clung to the cliff edge for many years, and in truth, it should have slipped to a watery grave a long time ago. But somehow the roots clung to the cliff, wending their way into the nooks and crevices, determined to keep the trunk firmly planted. If a tree could root out hope, perhaps a man could hunt for prospects, too.

He closed his eyes, sniffing, feeling the ocean's spray on his black nose. Circumstances would be better for Princess Scarlett if the bough broke and tossed his sorry lot into the sea, but the limb held firm and his dark thoughts fell short of wise answers.

Opening his eyes, he pivoted on the branch and glanced at the manor house instead, contemplating the woman inside. His tail swished back and forth; he opened his mouth, baring his teeth. *Smelling—* He couldn't escape the gnawing hunger that caused his mouth to water.

He growled.

Even from this precarious spot, he inhaled her red scent. He wanted the woman. He wanted her desperately. Not as a man desires a lady, but as a cat hungers for its prey. His appetite for meat gnawed at his gut. Saliva flowed, wetting his lips. He snarled at the night, revealing sharp white fangs.

The ravens heard his cry. Two hungry companions circled overhead, waiting for their feast to arrive at the forest table.

Nicolai snarled.

Not tonight, my friends.

Yet, he wasn't certain he could keep this meaty bounty from the black birds. He knew what would happen if he entertained Scarlett's company. Bedevilment held him within its grip. He could visualize her blood pooling on the floor.

Don't fool yourself, Nicolai, he worried, growling. *No good can come from this dark night.*

Cynara was a clever, crafty, and conniving bitch. The

witch played a cunning game, sending a feast of honey for a starving man to eat, but he was weary of this ugly business and didn't want to consume her evil any longer.

I must find strength to defend my heart, for if I eat of this table, my soul will be further cursed to the Netherworld.

Nicolai leapt to the ground and prowled toward his home. He couldn't help himself, eager, he stalked toward the copper scent of her royal blood.

Princess Scarlett

ALONE IN THE DINING HALL, Scarlett tapped her fingers against the edge of a rectangular table, while gazing at a silver candelabrum sitting slightly to the left of the middle leaf.

It was dark. Bands of light flickered throughout the room, their tiny flames illuminating the plate settings, pewter goblets, and fine art hanging on the walls, which made the portraits in the upper spaces appear all too real and sinister. One thought weighed heavily on her mind. Lord Nicolai would join her at this table, soon.

Her keen imagination assisted her stomach to twist into knots as the minutes ticked by with only the light of five candles to illuminate the chamber. Five tiny flames danced, but the fire on the wicks might as well have arisen from ghouls of the underworld. The flickering reminded Scarlett of her menacing circumstances and the man who could snuff out her life.

Frightened, she waited for the lord to arrive, hoping Bensen's plan might save them all from Cynara's curse. She didn't see how her assistance could make a difference, but the prospect of besting the evil queen influenced Scarlett's decision to remain at Nicolai's table. She wanted to win.

When Nicolai entered the dining hall, she twisted on the chair to observe him. Her mouth must have hung open in surprise, as even though she was frightened, she couldn't help but notice he cut a fine figure of a man.

"Good evening to you, Princess Scarlett."

She swallowed. The walls seemed to compress inward, the horror squeezing the sides of the dining hall with each stride from the man pacing toward her. She noted the stealth in which he walked as he sauntered forward with an animal's predatory pace.

"A good evening to you as well, my lord," she muttered, captivated by his heavy expression and his handsome face. Still, something inside herself warned—don't look into his eyes—but like a moth trapped near a flame, she held to his enchantment, hoping. She didn't know what would happen if she didn't remain alert.

"You look beautiful tonight," he said, pausing, standing near the entranceway.

She contemplated the curse whispering around him, a curse this man did not have the power to control or break, more so than his assessment of her person. "It's kind of you to notice, and I thank you for your compliment."

"I'll have you know, it's as if an entirely different woman sits beneath my gaze. Yet, I sense your apprehension, and understand your worry."

Scarlett took a slight breath. "I cannot know what you're referring to, as how could a woman change, other than her clothing of course, in less than forty-eight hours. I'm the same princess you met an evening ago," she responded, considering him further.

His silver embellished surcoat vested his form well; the breeches defined his waist, thighs, and legs like a second skin. Many women would swoon with desire observing him in this way, but as she beheld his dark beauty, Scarlett felt a fear so deep inside herself that her fingers trembled and her heartbeat quickened.

What was she doing, studying him for a moment longer than was wise? She must appear like a simpleton, sitting here, raking him with her regard. She must master her wits, control her statements and find her voice... "Even so, if we're conversing about our attire, you present a dashing prospect yourself."

A half-smile creased his face as he neared the table, and she noticed his handsome blue eyes, which challenged her perusal and never wavered from her gaze. "You stare at me with an odd intensity. Why? Do I disappoint you? My clothing not to your liking?"

Scarlett bit at her lip and edged her chair back from the table. "Did you not hear my praise of your wardrobe, my lord? 'Tis nothing like that. You're a well-dressed man," she responded honestly, "but I cannot help but notice that you seem deeply wounded, or maybe the angst I'm sensing arises from hunger. It is the dinner hour."

"Hmm," he muttered, then paused, considering, "a correct assessment. I am hungry."

She should have taken her chances and run, but she kept her promise to Bensen and remained in her seat, understanding this chiseled monster would give chase and satisfy his need, no matter where she fled.

"What are you hungry for?" Scarlett asked. Fear coursed through her veins and gave height to the anxiety thrumming inside her chest.

"The pretty bits and pieces that humans obsess over," he mused aloud. "A better quality of life, a companion for my needs, our dinner. But this show is not fooling me. I sense your trepidation."

"Minus the fear, I desire these outcomes myself," she offered, clasping her hands in her lap.

Nicolai broke off their eye contact, pulled out the chair on the opposite side of the table, and sat. The raw ire in his eyes conveyed to Scarlett that she must win this battle.

"Human beings desire a positive life situation," he acknowledged, placing his elbows on the tabletop and clasping his hands above his plate. "It's the motivation of your inquiry I question."

"Do you not trust me, Lord Nicolai?"

He studied her for several seconds. So intent was his scrutiny, a shiver threaded up her spine. "What reason could a man have not to trust a woman's company? I've naught enjoyed a lady's interest for years, so I do thank you for joining me at this table."

Scarlett pulled her chair closer to the table edge and took a breath for courage. "You would feed me, Lord Nicolai, or eat of me?"

He chuckled, but did not smile. "What? Eat you? Goodness, what sort of vile chinwag has Bensen been sharing with you? Dirty secrets? Dark stories from the grave? If I chose to disclose a sinful confession, what would the lady sacrifice for the information? I'm sure it would not be your virginal blood."

She grimaced, bit at her lip, and tasted sour acid building at the base of her throat. "I have been concerned that royal blood could be spilled, but I had not considered that you might prey on my maidenhead instead of my more fragile heart."

He reached for a tankard of ale. He swirled the amber liquid round and round, then stopped to take the slightest sip, his thin lips coming close to a grin, but Scarlett could not be sure if the humor burning within his eyes came from the drink or the suggestion.

"You are a presumptuous creature, and though I find your conversation titillating, I assure you, maiden fair, breaking through your virginal head should be the least of your worries."

"I can well assume. Bensen forewarned me that you have lost your taste for fleshy pursuits. Is it true? Do you prefer the animal hunt instead?"

Intent, he peered at her eyes and gestured to her with his left hand. "What else is there but the hunt? Some men say 'weak flesh and the hunted fox' belong to the same game. I can tell you; the hunt is only the beginning. Life changes with the capture."

Bensen came into the room just then, wheeling a cart that

held a large soup tureen. When he reached the table, Nicolai stood and assisted him, placing the tureen in the middle of the table, and then returned to his seat.

When Bensen removed the lid, the scent of cheese filled the room. Hunger stirred in Scarlett's belly as Bensen reached for the ladle.

"Princess," he remarked, filling her bowl, "we have simple fare in this home, and I can assure you, no animals were hurt or captured in the preparation of this evening meal. For your eating pleasure, I have cooked a simple cheese and egg potage."

He snickered and stepped toward the lord's side of the table, letting the ladle drip broth onto the wooden surface. "Let me tell you about the capture, Master. I stole into the hen's house with a stealth I didn't believe myself capable of, ruffled a few feathers with my fingers, and bagged half a dozen eggs. I didn't break them, not even one."

He stepped closer to Nicolai with an impressive grin. Scarlett watched him ladle a thick creamy broth into Nicolai's bowl.

"A cockerel in the henhouse was not the type of capture I was sharing with the princess."

Bensen grinned and ladled a second measure of potage into the master's bowl. "What sort of cockerel were you referring to, Master Nicolai?"

Scarlett watched Nicolai's blue eyes darken with gray, but his voice sounded smooth and calm when he spoke. "I know what you're trying to do, Bensen. A foul game is afoot here. Finish serving and leave us to play out our parts."

"As you wish, Master."

Scarlett sipped her wine, not knowing what else she could do. Bensen placed the ladle in the tureen, replaced the lid, and turned in her direction to smirk at her. A silent understanding passed between them.

"Bon appetite," he whispered, bowing to each of them. Then the butler left the room, leaving them alone.

"Bensen tells me," Scarlett whispered, placing her goblet on the table, "that you have a taste for wild meat. As of late, have you been successful at the hunt?"

Nicolai reached for his silver spoon and tapped the metal in a slow calculated measure on the table. She could tell the question angered him.

"As you can see by the simple fare on my table, I have caught little of consequence lately. What else has Bensen confessed to you?"

Scarlett reached for her spoon, dipped its rounded edge into the soup, and took her first taste. The cheesy flavor satisfied, and the allspice mixed with saffron was an interesting surprise for her taste buds. She was scared, but she tried to hide her fear by appearing confident in her manner. She spoke purposefully to her host.

"He said," she whispered, taking a breath for courage, "you're a beast."

Lord Nicolai sighed, then tapped his silver spoon against the table. If her statement had surprised his lordship, he didn't express his shock, but the candlelight illuminated the ire pinching his facial features, and she knew he was angry. Scarlett braced herself to run, waiting for the moment when Nicolai would lose control. It took courage to bend forward and take another sip of soup, while not losing sight of his perusal.

"He called me a beast. Princess, don't you think it's time you exposed your hand? What game is afoot here? Why did you agree to join me at this table?"

"You're right." She sighed, calmly placing her spoon on the table beside the bowl. "I owe my host the truth."

"Well, out with it," Nicolai demanded. "What game do you and Bensen play?"

Scarlett slid her chair back a pace from the table. "Bensen shared a tale with me. A story explaining the sad state of your affairs."

Lord Nicolai leaned closer to her. His eyes ablaze with an obscure yellow light. "A tale—tale of what? A sad story filled with a vengeful witch, a tender angel and a wretched black beast? Perhaps a few broken dreams that amounted to nothing more than dust and rot? Is this the story my butler shared with you?"

Scarlett took a breath for courage. "He shared with me, if I wander too close to you, you will hurt me."

Nicolai leaned backward on his chair, folding his arms. "And do you believe Bensen? Do you believe I will hurt you?"

Scarlett appraised Lord Nicolai, searching his glaring expression and the gray blemishes forming underneath his eyes. She placed both hands on the table. "Yes, I do. I do believe you will hurt me."

He chortled with laughter, and the cadence rang with ill vibrations. "You seem like a frightened child about to run. Where will you run to, Princess?"

Scarlett couldn't bear this predator and prey atmosphere

any longer. She rose from the chair and hurried toward the entranceway, but his maniacal laughter, devoid of human kindness, followed. She heard his chair legs scrape against the flooring. Slow and calculated, she listened to his footsteps beat against the wooden planks. She didn't know why she stopped at the archway, clutching at the column, to scrutinize his advance.

"Whatever happens now will be your fault. Did Bensen tell you my weakness starts when the chase begins? If you run, I will follow. I would not turn around again."

Scarlett didn't reply, but ran along the hallway to the end of the corridor as Bensen had told her to do. She didn't heed Nicolai's warning. Again, she glanced at him. Again, he followed. He didn't rush the effort, didn't hurry along. Confidently, he prowled forward.

"You're a beautiful woman, Scarlett. Did Bensen tell you what would happen if you ran? Did he tell you what would happen if I caught you? Remember our earlier conversation at the table? Life changes with the capture."

At the end of the hallway and behind the staircase, stood two large double doors. Breathing fast, Scarlett reached for the knobs. She twisted and turned them, right then left, but they protested movement.

"Open—damn it!" Scarlett cried out. Almost hysterical now that Nicolai stalked closer. She screamed. "Please open…"

"I don't like that room," Nicolai murmured. "I locked the doors a long time ago, ensuring no guest could ever walk inside that horrible great hall again. Try as you might, you won't get inside before I catch you."

Scarlett fumbled with the lock. She pulled on the doors and banged her hand against the wood in frustration. Bensen had promised her that the doors would open. She screamed when Lord Nicolai's hand found her neck.

"So pretty," he whispered, sliding his fingers along her neck and upward into her hair. The hairnet lifted away and fell to the floor. He played with her auburn strands before clutching her head. She felt helpless. *Would he snap her neck?* If she didn't know what his fingers were capable of, she would have enjoyed the touch. In her weakness, she angled toward his piercing stare.

"Don't hurt me," she begged, twisting toward the lord, pressing her back against large wooden doors. Escape was impossible. Lord Nicolai held her in his embrace.

When he closed the gap between them, the palm of his hand cupped her face. He seemed to sorrow for a moment, but then drew her mouth to his lips. She didn't do anything to prevent his intimacy, and permitted Lord Nicolai to kiss her.

He closed his eyes, pressing against her face, breathing her essence. "Grrr." A low rumble rattled from his chest, and when he opened his eyes again—they were not blue.

"What's happening?" Scarlett shrieked. Shocked, she pushed against his chest. "Who—what—are you?"

He purred; the sound rumbled in his throat. "Perhaps, Bensen didn't tell you his dirtiest secrets. I'm sorry, Scarlett. I am cursed, and I cannot prevent what happens next."

Scarlett screamed when Nicolai reached for the small of her back and roughly pulled her against him. His other hand threaded through her hair and drew her mouth to his lips. A dark passion devoured her mouth, bruising her lips, as if the lord had not touched a woman in a long time. He kissed like a man starved of affection, starved of love. She soon responded to his need, grasping his changing face, hungering for the passion he desired to the death. But then his lips changed, and he nipped at her skin, breaking through the flesh.

Red blood dripped from her lips to her chin while watching his transformation from a man to an animal. She screamed, pushing against his chest. A stab of pain— She tried to free herself from his grip, while witnessing his skin transforming to black velvet. His hands became large black paws. They rested on either side of her head. She screamed, fearing the coppery-yellow eyes of a panther.

I need, I need… to get through the door. But the panther breathed hot air against her face and nuzzled so close to her neck, she didn't dare turn around and lose sight of him.

Scarlett tried to reason a solution. There had to be something she could do to escape this horror. She scrutinized the panther's yellow eyes, searching for signs of the man who had stood before her moments before. Her courage mounted.

"Nicolai, are you inside this creature?" she said, her voice quaking. "Can you hear me? You must fight this curse. Do you hear me? Fight it!"

The door opened and Scarlett slumped to the flooring; the panther dropped to the ground, too, landing with a thump on either side of her feminine figure on four strong paws. She inched through the doorway, retreating from him, crawling backward, never taking her eyes off the beast whose hot breath fanned her skin. He roared like a lion, stalking toward her, baring his teeth. Long white fangs flashed inside his mouth.

"Nicolai— Please, don't hurt me."

Scarlett felt tears forming in her eyes as she inched farther backward, sliding across the flooring with her hands. Had Bensen lied to her? *Where was the cage?* But then her fingers touched the edge of cold iron bars, and she pushed herself inside. Now, if there was any hope for her survival and breaking this curse, the beast must follow her movements.

"Everything changes with the capture," she mumbled, sliding across a soft mattress, and soon feeling the bars on the far side. She propelled herself over them while the cat hesitated at the entrance. She told herself not to be afraid. He couldn't know the plan. She must act for both of them.

"Come forward, Nicolai," Scarlett urged. "Let's find an end to this curse. We must try."

The panther stalked forward. The menace needed to prowl one step farther.

The power of the cobra rose inside her blood. "A little bit more, Lord Nicolai, I'm waiting."

Without warning, the panther charged. But before he could reach her, both doors crashed downward, smashing to the ground, trapping his lordship inside. Scarlett heaved a sigh, and slumped to the planked flooring.

Breathing heavily, she scrutinized the animal held inside the cage. She took pity on him; she saw his coppery-yellow eyes were etched with a black appetite.

"Can you understand me?" Scarlett asked, wiping the blood from her lip. "Inside your black sheath, can you hear me? Regardless of good or evil, 'tis true that life changes with the capture. Still, I apologize for locking you inside another prison."

Feeling guilty, she gazed at the flooring. "I understand the unworldly misery that Cynara has committed you to, but the confinement inside this iron cell will be your last. I promise. We'll free you; we'll break this black curse."

Chapter Twenty-Three

LORD NICOLAI GRAYDON

Rage pulsed through two large veins and raced through Nicolai's heart, causing the chambers to flex faster than they had ever moved before. Trapped in what felt like a bird cage, he couldn't reach the traitors who'd conspired to place him here. He'd grasp their throats, starve them of oxygen, and steal their sorry lives if it were possible.

How dared they confine him to a darker place than the bleakness Cynara had cursed him to years ago. *Sarding nether land!* It was too much. He closed his eyes, fighting tears, suppressing his emotion, remembering the brutal tone of gates smashing against the floor. *Crash!*

A snarl emitted from his throat. An outward display of warning revealed itself to the culprits with the rise of black lips and the display of sharp, white fangs. He hissed at them, losing tears that secreted from the darkest reaches of his soul. Held in a cage no more than six cubits wide, he fought the confinement. He didn't want to be held in this place and couldn't accept being further damned. He paced wildly, his tail swishing. He hurled himself at the bars, careened his length against the iron, but the structure held firm.

"Calm down," Bensen scolded, staring at him. "You can't return to your normal self while fussing with your hardhead."

Traitor, Nicolai thought, while trying to stem the rage to lessen the impact of the curse's power. Yet, despite his anger, Bensen was right. Controlling his temper, his pride and his male ego, was the only way to return to human form. Even so, a growl rumbled from his throat and he bared his teeth.

"Stop it!" Bensen shouted, banging his cane against the bars. "I know you're angry. I sense the condemnation and can well imagine what you're thinking. Look, I had to do it. Confining you inside this cage was the safest path forward."

Unafraid, Bensen talked to him as if he were a mortal man, not a panther. *The stupid fool!*

"I take full responsibility. Yes, I built the cage."

What? When had he built it? And how long had the structure been housed here; an erection of iron bars, walls and a ceiling, the prison taking shape inside the great hall without his knowledge? He should have paid better attention to the daily activities of his butler.

Nicolai had never known forced entrapment such as this, and considering Bensen's skills, he wouldn't find a weakness in the iron.

Still, he'd survived sixteen years in an inescapable misery and he had no intention of spending one minute more, let alone the entire night, inside a second prison. He glared at Bensen while studying the princess, which only caused his ire to blaze stronger. He leapt at the iron again, not willing to admit defeat, but the bars held firm, unyielding to his posturing.

"Calm yourself," Bensen yelled. "You'll never return to your human form while howling like a banshee. Breathe through your anger."

Nicolai closed his eyes and pretended that neither Bensen, nor Scarlett, were standing near the cage. Bensen was right. He needed to assert a more peaceful mien. Weakened, he pivoted away from the princess to stem his behavior, as when he observed her feminine figure, hunger gnawed inside his gut.

Princess Scarlett

FEELING BETRAYED, Scarlett shifted away from the sorry scene. "You lied to me, Bensen," she accused, wiping the blood from her lips and pointing a trembling finger at the man who had come close to ending her life. "You told me Nicolai had a blood curse; a brain malady, and that when he hungered for a woman, his mind would shift. You told me he would become a hateful being, an ugly and vile man-beater. You *never* shared the lord of Drum Manor would turn into this, into this beast!"

"If I'd told you the truth, would you have acted out the same drama? Or would you have taken your chances in the forest, running for your life?"

"I don't know what I might have done," Scarlett replied, pacing, threading her fingers through her hair. "But I deserved to know the truth; the real threat I was about to face."

"Truth? I couldn't tell you the truth for fear you wouldn't enact the plan. Look at this creature," he said, gesturing toward the panther. "If I had shared Nicolai's catlike personality, you would never have pursued the role of curse-breaker, or helped me to lock him inside this cage."

Scarlett felt her lip with her tongue. It was impossibly swollen, but her injuries could have been worse. "He could have taken my life. He almost succeeded."

"Princess, let's not exaggerate the situation; you have a slight nick on your lip. Yet, I don't deny the threat. After all these years, I know what Nicolai is capable of. But here you stand, a slight injury, but otherwise alive and breathing. And with the bars separating the two of you, keeping each of you safe from harm as further transformations arise, our hope is restored we can put an end to this curse."

"I still don't know why you think I'll be able to assist."

"I have faith in the powers that brought you here." He winked. "Perhaps with safer conversations, you'll deduce the reasoning."

Studying the panther, Scarlett wasn't so sure. "The beast might be confined, but that doesn't mean I'll act on your instructions. I don't know if I can trust you."

Bensen's expression took on an aggressive guise; he sneered while grasping her hand. "You will do what I want, *Princess*, because you're the only key to my master plan. If you don't work toward the greater good, I'll open the door to that cage and loose the panther on you. I won't hesitate. It's do, or die. You recall the chase, yes?"

"You're crazy."

"Let me tell you something. I have been a loyal servant to this man for years. He might be confined inside a cage, but I don't intend to rob him of hope now. I've known you but a moment, but you will do as we have planned. If you won't try for Nicolai, try as revenge for the witch who put the master—and you too, I might add—in this situation in the first place. The other option is a shared dining experience—"

Scarlett sighed, then slumped beside the cage. She studied the panther who stalked back and forth, pitying the creature whose accusatory stare locked with hers. Did she sense a glimmer of longing, of hope, lurking inside the cat's sad eyes, eyes that belonged to Nicolai? His bleak situation mirrored her own struggle, and the similarities in their desperate straits earned a decision.

"All right," Scarlett said, yielding. "I'll try, since you give me no further choice."

Bensen hobbled across the hall and grabbed an armchair. Struggling, he slid the wingback across the open space to her. "Thank you, on behalf of two lonely men. Sit until the master resumes his normal shape. Don't go near the cage. His hands can change into paws quickly, and grab you, pulling you through the bars. He can't control the hunger."

"You didn't tell me about the hunger."

"You're safe, Princess. When the master returns, ask him about his darker tendencies. It's time he talked about his circumstances."

Chapter Twenty-Four

LORD NICOLAI GRAYDON

When the curse abated, Nicolai returned to his human form. The painful recoiling and compacting of his limbs lessened, and a wrenching illness in his head soon passed, too, but left him feeling like someone had struck him with a club. At the convulsing end, he crouched on the bottom of the cage, panting, collapsing on a mattress stuffed with feathers. Exhausted, he grasped a blanket and covered his nakedness.

He glanced upward, as if through a fog, and noticed that Scarlett was lounging on a chair near his prison, watching his movements. He pulled the blanket tighter around his figure, trying to dispel his anger, reasoning that this woman was responsible for his confinement. He harrumphed, knowing he presented a shameful image of immodesty, given he was unclothed, but he didn't care what naked bits she studied. She had confined him inside this place.

"Does it hurt?" she asked, her voice a whisper. "The change into a man?"

Defeated, Nicolai sighed, bent forward, and placed his head on the cage floor in despair and mistrust. "Yes, it hurts."

"I'm sorry," Scarlett murmured, "and sorrier still you're held within this prison, locked up like a caged beast. But you must understand, your stay is necessary."

Nicolai rolled to his side to entertain a more meaningful look at his jailer. Two details were apparent: the woman was beautiful, and the truth hurt. "I am a beast."

Nicolai could see Scarlett forgot herself. Curiosity compelled her to slip from the chair to sit on the floor beside the cage. Bensen had left her alone, and she observed him with a keen interest, as if studying a scientific experiment.

"You're not a beast. And I must say," she grimaced, leaning forward, "even in the shape of a panther, you're a thought-provoking study. But the scarier aspects of your life will keep me on my toes. I feared for my life."

He shook his head, gauging her soft expression. "I know you did. Especially when Bensen took a miserable time opening the door. I'm sure the latches have rusted."

"His late arrival nearly finished us both," she replied, touching her lip. Nicolai studied the puncture wound. The bloody remnants lingered on her flesh, and he could smell the remaining droplets, trailing a path down her neck. "I bit you, didn't I?"

She wiped her mouth and licked the blood from her lips. He watched her fingers slide across reddened and bruised skin, punctured from his teeth.

"Yes, you bit me. A moment more, kitty cat—I would have suffered a terrible fate. A moment less—I would have missed your kiss."

Nicolai grinned, chuckling at her comment. "I'm sorry, you have desirous lips, and I have missed a woman's touch. As for the bite, I can't control my actions once the curse takes hold."

"I've never been so frightened," Scarlett recalled. "You were a frightful man prior to turning into a monster. I'm not sure how I'm still standing here, listening to you, when you are safely locked inside this cage. I should run. I would run, too, but the options for which direction to travel leave me at a loss for decisive movement. And then there's your butler, a man who believes I might be the key to break your curse. I'm not sure I can help, but, he swore if I tried to leave, he'd lock me in the cage with you."

"My old faithful butler," Nicolai paused in contemplation, "Bensen has shared his interest in the possibility of ending this scourge, but I'm not convinced you can change my misfortune. The opportunities to end this madness lie with the woman who placed this curse on me in the first place. I'm sure she enjoys my discomfort and would never divulge a solution."

"I know Cynara is responsible. Why did she curse you, Nicolai?"

He seemed to contemplate her question. "I wouldn't— couldn't—give her what she wanted."

"And what did Cynara require of you?"

"My good name, my land, my heart—material possessions that all men own. But when I wouldn't yield to her demands, she cursed my heart and ensured through her black arts that no other woman could receive my passion."

Scarlett stood and edged closer to the cage. He watched

her movements. "I don't understand, and I need to understand to help you. What do you mean when you say: *she cursed your heart?*"

Nicolai regarded Scarlett seriously. He sat up. "Cynara wanted me to betroth myself to her. But regardless of the woman's obsessive desire and striking beauty, she was common. If I had owned a wealthy purse, I might have considered the match, but with my responsibility to protect my family holdings, I needed funds. I couldn't choose a woman of Cynara's social standing, and making that choice placed a rage so hot within her head, she shot her electric poison straight into my heart."

Contemplating his words, Scarlett placed her finger on her lip. "Perhaps you should not have dallied with her emotions, but it's too late to chastise you for what a woman perceived years ago. We need to focus on the ill effects of the curse. Please share what medium causes you to shift from a man to a panther, and the hunger you spoke of earlier."

"Women are the stimulus. They cause the curse to arise within my being and boil over to form the shape of the panther."

"How does it feel to be the panther?"

"How does it feel?" He looked to a place she could not see. "Sometimes the creature's stealth gives me morose satisfaction. I'm king of the forest, and with the exception of one woman, not too many predators can hurt me. The animal strength empowers. I take shape without provocation. However, if I contemplate the passion of a woman, *a beauty such as yourself,* my heart beats faster, my blood rushes through my veins. I turn, not to passion or love, but to an evil hunger that causes me to transform. I don't have to tell you what the panther does next."

"Oh my," Scarlett whispered, touching her lip. "You would have done more than bite me. You would have taken my throat. Now I understand why Bensen wanted you inside this cage."

"He's a crafty old creature, and wise, too. I know he only wanted to keep you safe."

Scarlett knelt so her knees rested on the floor beside the cage. She grabbed the cold iron bars with her hands. Nicolai edged closer, too. The blanket tumbled to his naked waist, but he didn't care. He only had eyes for the princess, and with the bars between them, she was possibly safe.

"When did Cynara wreak this havoc on you?"

"Sixteen years ago, when I betrothed myself to Lady Alexandra. So many years have passed..." Nicolai recalled. "I was betrothed to marry a woman with social standing and wealth. I do confess our match was not born of love. I would have married any well-to-do lady to save my beloved Drum Manor. Alexandra's family possessed wealth beyond compare, and with her dowry, I could have returned my home to its former glory. She seemed like a good prospect at the time."

Nicolai felt downhearted while studying the hall. He gestured with his hand. "But instead, I have managed to bring this once beautiful mansion from promise to ruin."

"Did you love her, the Lady Alexandra?"

He smirked, reached for a black bar and slid closer still. "Did I love her? What does a man know about love? She was the answer to my prayers and nothing more."

Nicolai reasoned that his response to Scarlett's question

met with her displeasure. Her face wrinkled in disapproval. She shook her head.

"Sounds a bit one-sided and selfish. You forgo the love of one woman for another flame, and then you deny the new flame a wick in which to burn. Lord Graydon, this is not gentlemanly of you."

"Scarlett," Nicolai protested. "I never had the opportunity to light the flame you speak about. Please let me assure you, I am a gentleman."

"If what you say is true, you leave me curious. Although, I'm not sure I want to know the answer to my next question. What happened to Lady Alexandra?"

Nicolai grew pensive, quiet. He stared at the floor. "She met with a disastrous fate."

"Did you…?"

"No! I have never harmed a woman. Cynara stole her life. I might share some fault in her death, but I never wanted my future wife hurt; our mutual feelings could have grown in time. At any rate, I don't deserve to live my life this way. The price is too high."

"I agree, the cost is great. 'Tis sad Lady Alexandra suffered an unkind fate. I wonder what sort of action could break the curse," Scarlett said, thinking aloud. "Obviously, passion is out of the question."

Nicolai stared at Scarlett in complete disbelief. He grimaced, then chuckled softly, surprised to hear such a statement slip from her lips. He barely knew her. He stood, holding the blanket to his waist, knowing she could see his advantages quite clearly.

"I don't know." Nicolai leaned against the iron bars. "But

I would think passion would be fraught with difficulty. Simply staring at you, breathing in your scent, ignites turmoil inside my head and my loins."

Scarlett stood and placed her hand to her lips. Nicolai was amused when her pale cheeks flamed with a delicious cherry red. She dropped her hand and leaned away from the bars, placing both hands on her hips.

"Don't stare at me then," she ranted, obviously flustered. "Don't smell me either. Look away while we consider our options. There must be a way to end this curse. Cynara is not infallible. A crack must exist in her defenses, and we will search until we discover the flaw, shattering the weakness —together!"

Nicolai was amazed at the hope Scarlett tried to offer, no matter that the possibility of changing his circumstances were slim. Amazing that the woman cared about his plight when she was meant to be his next victim. Whether she meant her words or not, the sentiment touched him.

"What are you thinking, Scarlett Princess?"

"I'm thinking, Nicolai," Scarlett whispered, stepping closer once more, "to break the curse you should face the woman who afflicted you in the first place. Give her your heart. Give her what she has longed for all along. She is a woman alone, without the love of a man now that my father has died. Perhaps she still has a weakness for your heart."

Nicolai harrumphed. "She'd dice it up and eat it. Raw. The woman has hurt me enough, and I don't fancy further pain and anguish. In fact, I don't want to see the witch ever again. And entertaining a new liaison couldn't possibly bring a positive result."

"How do you know unless you try?"

"Cynara would sooner thrust her evil fingers inside my chest and pull out my beating heart from the cavity, grinding the appendage into the floor with her foot. I promise you, Scarlett, no quarter can be gained from an evil witch's lair."

Scarlett lunged toward him. She grabbed his naked shoulders and pulled him toward her.

"Then we have no other choice."

"What are you doing?" Nicolai keened. "Bensen warned you to stay away from the cage."

The light didn't leave her eyes. Nicolai could tell she would not be swayed from her actions.

"There's only one way to break this curse, Nicolai. I think you know what it is."

"Enlighten me," he whispered, stroking the side of her hand. "I know not what you attempt."

"The only way to break the curse must be to educate your heart and add some light to the source. Nicolai, you must learn to love. Only light and love can send this blackness away."

She reached for his head with her hands and threaded her fingers through his hair, gently pulling him closer to the edge of the cage where her lips waited. He didn't want to linger too close to the iron bars. He knew what would happen if he approached. He tried to look away. He dared not peer into her eyes, but she shifted him toward her golden-brown allure and forced his attention to her beauty.

The hunger initiated almost immediately. The hope shining in her eyes was a beacon he couldn't help himself from following. His hands reached through the bars, barely touching her shoulders.

"Kiss me, Nicolai," she implored, studying his eyes with a keen interest.

He found her lips as black patches formed beneath his eyes. Before he transformed, he found the supple flesh wanting, sweet with scientific purpose.

But passion would be denied. A walking stick struck the cage with a resounding thwack, startling the pair and forcing them apart.

"No!" Bensen yelled. "I warned you, Princess. I told you what would happen if you went near the cage. He will cut you apart to get you inside."

"It's a chance we must take," Scarlett cried, pushing away from the bars in frustration. "It's the only way to end this curse. Come what may, your master must learn to love an authority greater than himself."

Bensen struck the cage again. Lord Nicolai backed away, not wanting either of them to see the bits of black velvet that had sprouted on his cheeks and chin.

"Love is not born of lust," Bensen appealed, maneuvering Scarlett away from the cage. "If my master is to break this curse through love, then you must teach him romantic language without ever touching him. Do you understand what is at stake?"

"Yes," Lord Nicolai and Princess Scarlett replied at the same time. Scarlett, in sad defeat, slumped in the chair.

"Promise me you won't make the same mistake again."

Nicolai contemplated Scarlett, who appealed to Bensen with both hands, palms up. "I can make no such promise.

Regardless of your warning, I must play with this curse to glean its strengths and weaknesses. Love is found in words and deeds, and the master is weak, which is why he was vulnerable to the curse. I will do as you say and reflect on a possible solution."

Bensen nodded.

"However," Scarlett said with a heavy sigh, "Lord Nicolai must be hungry, and it would be a shame to waste your cheese and egg potage. You will feed him, and I will retire for the night. We have much to consider and I require my rest to resolve the possibilities."

Nicolai watched Scarlett walk around the cage, assessing him as she moved past his bleak prison. He was certain her mind was already searching for answers to quell his rabid curse—a misfortune that would keep him imprisoned, since he didn't believe she'd be successful, but he admired her determination all the same.

Soon she had left them alone in the great hall.

"The princess is a bit of a bossy woman," Nicolai chuckled softly. "Bensen, she addressed you as if she already managed the lead role of lady of the manor."

The butler's eyes lit with wisdom. "Good looks, a stern backbone, and strong birthing hips. The promise of a new fortune should you ever kill an evil queen. She'd make a fine wife for you, Master."

"I don't deny it," Nicolai said, considering. "I am ravenous with hunger, Bensen. All this chasing around the house has ignited a hunger within my gut. Will you attend to my needs?"

"Don't I always?" Bensen sniggered. "I'll return shortly

with your cheese and egg potage, but somehow, I don't think the soup will satisfy your appetite."

The image of Princess Scarlett reignited in Nicolai's mind as he watched Bensen take his leave. The old man was correct and wise to a fault. Regardless of the blood that had been spilled, the kiss had been worth the risk.

Chapter Twenty-Five

BENSEN

Fruitless days stretched into endless nights, and nights yielded to the failure of more ineffective days. Their efforts were a circular round of 'begin and end' with nary a chance of success. Bensen grew weary of the repetition as the three inhabitants of the manor accustomed themselves to an uncomfortable routine.

"What do I do?" Bensen fretted. He knew Nicolai was growing weary of his confinement, but the iron cage kept the inhabitants of the manor safe. He remembered building the cage years ago, bar by bar, worrying his secret might become known. But undisturbed, he'd gone about his construction in the morbidness of the great hall, thinking he might need its protective walls for himself.

At the arrival of the princess, he had welcomed the opportunity to put the cage's strength to the test, arranging a tight but comfortable living space for his lord and master. Yet, he felt guilty for Nicolai's lengthy stay and the certain knowledge that they were failing.

He stoked the fire each morning, preparing the foodstuffs that would satisfy their hunger as Master Nicolai and Princess Scarlett attempted to undermine the curse. He could see their relationship was growing closer with each passing day as each of them had a stake in ending the nightmare.

Master Nicolai wanted his life back.

Princess Scarlett desired a new life, too.

Bensen hoped if a cure could be found, he could move forward with renewed purpose. Perhaps his wounds would heal as well.

He'd held out for hope for so long, it hurt to watch possibility slip further away.

Even so, no matter the conversation, they came no closer to breaking the curse. Bensen was beginning to believe that this blight, this long dark night, required a force greater than a princess to finally conclude.

Frankly, he had begun to believe that witnessing an ending to this damn malady would not be possible. If a resolution didn't transpire soon, he'd have to send the princess away and set his master free.

Chapter Twenty-Six

PRINCESS SCARLETT

Scarlett retired to her bedchamber earlier than usual with her head aching from the constant weighing and examining every probable solution to Lord Nicolai's dilemma. One vital question repeated itself, over and over again: "How do we put an end to this curse?"

Feeling anxious, she worried her lower lip with her teeth while lying on top of cushioned layers of bedding. Attempting to relax, she pulled the coverlet up to her chest, not bothered by the lingering smell of mold and mildew.

Try as she might, Scarlett had come no closer to solving the riddle, and a fortnight had already passed since they had successfully locked Lord Nicolai in his cage. It was a cruel punishment. If a solution could not be found soon, she would be forced to leave Drum Manor, thereby freeing the man from at least one misery. She wouldn't keep Nicolai confined in an iron cage longer than was necessary.

But where would she go? She couldn't stay in this house if

the curse couldn't be broken, but she didn't want to leave anymore, either. This problem kept her thinking about probable solutions during her waking hours. How could she undermine the witch? There must be a way.

Cynara had placed the curse on Nicolai in anger as a penance for wronged affection, but regardless of the enchantress's emotions, the pair had shared a one-sided relationship. Nicolai had not loved Cynara, nor had he loved other women. In many ways, he was a helpless beast who had used passion to stoke his advantage.

If insincere affection had placed Nicolai in this predicament, could learning to love break the curse? Scarlett could not be sure. They had broached the subject of love shattering the darkness, which might dissipate the curse, but could such an action provide a lasting cure?

How could one teach a man to love? Scarlett had never experienced such affection, and she didn't know how to offer the education. Rational fear prevented her from venturing too close to the object of her discovery. She had experienced his teeth, and the scar at the corner of her lip reminded her of his bite.

Frankly, Scarlett didn't love Lord Nicolai. Sure, she felt a token bond of camaraderie as they shared a common foe, but none of her female emotions equated to something more romantic. Some women believed they felt sensual stirrings at the first sight of their future mate; *however*, meeting Nicolai had earned a different reaction.

A dangerous attraction had existed from the start, but now that she had witnessed him changing into a panther, the transformation itself challenged her feelings for the lord, feelings that must be explored in order to respond to the question of the curse.

Still, she was beginning to feel a token friendship for Nicolai. They faced a similar nemesis and the same problem, in the name of Cynara Musadora.

Scarlett rolled onto her stomach and punched her pillow in frustration. She understood that to break this curse, she had to pursue all avenues of possibility. No other option existed. She needed to know the man better in order to pursue means and methods, but developing a closer relationship with Nicolai was a dangerous gamble, regardless that he was locked inside a cage. Simply studying Nicolai ignited turmoil in her gut, and she had to admit the truth of the situation. He modeled a stimulating image of a masculine man, and she didn't mind perusing his handsome physique. Therein lay three constant difficulties: sight, touch, and smell.

Sight. Nicolai possessed compelling blue eyes, but seeing a woman through his human lens held the first complication of the curse. Sight triggered a sexual interest in a woman, which in turn caused a switch to ignite in his mind.

Bensen had blindfolded Nicolai in the hopes that limited sight would prevent the shift from man to panther. However, as soon as Scarlett touched Nicolai, *anywhere*, the black scourge willed itself to begin the transformation.

Touch. Scarlett was drawn to Nicolai's hands, but touching them had encouraged a secondary demon to present itself. Touch ignited an electrical current that journeyed from his brain to the rest of his human form, triggering the blood change to begin. She had experienced as much during their first kiss, and continued scientific explorations always led to the same result. Black transformations. She'd given up on affection through physical caresses.

Smell. Scent triggered the desire to kill, in that the nose begat a hunger, which in order to be fed required the taste of blood. But no matter what method Bensen and she used to bind Nicolai's nostrils, his sense of smell could not be abated, or thwarted from scenting her blood. A garment could be held in front of the cage, held from a distance across the room, and Nicolai changed.

The poor man was tiring of this game.

If anything, an evil desire for the opposite affection, *hate,* grew stronger within Nicolai. If she left the manor, permitting Bensen to release his master, would that lifeblood-desire lead Nicolai to hunt for her on whatever path she travelled, no matter which way she walked? If so, she'd die anyway.

Scarlett had hoped the curse might be thwarted by denying the three senses, but attempting to do so had failed.

How could lessons be taught if most mental capacities were turned off?

This left the benefit of hearing as the only means left to her to play with the possibility of a kind education, and she was beginning to believe that *love* wasn't the solution at all. A stronger quotient, perhaps a magical ingredient she couldn't quite determine or define, waited to be found.

"*Love,*" Scarlett sighed, rising from the coverlets. "I want to experience this tender emotion, but I'm not sure if Lord Nicolai could become a lady's partner, even if he offered more than black desire. What happens if Bensen and I fail?"

Scarlett gave up on her need for sleep, rose from her bed in her nightclothes, and left the lady's bedchamber. Perhaps the answer lay hidden somewhere else.

Though eerie sounds hooted in the night, the light of a full moon guided her passage as she left her bedchamber, carrying a lit taper. She descended the staircase, being careful not to trip as she made her way. She soon found herself standing in the middle of the library, studying a myriad of books.

Scarlett observed the storied surroundings as a single flame lit the space, still forlorn in its dilapidation. She sighed, stepping forward to study spent books, black spider webs, and coats of dust littering each surface. Would this pitiful sight ever change? Scarlett hoped so for Bensen and Lord Nicolai's sakes.

She approached Nicolai's desk and permitted her fingers to slide across the wood-grained surface, trailing a path through the grime. She placed her lit taper on the desk, complete with porcelain stand, and then sat on the leather seat. She leaned forward, resting her elbows on the wooden surface, and placed her hands beneath her chin.

"Hmm," Scarlett mused, considering, finding the gems that decorated her neck. She touched the sapphires, rubbing the blue and white stones between her fingers as she struggled to find answers.

A book fell to the ground. The resulting thwack frightened Scarlett to alertness. She rose from the chair and peered across the library to the nearest bookshelf, noticing that a novel had fallen and now lay open at an awkward angle. She stepped toward the volume, seeing that a particular page sought her attention. Scarlett picked the book up and read aloud:

> *"Ah!" she said, when she went at night to bathe her arm, now much reduced in size, "little did I ever think this house, once so peaceful, would be so changed." "A merry place, 'tis said, in days of yore, but something ails it now— the place is curst," was the mental comment of Constance.*[1]

"What foul happening is this?" Scarlett wondered aloud, closing the book. Yet she chose to believe the novel's movement to the floor was an accident. Perhaps a rodent had crawled among the shelving, causing the volume to fall. Not feeling up to reading, she placed the book on the shelf, sliding the leather tome in between two volumes of similar size. She returned to the desk, only to hear something bang to the flooring again.

Scarlett pivoted, staring at the bookshelf in surprise, shocked to witness the same novel lying open on the floor. Shivers crawled up her spine. Hadn't the book falling to the floor been an accident? What had caused this disturbance? Tentatively, she approached the book, but as she neared its resting spot, the pages flipped, feathering back and forth as if a real person was flipping the pages, until the movement quit at page 251.

"What just happened?" Scarlett fretted, reaching for the book. Grasping the intended message in her hand, she read from the volume again.

For who with clear account remarks, the ebbing of his glass, when all its sands are diamond sparks, which dazzle as they pass?[2]

What could this tomfoolery possibly mean? Was someone attempting to send her a message? If so, who? She closed the book to peer at the main title. "*The Wife's Trials,*" she whispered, "authored by Wife?" Scarlett held the book while contemplating the library. What else hid among the cobwebs? Surely not a ghost? A cold shiver ran up her spine as if a finger had touched her, then fingered the length of her back to the top of her neck. She shook off the sensation, considering the possibilities, but she knew with a certainty that something had flipped the pages. Pages did not turn by themselves.

Scarlett returned to Nicolai's desk and placed the closed book on its surface. She scrutinized the volume for several seconds, waiting and watching for another magical event to occur. She stepped away in amazement when the book opened and the pages flipped again.

Our remedies oft in ourselves do lie,
　Which we ascribe to heaven.[3]

Scarlett reclaimed the book and concentrated on the passage, understanding that in this mystical action, some unearthly force was attempting to deliver a message. Though shivers whispered along her spine, she tried not to be afraid. She had witnessed a man transforming into a panther. Surely a ghost could not harm her.

"Our remedies oft in ourselves do lie?"

She could only ascertain one meaning from the quote: The remedy or solution to the curse must come from her. She shook her head, not knowing where else she could dig to find an answer. Perhaps it was better to set her feet to bed and leave her worries to revisit on the morrow.

Scarlett contemplated the book in her hands, wondering what she should do with the volume. Should she place it on the shelf, where it might jump off again, or bring it with her to her bedchamber? She decided to do the latter. Perhaps she'd place it underneath her pillow, where the pages would be silent, unable to turn again. Or maybe the words would somehow find her in her dreams?

Scarlett sighed, finally feeling the weight of her fatigue. She retraced her steps to her bedchamber, climbed into her bed, and tucked the book beneath the covers. "It's ironic," she mused, "*A Wife's Trials* by the authoress, Wife. Nicolai does not have a wife."

Scarlett tossed and turned for a time, but she soon succumbed to a restless sleep. Among the shadows of Drum Manor she walked. Leaving her lady's bedchamber, she moved from the top floor to the landing, where she studied the dreary paintings of the past. She soon found herself entering the great hall. A crowd of rich people wearing elaborate finery had gathered in the space. Their presence surprised her. *Were they waiting for her? Why were they here?*

Scarlett retraced her steps to the entrance of the hall, only to realize that the large iron cage no longer sat at the entrance. The realization frightened her, and her heartbeat quickened in response. She scanned the hall, turning this way and that, searching for the lord of Drum Manor, but he was nowhere in sight. And the ballroom differed from the shabby space she had viewed hours before. Lit with a warm golden light, the hall welcomed her inside, and an unknown entity urged her to come closer.

She was surprised that nary a speck of dust lingered on any surface. No grime settled on the lounge chairs along the walls or on the banquet tables that held a bounty of finger foods. She searched again for Lord Nicolai, expecting him to greet her with his dangerous charm, but instead, a woman's birdlike twitter caused her to pivot toward the sound.

"Princess Scarlett," a woman murmured, "how nice to meet you."

Scarlett scrutinized the complexion of a pale white angel, whose long white hair fell past her shoulders, tangling at her waist into a matted nest. Dewy blue eyes stared at her, emitting a cryptic white light. The helix shone so bright that the room no longer held interest; the faded blue surcoat hugged the angel in a familiar style.

"Do I know you?" Scarlett asked.

The woman glanced away demurely and then peered at her in appeal. "We're not acquainted," she whispered. "Before now, the ebb and flow of our lives made it impossible for us to meet."

"How did our meeting become possible?"

The angel tittered nervously; her hand floated to her neck.

"You're wearing my jewels. I suppose the blue gems linked with the spirits to help you with the remedy you seek."

"My remedy?" Scarlett gaped at the woman, confused, but then a memory surfaced. "Oh yes, the question about the curse. Can you help? Do you have information about the curse?"

The angel smiled thinly, nodding. Her tiny hand flitted to her neck once more. "I know how you can end the curse." She trilled a second time.

Scarlett cringed at the shrill note puncturing the air in the room. Its vibrancy was so stark and piercing, the sound hurt her hearing and almost gave her a fright. She cringed from the vibrations.

"How? What do I need to do?"

The woman reached toward her and clasped her hand with icy cold fingers, fingers that compelled her to rush across the great hall at an abrupt pace. Just as quickly, she stopped. Extending her right hand, she pointed at the wooden flooring. She bore a grave, sad visage.

"Do you see the spot?"

Scarlett's eyebrows rose, for nary a spot existed. "I don't suppose I do…"

"Look closer," she urged. "You will notice diamond sparks floating across the floor. Look at the spot with your third eye. Search the space. Look hard. Do you see the light?"

Scarlett took a step closer. She saw by the angel's serious expression and by the firm tone of her voice that her message waxed important. Scarlett searched the space, seeing only a parquet wooden floor. She knelt on the wood and cautiously drew her fingers through the airy space. Still, her vision came up blind.

"No," the woman cried, shoving Scarlett's shoulders with all her might, forcing her to fall backward, away from the spot. "You will disturb the particles. You must not disturb the particles."

Pain reverberated through Scarlett's back and lower extremities. Anger suffused through her. She lay on the hard wooden floor, gazing upward at a ghost of a woman whose eyes had changed from white light to an ugly gray. She shivered, noting the angel's leathery skin with dark smudges underneath her eyes and lips so cracked and dry, they could bleed. A dry, dead ghost stood before her, certainly not an angel. The sight frightened Scarlett so much that her anxiety rose and her heart raced with fear. She slid backward, trying to retreat from this nightmare.

"Madam, you're crazy. I have heard enough. Stay away from me."

The ghost moved swiftly and grabbed Scarlett's wrist. Unimaginable strength yanked her forward, forcing Scarlett to kneel. The ghost grasped her head, almost extracting her auburn hair from its roots, drawing her to the spot, forcing her to see whatever magic the spot held.

"Look closer," she demanded. "The diamond sparks appear on that spot, dancing, assuming a circular bend on the floor like a constellation of stars in the night sky. Remember: *When all its sands are diamond sparks, that dazzle…*"

Scarlett burned with anger, her memories clouded, but somehow, she recalled the mark on the floor. At first, she refused to search, but as her curiosity took hold, she did peer at the spot and the tiniest glimmer of light met her observation. The glow was faint, and not at all the behavior of sparkling diamonds, appearing more like white energy or an inner light. A chakra. Astounded, she forgot to be angry and leaned closer. She could see the light. Finally, she could see the diamonds dancing, as they radiated and swelled into the image of a tiny sparkling woman—on that damnable spot!

"Oh my," Scarlett whispered, leaning closer, appealing to the ghostly angel with an extended hand. "I see it."

"Good." The woman sighed heavily. "Now, listen carefully. To break the curse, you must remember each detail I share with you. If you forget anything I say—miss a step or an ingredient—this conversation will have been for naught."

"I will remember."

"I hope so. You must first find a pint crock with a serviceable lid. Once found, bring the pint to this spot, and gently sweep the diamond glints inside the container. Be gentle. Be careful! If some are lost…"

"I'll be careful," Scarlett promised. "Please continue."

"I will do everything possible to help you see my spirit glowing. Once the diamond shimmer is contained within the crock, you must add to the light one full cup of liquid blood. It must be human."

"Human blood? Where will I get that?"

"Slit your wrist if you must, but the blood must be human."

Scarlett frowned. "It will be human."

The ghostly angel sighed, seeming to struggle with her breathing, her instructions continuing. "Stir the diamond light and the human blood with a wooden spoon. The spoon must be made of wood, for wood represents the earth. Do you understand?"

"I understand. What do I do with the blood drink?"

"You take the crock and its contents to Lord Nicolai. He must drink it all and not spill a single drop. He must not be sick. Don't tell him that it will make him ill and gravely so."

"Why should I feed him this concoction if the blood will make him sick?"

The ghost raised her hands in appeal. "Because the illness is a manifestation of opposing forces, good and evil, fighting to extricate this black curse. I will win. I will rip the scourge from Nicolai's black heart."

Scarlett searched the woman's face. Curious to learn more information about the woman she was conversing with, she rose from the floor and stood on her feet again. "Who are you?"

"I am Lady Alexandra."

"Lady Alexandra?" Scarlett shrieked in surprise. "I thought you were dead. Why would you assist Lord Nicolai with an ending to the curse? He showed you little love."

Lady Alexandra stepped toward Scarlett, and reached for her hand. "I do not act for the man. I don't care about the man. The death of the black curse will result in my human resurrection to new life. I will live again."

"New life," Scarlett said in a whisper. "You will live again. Walk again. But how can this be possible?"

Lady Alexandra drifted farther away. Scarlett watched as her feminine form blurred, transforming into a rainbow of glistening beads, awaiting its ocean. However, Alexandra's voice lingered. "You must wait and see. Now, repeat my instructions."

Scarlett searched inside her mind, remembering. "A pint crock, this spot on the floor, diamond dust, human blood, red blood, and Nicolai. Make him drink, and don't spill a drop."

Scarlett awoke in the morning with the words slipping fresh from her lips and *The Wife's Trials* held firmly in her hand. "Make him drink!"

"A dream, only a dream," she whispered. But the drama-filled scene playing in her mind had felt real. And if it were true, then Lady Alexandra was alive.

Perhaps a crazy reality toyed with her mind, but the realism compelled Scarlett to act. She threw off the covers and jumped from her bed, running to the large ivory door. Unlocking it, she reached for the handle and pulled on the knob. In her haste to leave the room, the door banged against the wall.

Down the flight of stairs she raced, wearing only her linen shift, running as if her life depended on the action. She rushed to the doors of the great hall, which barred her entrance. Standing before the two large doors with her heart racing, she reached for the right handle, but the knob refused to turn.

I must get inside.

She tried to turn the knob again. Evidence was waiting and she must view this diamond spot during the daylight hours.

She must see it now.

1. *The Wife's Trials, Volume III*: By Wife. A novel. 3 vols. (London: Hurst and Blackett, publishers 1855) p. 149.
2. *The Wife's Trials, Volume III:* By Wife, p. 25l. (Lady Anne Hamilton. William Robert Spencer. Poem. 1770–1834)
3. *The Wife's Trials, Volume III*: By Wife. p. 219. (*All's Well that Ends Well*. William Shakespeare. Play. 1602)

Chapter Twenty-Seven

PRINCESS SCARLETT

"Princess Scarlett," Bensen called from somewhere behind her. "What's gotten into you? Have you forgotten that I lock the door for your own protection?"

Scarlett didn't turn around. Determined to access the great hall, she held the knob in a firm grip. "You don't understand. I have to go inside the hall to speak to Nicolai. It's urgent."

"Why?" he asked, shuffling closer. "Has something changed?"

"As a matter of fact, yes!" Scarlett proclaimed, pivoting to face the butler, pressing her back against the door. "A disturbance occurred during the night that may have provided the solution we've been searching for, but I won't know until I'm able to enter the hall."

"I can see you're anxious, Princess. Why don't we talk about your reasons for entering the hall before we disturb Master Nicolai? Perhaps while we prepare the food to break his morning fast?"

Scarlett banged the wooden door with her fist, but as Bensen held the key to her entry, warring with the man wasted her energy. Sighing, she admitted defeat, pushed away from the double doors, and stepped toward the old gent instead.

"I suppose you leave me no other option. Lead on to the kitchen, but permit me to bend your ear while we make our way."

He had the nerve to gawk at her with a raised brow. "Perhaps after the princess changes into a garment more—suitable for daywear?"

When Scarlett realized she was wearing little else than her linen shift, her face blazed pink. She crossed her arms against her chest.

"Oh dear," she muttered, self-conscious in her night clothes. "I'm sorry, Bensen. I will change into clothing more appropriate and meet you shortly."

"Do hurry," he replied, "you have gained my curiosity."

"Yes, of course," Scarlett agreed. She hurried to her bedchamber, retracing her steps up the staircase with a purpose to dress in more acceptable clothing. Once inside the chamber, she attended to her toilette, dressed in a modest forest-green surcoat, and bound her hair in a matching snood adorned with tiny white pearls.

Normally she would check her image in the reflecting glass, but she had little time for vain tendencies, given the developments during the night. Instead, she collected *The Wife's Trials* from the side table and hurried through the doorway.

When Scarlett entered the kitchen, she noticed that

Bensen had stoked the fire. She accepted the stool he had placed before the counter's edge. A seed of truth lingered from the female visitor who had occupied her dreams the night before, and Scarlett hoped the butler would believe the fanciful story.

Scarlett told her tale while Bensen worked at their breakfast. He said little while she recollected her experience in the library. He was quieter still as she shared the elements of her lifelike dream. She watched him add a healthy dollop of lard to the hot skillet. The fat melted and then slowly slid, sliding around the cast iron pan.

When Scarlett mentioned the spot on the floor where diamonds were clustered in the shape of a woman, he stopped to stare at her.

"You don't say," he paused, dumbfounded, then returned to his work. Half a dozen eggs in quick succession hit the skillet's side and fell from his hands into the pan. Bensen soon had them bubbling above the fire.

"She told me I would require a full pint of a human's lifeblood. Where will I—will we—find a pint of blood?"

"A curious prospect," Bensen snickered, adding a handful of mushrooms to the pan and then stirring them with a wooden spoon.

"Bensen, I see that look in your eyes. You don't believe me, do you?"

He sighed and laid the spoon on the countertop as his mixture bubbled away. "Do you believe this story has merit? Or are you toying with me? It sounds like a child's tale weaved with a woman's keen imagination."

He picked the book up and fingered through the first few

pages, seeming to find little of consequence. "Doubtful," he stated, returning the book to its resting place.

"But both experiences seemed real; neither could be a dream," Scarlett urged, touching his wrinkled hand in appeal. "Bensen, my experience was genuine."

He guffawed. "You think Lady Alexandra appealing to you from the grave was factual? I watched her die with my own eyes."

"I know this story sounds like an outlandish tale, and I know not how or why, but Lady Alexandra is not dead. She lives! Somehow, she is caught between this world and a Netherworld."

He chortled with laughter. "She is caught in the hold of your imagination."

The humorous inflection in his masculine tone infuriated Scarlett. She grabbed a knife from its wooden sheath and stabbed the sharp blade into the wooden counter beside his hand.

"Bensen! I don't have time for your ill humor. Neither does Lord Nicolai. After a fortnight of frustration, please respect the ghostly spectacle I experienced. Books don't fall from shelving by accident and pages don't turn without assistance from someone or something, which leads me to believe the enacted drama was real. It was real!"

He considered her thoughtfully, amusement creasing the corners of his silvery old eyes, but she also saw that his curiosity had taken hold. "You're serious? You're not toying with me?"

"Bensen," Scarlett begged. "This could be the break we have been waiting for."

He left the knife where it stood on the counter and brought the skillet forward from its perch above the fire, holding eggs nicely cooked.

"My master will be hungry. Perhaps we'll share your tale while we break our fast. Make yourself useful, Princess. Gather the plates and the cutlery. We make our way, from this point forward, together."

"What about the knife?"

He chuckled again. "Bring it. Later, we shall use it to acquire your blood. Bring the book, too, if you have the mind. The master enjoys a good read."

Chapter Twenty-Eight

LORD NICOLAI GRAYDON

Nicolai fidgeted inside his cell, mentally wounded from living his life in forced entrapment, whether the confinement came about from a curse long suffered, or a cage. His captivity might be necessary, but the stay caused him fatigue, hardened his heart, and filled him with a sense of impending doom. There was no escape from this bloody rune.

The cage's width, not much greater than his physical height, robbed him of independence. The space barely allotted enough area for a mattress, let alone a stool. He grabbed a black rounded bar, feeling the steely cold beneath his fingertips while perusing the hall.

"Look at what I've become," he said, studying a sea of dusty spoils. "Not pretty, not pretty at all. The view becomes graver with each passing day."

Nicolai sighed, released the bar and wiped at his brow. He prowled across the abysmal length, likening his step to how a cat would seek, never losing hope that a weakness or a way out might be found. The exertion only increased his anxiety. He slumped to a wooden stool.

"Damn you, Bensen."

Nicolai hadn't known his servant could be so crafty, but he should have recognized his skills as in many ways, each of them had been forced to suffer similar circumstances. One of them on the inside of the curse, the other forced to respond to the consequences.

When had Bensen built this monstrosity? It seemed like a waste of effort. Freedom didn't seem likely for either of them, and his trusted butler was too wise to permit avenues of escape before the timing was right, if the timing could ever be opportune.

I must be patient, Nicolai reasoned.

The hall door opened and Bensen entered. Princess Scarlett followed close behind him, carrying plates and cutlery. She appeared as anxious as he felt inside.

"Breakfast is served, Master Nicolai. Princess Scarlett and I have come with more than your morning meal. The princess has shared an amusing tale with me. In fact, she was anxious to see you earlier this morning to discuss her interesting imagination."

Nicolai watched the pair walk around the cage. He saw how Scarlett's brow creased with annoyance at his butler's comment, which made him curious to learn what this was all about. She placed three plates on a small side table. He was hungry for the food and hungrier still for her feminine charm. Perhaps further scientific experiments, too.

Nicolai snickered, studying the princess. "Don't keep a captive audience waiting. I enjoy a good story."

She took a deep breath and sighed heavily. "Last night, Lady Alexandra visited me in the library, and then she came to me in a dream," she began, rising from her task. "She told me how to end the curse."

Nicolai grabbed the bars, grappling with the news Scarlett had shared with him, but he didn't express outward signs of believing her. How could he? Good could not be found in death, and Alexandra was deceased. Frankly, dead women did not tell their tales.

He shook his head in disbelief at her disclosure, but boredom intrigued him to ask questions. "Alexandra has come to you, and in a dream? Tell me, Scarlett. What has she revealed?"

Scarlett faced him, serious in her expression. Her beautiful golden-brown eyes fired with emotion. "You won't like it."

He smiled slightly. "I don't like being locked in an iron cage, either."

She stepped closer. "Lady Alexandra shared startling information with me, but more importantly, she said to escape the curse, you must drink a cup of lifeblood—human blood, no less—mixed with her spirit."

He raised his brow in bemusement and leaned against the iron bars. "What? Scarlett, I see how this story has excited you, but there's no spirit left to mix with bodily fluids. Cynara took her care to burn all human trace, nothing remains of my former fiancée."

"I thought you'd believe me. Despite two men's disbelief, I'm not making this up. Something remains!" Scarlett asserted, appealing to him. "I have witnessed diamond sparks with my own two eyes."

"What have you seen?"

Scarlett turned away from him and crept across the flooring, taking her time to investigate a path that for all intents and purposes, didn't give off much of anything.

"Her remains," she ground out, moving methodically, as if searching for a lost piece of jewelry. He was interested in her pursuit and was keen to see if she would make a discovery.

"I have to be careful," Scarlett said, taking tentative steps forward while searching the ground. "The orbs cannot be disturbed until I seek to remove them. And they must be captured together and stirred just so. With a spoon of the earth—a wooden spoon."

"Most interesting," Nicolai whispered, disregarding her exploration. He contemplated his fingers, then sought his butler's attention. "Bensen, what do you think of this story? I don't see anything but dust and ashes."

Bensen raised his brow and plated a helping of eggs. "I think you should eat, Master Nicolai, while the princess takes up her study. Might as well not go hungry while we're waiting for results."

Bensen passed the plate through a small opening in the bars into Nicolai's outstretched hands. A fork soon followed. But Nicolai's attention focused on Scarlett. She had become quiet, intent on her discovery.

He watched her kneel on the dust-strewn floor in a simple dress, a forest green as lovely as the leaves that used to grow on his favorite tree. She was beautiful. The woman had certainly captured his interest in the passing weeks. He wished he could taste her sweetness without regret. Regardless of whatever scientific discovery she explored, the panther always came forth and he was certain the scent of her blood still lingered in his nostrils.

"What do you seek among the dust piles? Surely nothing of consequence can be found on the flooring?"

"Quiet, Nicolai. I must locate the diamond orbs. If I don't see their glow, then perhaps you're right, and my visitation was no more than a dream."

Nicolai sat on the stool. He took a forkful of eggs and enjoyed the first bite. Bensen had become a satisfactory cook. He consumed a second helping while watching Scarlett scour the floor, intently searching. She seemed to sadden as the minutes ticked by.

"Bensen," he muttered between bites, "it appears I will be locked inside this cage for an eternity."

When Scarlett squealed with delight, Nicolai refocused his attention to where she sat on the floor. He heard her laughter rippling like a sweet breeze rushing in from the ocean. He watched the breath from her lips cause the dust motes to float into the air. She stood slowly and stepped away from the spot on the floor. She brushed the dust from her knees and returned to his prison with a satisfied expression and a beatific smile on her face. Bensen made to hand her a plate of breakfast, but she dismissed his offering with a haughty wave and grabbed the bars of Nicolai's cage instead. The appeal in her eyes gave him hope.

"I wasn't wrong. I have seen them again. I swear by all that is righteous and holy that the sparkling diamonds I observed in my dreams are alive, dancing on that spot over there."

When Scarlett pointed in the general direction she had just left, Nicolai had a memory. Bensen dropped his fork on the floor.

"That particular location?" Nicolai whispered. "It's the same spot that Alexandra met her death."

Princess Scarlett clapped her hands. "It's real, don't you see? Lady Alexandra has come to me. She will be your salvation, Nicolai. She will end this curse. All you need to do is drink her aura mixed with blood. But therein lies a problem."

Nicolai stood. "It's not a problem. I'm accustomed to the taste of blood."

Scarlett grabbed the iron bars. "But we require human blood. Where will we find the blood we need? It can't come from me."

Bensen chuckled, and Nicolai smiled in mutual understanding. "If blood is what I require, of course it can be filled by you. You want to help me, don't you?"

Bensen grinned. "We know all we need to know. You had best eat, Scarlett; you will require your strength."

Scarlett sighed and reached for the plate that Bensen had previously offered. She leaned against the iron bars and ate reluctantly while Nicolai watched her, shaking his head.

"Stop it. You're both staring at me as if I'm the next course."

When she finished, Bensen took her empty plate and placed it on the floor. He pulled a small knife from his pocket. "You are the next course, and we thank you for being the mark to end this infernal curse."

Scarlett jumped when Bensen grabbed her left wrist. "What are you doing? How dare you!"

Nicolai watched the princess fighting, twisting to and fro, trying to free herself from his wily old butler, who conveniently maneuvered her into contact with the cage. He grabbed her free wrist and held her still.

"We have need of your blood," Nicolai stated. "It's required, according to your conversation with Lady Alexandra."

He could tell she was afraid, but she had shared the possibilities when she recollected her dream. She had instigated this journey and would have to see it through to the end.

"Wait! I'll give you my blood, but there's a factor you need to know first."

"What more do we need to know?" Nicolai said, reaching through the bars again and wrapping his arm around her waist. And although the bars separated them, he pulled her closer to his chest, breathing hot air against her ear. "Tell us, Princess Scarlett. Tell us what we need to know."

"I carry the blood of the cobra," she hastened to say, her heartbeat rising. "I will gladly offer it up, but I warn you, I don't know if you'll survive if you consume my blood."

He pulled her left arm to his face and nuzzled her flesh against his skin. He felt the black curse raging hot within himself. "Is this the real reason Cynara sent you to me? To kill me with your blood?"

"No," Scarlett cried out, trying to escape his grip. "At least, I don't think so."

Bensen released her other hand and approached the spot she had investigated moments before. "I don't see any tiny bits. Nothing unusual sparkling here, Master Nicolai, no diamond bits shining anywhere."

"They are there," Scarlett said, angering. "But they're difficult to see."

Nicolai felt the urgency in her voice. He was tired of living this way. It was time to believe, time to take a risk. He grasped her hand tighter, but he needed to know one more detail.

"Why do you think Cynara sent you here?"

"To die! 'Tis obvious."

She managed to shift in his grasp and pivot toward him, and stared at his eyes in an earnest manner that caused his breath to quicken.

"To die?"

"Yes, to die. It's a long story, but after the cobra bit me—"

"—Princess, we don't have time for long stories."

"She sent me to you, so you could complete what she couldn't finish herself."

It was time to trust someone, and in that moment, Nicolai chose to place his trust in Scarlett.

"I believe you. I'll drink from your cup. If I survive your poison, I could reap a larger reward. Maybe I'd be immune to her witchcraft, too."

"Bensen," Nicolai said, grimacing, "do you have the vessel in which to catch the blood?"

"We require a pint crock. Is that correct, Princess?"

Scarlett squirmed in his embrace. "Yes."

"Get the crock, Bensen," Nicolai demanded, "and bring the knife, too."

Scarlett shrieked when Bensen left the hall. "What are you

going to do? Nicolai, you're hurting me. Please let go of my wrist. You'll turn…"

"We're going to take your blood," Nicolai said, smelling the scent of her skin and the red that flowed beneath.

She twisted and tried to escape his grasp, knowing as he knew that the beast threatened to rise. But Nicolai held tight to her arm.

"But my blood might cause you harm."

"It might also give me a chance at life and make me immune to Cynara's spells. That's a gift too precious to refuse."

The butler returned, huffing and puffing. Nicolai pressed his face into the layers of her auburn hair and breathed deeply. The curse warred inside him for change, and he fought hard to remain standing as a man.

"Bensen has repeatedly warned you not to get too close to the cage, but you refuse to listen. But don't worry, darling, you won't linger here for long."

Nicolai felt the cold steel of a blade placed against his palm. "May the gods forgive me."

Scarlett screamed when Nicolai slid the knife across her wrist, but she held still in his grip. A rain of blood sprayed forth and Bensen captured it in a solid pint crock. Nicolai couldn't sense her emotion or guess at the fear she might be experiencing. But he did sadden when she slumped on the other side of his iron prison and slipped into unconsciousness.

She had paid a price. He'd have to pay a price, too. Time would tell if the outcome was worth the cost.

Chapter Twenty-Nine

PRINCESS SCARLETT

When Scarlett opened her eyes, she was lying on the sofa in the drawing room, surrounded by shadows. At first, she didn't know where she was or what had happened to her hours before, but her memories were soon restored with shocking clarity. Lord Nicolai had withdrawn her blood and she had fainted in the pain of the moment.

In the hours that had passed, the sun had slipped beneath the horizon, giving way to darkness. She turned her head to the side, glimpsing a candle burning on the side table. Beyond its tiny, flickering wick, a fire burned in the hearth. The heat alerted her to the tingling pain in her wrist.

Scarlett gently lifted her arm and saw that her wrist had been bound tightly with a cream strip of cloth. Sighing, she supposed she should be grateful to the lord of the manor who had taken care not to let her bleed to death. Apparently, the beast with sharp teeth also had some talent with a blade.

"You're awake," she heard Nicolai whisper. She laid her aching arm against her chest and turned her head slowly to

"

her right side, focusing across the drawing room to where he sat. He was dressed comfortably in a white tunic that hung casually past his waist and draped over black breeches. She was hopelessly drawn to his blue eyes. She was not afraid.

"You're not locked in your prison," she commented. "Bensen released you from your cage?"

"Bensen felt he should release me, given that I'm about to risk everything to end this curse—my breath, my beating heart; my life."

Scarlett regarded him where he lounged in his chair with his right leg crossed over his left, his booted foot resting on his knee.

"You appear as if you're at peace with your decision."

"I'm ready for a change."

She knew she should be afraid of this handsome man, this dark beast who could change into a monster in a moment's fancy. Twice he had hurt her, but strangely, she felt comfortable in his presence. Somehow, they were equals.

"So," she whispered. "You will drink my blood?"

"I will be honest with you, Scarlett. I don't believe there's a chance that the curse will be broken," he said with a grimace. "I think it's more likely your tainted blood will kill me."

"If you believe that," Scarlett said, sucking in some air and breathing through the pain, "then why would you take the risk of consuming my lifeblood?"

"I'm tired. Tired of living my life this way. If I die, my suffering will be over and the curse will be broken. I can accept the cost."

Scarlett slowly pushed herself up, rising to a sitting position on the sofa, and placed her feet on the floor. "I don't want you to die, Nicolai."

"Scarlett, I have lived with this infection for too long now. Should you be right and I break free of this curse, to live, to breathe another day, then hallelujah. If not, may the gods in the Otherworld forgive me for my crimes."

"What if you live?" Scarlett asked. "What would you do then?"

Nicolai's smile stretched wide, and his eyes shone bright with hidden possibilities. Scarlett wasn't sure she wanted to know where his thoughts lay.

"It's been so long since I've enjoyed a real life," he sighed, purposefully gazing in her direction, "I'm not sure I would know where to begin."

"Would you search out another wife? Perhaps another female victim to serve your financial interests?"

"You're the only victim in my presence. This man can only hope the princess will lead him on a merry chase to victory."

Scarlett blushed. "Lord Nicolai, you must be cautious about speaking such words at this late hour, as it would be dangerous to awaken the beast. You're no longer locked in a cage."

"At this hour, I only have the end game in mind and not passion. It's time we accepted the drink. My soul has already lain rotten too long in this black night."

Scarlett watched Nicolai rise from the chair. He walked toward her with an outstretched hand. She took his fingers with her uninjured hand and permitted him to help her rise to her feet.

"Come with me to a once grand hall, my Scarlett

Princess. Perhaps if your diamond orbs stir well inside your potion, we can make it grand again, a great hall fit for a princess."

"I don't know." Scarlett sighed, her fingers lingering within his grasp. "Currently, I'm bereft of a crown, so there's little gold to offer your treasury."

Nicolai chuckled and squeezed her fingers. "When we win this battle and remove Queen Cynara from her throne, there will be plenty of gold to aid my purse. And you know, Scarlett Princess," he winked, "how I like a fat purse."

They walked beside each other; their fingers almost touching. She feared the trouble that lay ahead, but she wasn't afraid. "I have not said that I would consider such an offer."

He laughed again, touched her chin with his free hand, and urged her face upward to meet his questioning glance. "You have not said you would refuse me, either."

Chapter Thirty

BENSEN

The midnight hour had almost arrived when the princess began stirring her lifeblood and a disembodied soul inside a crock with a wooden spoon. She sat on an armchair with the master nearby, and Bensen saw she was recovering well from the bloodletting. Her return to good health had surprised him after the amount of blood loss, but he understood her strength rose from a unique blood matrix, thanks to the bane of the snake world.

He glanced away from the princess to concentrate on His Lordship, who sat on a leather-covered bench in a once great hall, the poorer lord waiting for his unnatural drink. Bensen had never seen him so contemplative, or so quiet. He hoped in the coming hours the master wouldn't become quieter still —or, gods forbid, perish from this taint.

"It's surprising," Bensen mused, staring at the crock pint, "that cobra venom, a toxin that reliably kills its victims, could save a woman's life—and potentially my master's—from another woman's evil. If the choice were mine to make, I wouldn't have the courage to face such a bite."

"That's not true," Nicolai said, seeming genuine. "I know you're a brave man. You've suffered worse fates, showing concern and kindness to me."

"I had a job to do."

"You could have sought employment elsewhere, like the others. You're a good man, a loyal servant and a friend. I appreciate that you've stood by me all these years. I'm grateful to have had your company. If I should die…"

"Don't," Bensen stated, staring at the flooring. "I don't want to hear talk about dying. I hope to witness an ending to this curse so a new life can begin—whatever the 'new' might be. And should your sacrifice prove winsome and the scourge be broken, maybe the spoils of success might shine on an old butler, too, perhaps healing my war wounds as well."

"Benefit both of us? I had not considered that drinking this concoction might have a dual effect. Gives me more than one reason to take the risk."

"Three reasons, if the results surmount an evil queen's scheming," Bensen replied, gesturing toward the princess. She stood in front of Nicolai as if she was afraid to pass him her fluid.

"The mixture's ready," Scarlett said quietly. "Are you sure, Nicolai?"

"The hour grows late for conversation. Give me the remedy."

Bensen watched Scarlett approach Nicolai. She was soon sitting beside him on the bench, but she didn't rush to pass him the fluid or urge him to drink it down. Perhaps her hesitation was a good sign that each of them could trust her. She seemed frightened even though the potion she held could change everything.

"You're a brave man."

"I'm not brave. I'm just weary of this life. Unhand the brew, Scarlett."

Bensen watched as the princess passed the crock pint into the master's hands. He wasn't a praying man, but he mumbled wishful words of anticipation to whatever presence might hear his plaintive call, that this brew might deliver freeing results.

"You should know, Nicolai, before you drink this fluid, I can still see the orbs shining through the red. You're about to drink magic."

"I don't see magic. But I accept what cannot be seen and hope for what might be possible." He took a tentative sip.

Bensen cringed when the master's facial expression soured and his lips wrinkled in distaste. Clearly the brew was foul.

Nicolai grimaced, making a face. "It tastes awful. What horrid flavor fouls your blood, Princess?"

"You know very well," she said, shaking her head.

Bensen understood that only a determined man would lift misery to his lips and drink of it again. He crossed his fingers while Nicolai drank, quickly and deeply, as if the action assisted the noxious bleed to leave his taste buds faster. When he was finished, he wiped the remaining red from his lips with his forehand, then tossed the crock to the floor.

"Awful," he winced, his facial expression pinched while placing his hand at his throat. He was soon belching. "I'm going to be sick."

Scarlett clung to Nicolai's arm. "You must not be sick.

You must keep this elixir inside your gut and permit Lady Alexandra to do her work."

"What are you talking about?" Nicolai responded, burping, urging her hand away.

"Lady Alexandra is alive inside of you. Now she will fight to break this curse."

"What menace runs amuck here?" Bensen asked, cringing as Nicolai reached for his stomach. The tight expression on his face changed to one of agony. "What do I do? How do I help?" he asked, stepping closer to the pair, watching the toxin take effect.

"Scarlett, what have you fed me? What have you poisoned me with?"

"I'm sorry," Scarlett said, her hand flying to her lips in obvious fear. "She told me not to tell you."

Nicolai pulled his knees upward. "Tell me what?"

"That you would be sick, Nicolai, and gravely so."

Bensen grabbed the princess and ushered her away from his master. He didn't care that she stumbled and collapsed on the flooring, or that her shocked expression conveyed her anger. His only consideration was for his master's well-being, not the princess who had fed him her concoction. Uncertain of what his action should be, he watched Nicolai's coloring fade, his skin bleaching to a clammy white and soon changing to a frightening shade of gray.

"What have you done?" Bensen shouted. "You have killed His Lordship."

Scarlett scrambled away. Her fingers flew to her lips. Tears filled her eyes. "She told me not to tell her secret. She told me

Nicolai would not drink the liquid if he knew the consequences, and I warned you about my blood."

He turned away from her excuses and watched the light further diminish from the master's eyes. Nicolai's breathing quickened; perspiration soon beaded on his forehead.

"Bensen," Nicolai appealed, his hand reaching for his throat. "I can't breathe. I can't breathe…"

Bensen scrutinized the princess, not sure how they should manage the situation, but the princess appeared as helpless as him. A tear slipped from her eye.

PRINCESS SCARLETT

SCARLETT HEARD the trill of a lady's voice. She searched for the sound. "Bring on the curse, Princess Scarlett. Now! You know what to do. Kiss Lord Nicolai."

"What's happening?" Nicolai moaned, writhing on the bench.

Scarlett scrambled to her feet, but Bensen wouldn't permit her anywhere near Nicolai and blocked her approach.

"Move aside, Bensen. Only a woman's kiss, my kiss, can help Nicolai now."

Bensen guarded Nicolai like a soldier and the old mule refused to budge. "Your kiss further poisons the situation and could force him to his death bed. I will protect this man with my life."

"Don't be an ass, Bensen. Look at him, he's in trouble.

Please— A kiss can't hurt a man. If a mark of affection helps the situation, you must let me try."

At first the butler seemed uncertain, his facial features contorted with indecision, but when Nicolai made a grimace and groaned in anguish, he relented and stood aside.

Scarlett dropped to her knees, leaned against the bench and reached for Nicolai's head. Combing her fingers through his hair, she scrutinized unfocused eyes. Tentatively, she kissed his lips, but she sensed the poor man didn't even know she had touched him.

"Can you hear me, Nicolai?" she asked, cheek to cheek, whispering in his ear. "We must bring on the curse. It's the only way to save your life."

She leaned closer still, and pressed her lips against his mouth, kissing him again, still afraid of what he could become, but when no reaction occurred, she kissed his lips a third time. She withdrew to study his eyes, which seemed to roll backward in his head.

No response; no black curse.

Nicolai moaned. "Scarlett, I'm dying…"

She clutched him, forehead to forehead, she stared at his eyes. "You're just weak, Nicolai. You're not dying. I won't let you die."

Yet, Scarlett saw that Nicolai was in desperate straits. She grasped his hand and squeezed his fingers, and rose upward, appealing to Bensen, who didn't seem to know how to respond either.

"It's the snake blood," she remarked, shaking her head. "I feared the blood would either kill him or counteract the curse. Bensen, Lady Alexandra asked me to bring on the curse, asked me to kiss Nicolai, but the curse must be weakening, lessening the chance of passion and bringing the lord closer to death instead? What do I do?"

Bensen seemed miserable, but one brow rose upward. "There's only one place I can think of where blood flows to passion. Princess," he whispered, gazing downward, "I think you must dally with the master's carnal desires. That is where the heart of the dark curse resides."

"I don't understand," she said, confused. "Where might that be?"

Bensen pointed at Nicolai's crotch.

"What? No…" Scarlett muttered, objecting. "Bensen, I will not humiliate myself, or Nicolai, by touching His Lordship in such a sensitive spot. It seems too daring of an exploit for a woman of my sensibilities to undertake."

"It's no more than a male organ," Bensen barked, "an instrument of desire. How does touching him matter if the contact saves his life?"

Scarlett swallowed, hesitated, her mouth fully open. A voice intruded in her mind: "Do it! Touch Nicolai! He's dying." Scarlett searched the space for the voice, but saw no one.

"I know you're a lady of gentle birth," Bensen said, grasping her shoulders and urging her to the source. She quivered beneath his maniacal conviction, her hand on Nicolai's thigh. "I see your hesitancy. But sometimes we must act in uncomfortable ways and do what must be done."

"All right." Scarlett responded, blushing furiously as she caressed Nicolai's soft tissues. She stroked tentatively at first, and then more aggressively when her massaging didn't yield a response.

"I'm failing." She shook her head. Her eyes filled with tears.

While waiting for signs of beastly transformation, Scarlett kissed Nicolai's lips, rubbed his arms, squeezed his hands, and tentatively cupped his groin. Nestling as close to his skin as she could get, she whispered sweet nothings: "My lord; my darling, my love, I'll give you the kingdom if it's ever in my power to gift to you. But please, Nicolai, don't die."

Scarlett searched Nicolai's facial expression for signs of the curse coming forth. When black smudges appeared underneath his eyes, she shrieked with joy.

"Now away," Lady Alexandra cried from somewhere. "But be ready with the crock."

Scarlett scrambled to the floor. She searched for the crock and held it in her hands.

Nicolai panted in earnest. He slipped from the bench, falling to the floor.

Scarlett dropped the crock. Nestling beside him, she reached for his hand and found the appendage cold and limp. Tears filled her eyes as she held his hand to her heart, fearing he would die.

"Live!" she retorted, squeezing his fingers. "You will live, Nicolai."

He curled into a fetal position. Groaning, he clutched his stomach. Finally, he trembled, then relaxed and lay silent. Still.

"You have killed him," Bensen exclaimed, raising his hands in an accusatory stance. "Move away from him."

"I will not leave him!" Scarlett blurted, refusing to break away. She grabbed his hand, feeling for a pulse. She listened to his chest, searching for a heartbeat. Bubbles of air slipped from between his lips and his hands felt numb with cold.

"No… Don't die," she cried out, grasping his head, his shoulders, shaking him as if the action might help, but when the pressure rendered no results, she pulled him closer still.

"Nicolai, can you hear me? You must fight to live. Fight for every breath inside your lungs. Don't give up. I've promised you the moon."

Nicolai did not speak, and his skin altered from a hue of pink to a grayish blue. A feminine voice yelled inside her head.

"The curse is caught. Tell Bensen to push against his chest and restart his heart. Hurry!"

"Bensen! Nicolai needs our help. Push against his chest and restart his heart. Do it now."

Bensen didn't question her instructions. Scarlett moved aside as he grabbed Nicolai and placed him on his back. With both hands, one on top of the other, he pushed against Nicolai's chest, directly above his dead heart.

Nicolai soon convulsed and vomited up fluid as if he had been drowning. He seemed confused when he opened his eyes. Again, he labored to breathe.

"I'm going to be sick," Nicolai moaned, the color returning to his face.

Nicolai expelled his stomach contents. A bodily stream of fluid and human skin slipped from his mouth, flooding to the flooring, but soon the liquid molded into the solid shape of a woman. Scarlett could only gape in wonder at how such a shape-shifting event could be possible.

Alive, Lady Alexandra lay on the floor, wet with disgusting green bile, her tiny hand still locked inside Lord Nicolai's jaw. Scarlett didn't know how she kept her own stomach contents from spilling with the sour smell filling the room. She was further grateful that she didn't succumb to a dead faint as she swayed on her feet in astonishment.

Lord Nicolai was alive and it appeared the curse was at an end.

LADY ALEXANDRA VON KAMPEN

"The crock," Lady Alexandra called, coughing fluid from her lungs. "Pass it to me. Hurry!"

Scarlett reached for the container lying on the floor, and Bensen grabbed the lid as a black shadow emerged from Nicolai's mouth. Lady Alexandra did not waste any time. She grabbed the crock and shoved the floating mass inside. Bensen readied the lid and slammed it on top.

Wet and relieved, Lady Alexandra collapsed to the floor, taking the crock in her quivering hands. Too many years had passed since she had breathed real air. The inhalations were difficult, painful, but the discomfort reminded her she was alive, and being alive filled her with joy.

"He will live," she said, sputtering. A glimmer of a smile played on her lips. "He will live."

Lady Alexandra glanced at the princess while holding tightly to the container filled with an evil scourge. Scarlett collapsed to an armchair.

"You did well, Princess," she said. "Very well."

"I can't believe what I've witnessed," Scarlett replied, her expression dazed. "You're alive, when everyone thought you were dead."

"I can assure you," Alexandra began, "I never died. I was confined to a space between life and death. I could see and hear everything happening around me, but I couldn't communicate until you arrived at Drum Manor. If not for you, I would still be banished and Nicolai would remain cursed. You have saved my life and the life of this lord, Princess Scarlett."

"I don't know what to say."

"You don't have to speak. It is I who must express consideration. Thank you, Princess Scarlett."

"What will you do with the crock and the contents inside?"

Lady Alexandra rattled in her laughter; a rasping sound due to the liquid sitting in her lungs. She gazed at the container as she moved to her knees, struggling to rise from the floor to her feet. When she successfully stood, her legs shook unbearably.

"A gift fit for a witch is locked inside this crock. When the time is right, I will release the shadow inside and return it to its rightful owner."

"Queen Cynara?" Scarlett asked. "However would you accomplish such a thing?"

"Don't worry your lovely head. Leave it to me."

Alexandra watched as an incredulous smile grew on Scarlett's face. "Alexandra, you have gained some strength."

"Fighting darkness for the better part of your life does

force a woman to come out of one's shell and gain some courage."

Nicolai groaned from the ground. "When did the flighty sparrow transform itself into a bird of prey?"

Alexandra watched Nicolai where he lay on the floor. She wasn't sure why this man had caused her anxiety levels to rise years ago. He was only a man and no longer a dark soul to fear. "Long after a spurned lover cursed you, Lord Nicolai."

Alexandra watched Nicolai stir further. "We're in a difficult situation. We're still betrothed, Alexandra."

"Darling," she giggled, "let's not curse each other any further."

Chapter Thirty-Two

QUEEN CYNARA

Queen Cynara was asleep in her bedchamber when a dark mass floated through the open window. The churning miasma drifted toward her, rising and falling as it made its way across the chamber to her bed. The evil spirit soon lingered above her sleeping form, blanketing her scantily clad figure.

Cynara rolled in her sleep and breathed deeply of the essence, which threaded its way to the furthest passages of her lungs. Her face took on a quizzical expression and she unknowingly inhaled further vapors.

She curled into a fetal position, unconsciously trying to protect herself, but the curse she had weaved on Lord Nicolai and Princess Scarlett had rebounded, and it stretched like an elastic until it gave way, snapping against her flesh.

Lightning lit the room with punishing white-hot flames, striking her skin like a whip as the thunder sounded. A sting of light repeatedly struck her arms, her legs, and her face; burning deep scarlet marks into her skin.

Cynara awoke screaming, shielding her eyes with her hands as lightning whipped her skin again and again from above her royal bed. By the time her lady-in-waiting responded to her screams of distress, the black mass had disappeared.

"Help me, Eliza," she croaked, trying to cough up a heavy weight sitting in her lungs. Her lady, obviously frightened, didn't move.

"Don't stand there, you simpleton," she hissed. "I'm burnt. Get the physician."

"As you wish, Your Royal Majesty," Eliza stammered, soon fleeing from the room.

Cynara examined the injuries to her arms and legs, and saw the lightning had left a red-feathered tattoo on her skin. She cringed, realizing that her lungs were aflame with injuries, too. She quickly understood the meaning behind the wounds as she tried to breathe.

Somehow, in some way, Nicolai had broken free of the curse. And the two people she most wanted dead in the Kingdom of Velez were alive.

And now she was marked—by *the Scarlett Mark*!

She was seized with anger but was helpless to act. For now, the pain was too great.

Chapter Thirty-Three

PRINCESS SCARLETT

A week had passed since Nicolai's curse had been broken, and since that time the dour mood at Drum Manor had brightened considerably. A formidable lord no longer existed. A gentleman emerged; a better man with a sunny disposition whose merriment and laughter carried to anyone who came into contact with him.

Nicolai worked from sunup to sundown, restoring his life. The first act he had embarked on was to take Bensen to the village where he rehired former household servants. It took a great deal of conversing to convince former household staffers that he was no longer a threat to them, but with Bensen's skin healing, the butler walked with verifiable proof that the curse had been broken.

The manor house appeared different now. The outer structure still required repairs and the shrubbery beside the manor required a severe pruning, but at least broken panes of glass had been replaced. The inside chambers had fared better, having been swept clean. The linens were washed, and all traces of spiders and their terrible black webs were gone. The fresh scent of soap lingered in the air, but something about the cleanliness and the violet smell triggered depression and sadness in Scarlett.

The transformation of Nicolai's life and his manor was an irrefutable sign of change, one which she was grateful to bear witness to, but her own life situation was still layered in threat.

Irregardless, she was happy for Nicolai. It was amazing to witness his life returning to normal. He had a second chance. Who wouldn't welcome a second chance? She hoped he used this opportunity for the greater good and didn't forsake it. But while the future seemed brighter for Nicolai, her life circumstances were no different from that first day, the day she had arrived at the manor. She wished she could envision a positive ending to her own circumstances. She knew horror and further challenges lingered on the horizon. A reign of blood and magic was not at an end.

Knowing this, the cheerful atmosphere became too much to bear, so she escaped the inner workings of the household staff, choosing to leave the manor to explore the seaside. She tracked a path at the top of the cliff edge and traversed a narrow walkway, until she took a final leap to a sandy beach. She trudged through the grit, trying to reach the sea, soon meandering beside the peaceful lull of the ocean.

The water should have buoyed her spirits. It didn't. Miserable, Scarlett stalked along the shoreline. The sunlight heated her face, causing her cheeks to flush. She removed her shoes to feel the sand beneath her toes, and the ice-cold flow of water as it drifted in and out, caressing her ankles in an invigorating way. From time to time she stopped and stared at the sea. What lingered on the opposite shore, a shoreline she couldn't see? Like the uncertain waves of her life, she didn't know what further trials lay in wait. She gripped her skirts and considered her sisters in this regard. Then she released the fabric, permitting it to trail behind her.

A bed of rocks was situated on the farther side of the shoreline. Scarlett found a spot on the sand beside a particularly large boulder and leaned against its hard form. Closing her eyes, she listened to the ocean, swell and retreat, in and out, while the sea breeze caressed her skin.

The sadness consumed her for the battle that had not been won, that might rise again, compelling tears to slip from beneath her eyelashes. When Nicolai approached her, she didn't hear him.

Lord Nicolai Graydon

When Nicolai found Scarlett, she was lying in the sand with her head resting against a stone pillow. Her eyes were shut. Her fingers sifted through grains of sand. He considered her actions while studying her beauty, watching her chest rise and fall. He tentatively approached her beach sanctuary, not wanting to intrude on her privacy, but his interest had been aroused days earlier, when her actions had saved his life.

His life—

She'd given him more than a man could ever hope for. A

wealth that couldn't be repaid through monetary means. How did one compensate such an endowment; how did one thank a woman for it? He existed in a state of wonderment he'd never be able to reimburse, so great was her gift to him.

The princess was a desirable woman. He contemplated her beauty without her knowledge, his awareness of her cultivating a stronger relationship with each passing day. He longed to comb his fingers through the chocolate waves falling around her shoulders, ached to succumb to her embrace, while waiting for her to open her eyes. Yet, as he stepped closer, he recognized an unsettling poise when a weakness revealed itself, simply by the way in which she lay in the sand.

Scarlett's facial features seemed to quiver with hidden emotion. Her face pinched, expressing sadness. Was she upset?

Perhaps hearing him, she opened her eyes. "I don't mean to intrude on your seaside pleasure, but I was hoping to talk to you. Bensen told me you went for a walk beside the ocean."

She blinked, and he could see her eyes glistened with unspent emotion. The sight of her sorrow caused his breath to catch in his throat, and his insides to wrench. "Scarlett, have you been crying?"

She raised her hand to shield her eyes from the sun. "No, of course not. What sadness could compel me to cry?"

He stepped closer. He knelt on the sand beside her. He drew his pointer finger through the liquid beneath her golden-brown eyes. "I'm not imagining this. These are tears beneath your eyes. Is it only the saltwater, fresh from the sea that causes this weakness? Or is there some hidden upset you'd like to share with me?"

While she attempted to smile, whatever sorrow she was experiencing caused her to glance away, and further tears leaked from her eyes. Nicolai worried. He didn't like this situation; he didn't know what to say in response. He stretched beside her, clasped the side of her face and gently urged her attention back to his sight. He responded to Scarlett in a manner he had never extended to another woman; he cared about her well-being and responded through compassion.

"I think I know what causes this sorrow, but don't hold this burden inside. Tell me your worries. Let your burdens go."

"I'm happy for you, Nicolai," she breathed, her voice waffling. "But nothing has changed for me. Nothing has changed."

She lay so close to his face that he could see the whites of her eyes. He wanted to kiss her sorrow away like she had awakened his sorrow to joy, but this was not a moment for flirtation. He pulled her into his embrace, giving her head a softer pillow to lie on. She accepted his offering and lay where his heart beat strong. He wrapped his arm around her, pulling her closer still, his fingers finding her waist.

"Something has changed," he whispered.

She raised her head; she studied his expression, searching. "What has changed, Nicolai? Tell me."

"You have earned yourself a champion, my Scarlett Princess. I don't know how I might assist you yet, but I will try."

"What do you mean?" Scarlett asked. "How could you help me?"

Nicolai placed his fingers on the side of her face and found her skin warm to the touch. He drew his fingertips along the soft plateau of her temples, wondering at the slight intake of her breath. "We've only known each other for a few weeks, but in this time, you have set me free. Such an action from a woman does cause a man to stop and take notice."

"Notice of me, Nicolai?"

He smiled, studying her expression. "I want to kiss you, but I've lacked feminine affection for some time. I fear what will happen should I press my advances against your lips."

Scarlett's frown shifted into a slight smile. "I don't think we have to fear tender embraces such as kisses, anymore. The curse is broken."

He stroked her rosy lips, exploring the soft, warm flesh with his thumb, his only desire on this earth to kiss her mouth. "Is that an invitation?"

She pushed against the sand, moving up his chest until her eyes searched his earnestly. Hidden emotions lingered within her eyes. *What thoughts consumed her?* No one had stared at him in such a way. Like someone might want him, too. Still, he didn't press his advantage and let Scarlett nestle closer to him.

"It could be." She touched his lips with her fingers, a casual quest of affection sliding across his mouth, a sweet exploration that provoked a lower primal ache and a heated discovery when she abandoned his skin too soon.

"I find you appealing, Nicolai. I can see why you were a

great temptation for many women. You are a handsome man."

"I want to be your temptation and I'll die if you don't kiss me."

She pressed her lips slowly against his, closing her eyes. A soft embrace, a sweet kiss that lifted away too soon. He hardened with the pleasure, but he must not fall prey to a sexual appetite. After all, he had come to her with a purpose in mind.

"Scarlett, I wanted you to know I was serious when I said I would be your champion. I want to see this battle through to the end."

"What do you mean? What are you saying?"

"I'm saying that until you are safe from Queen Cynara, and we can locate your sisters, I will be your lord."

She kissed him again, a simple peck that left him breathless. "You will be my lord? Are you proposing to me, Nicolai?"

He chuckled, hearing the surprise in her voice. "I have not promised to love, honor, and obey," Nicolai amended. "However, I do commit to serve and protect, if I can."

"Oh Nicolai," she said. Her tears falling afresh. "Perhaps as we get to know each other better, I can teach you how to love in return."

Nicolai rolled Scarlett over onto the sand so that she lay flat on her back. He lay above her gazing at her eyes, wiping fresh tears away before replying.

"I give you permission to begin instruction right now. I'm open to all manner of scientific discovery."

"Permit me to test the limits," Scarlett breathed, entwining her fingers in his hair and pulling him toward her mouth, inviting his exploration of her lips. She did not protest his advance, his embrace, or his kiss.

Nicolai kissed her soundly and enjoyed her company for the better part of the afternoon, but he did not take advantage of her fragile emotion.

Hours later he found himself alone in his bedchamber, gazing at the secret passageway from where he lounged on his bed. "Why did you choose to be a gentleman, Nicolai," he wondered aloud, "when you wanted her sweet loving so much? It's been so long."

A seed of a new relationship had begun and deeper desires would only be permitted when the lady deemed it appropriate.

"I can't believe it," Nicolai muttered, understanding that a new emotion had roused his interest. Every part of him vibrated from a woman's sacrifice. There was no doubt in his mind that the transformation taking place inside his heart and mind, strengthening and warming him, was rooted in love.

Why hadn't he told her?

Epilogue

GARRETT MORRIS

Garrett sprinted up the staircase inside the northern tower of Camden Castle, flanked by his fellow warden, Theodore Wilkins. A new mission was underway, thanks to the queen's ailment. The alliance suspected that Princess Scarlett had survived the queen's banishment and while there was no way to prove her success or failure, if it was true, the ending of one threat meant that the princesses Ruby and Rose were no longer safe. They needed to be chaperoned to safety.

He opened the wooden door to their prison and hurried inside the chamber. Rose rested on the bed, a bed the princesses had been forced to share, given that there was only one. Reading, she was always reading. Ruby, unlike her peaceful sister, paced.

"I told you to be ready. The time has come for us to escape this place."

Ruby placed her hand on her royal hips, which were beautifully swathed in a purple surcoat. As always, she was difficult.

"This kingdom is my home, Garrett Morris. I'm not a threat to the queen and I'm not interested in abandoning my royal title. 'Tis my right to demand an audience with Her Majesty to present my case."

"That won't be possible," Garrett stated, angering at her naive remark. "Scarlett has somehow set her mark on the queen, we think, and the action has incapacitated the witch for the time being. But she'll regain her strength, and when she does, the witch will be furious."

"Scarlett has done what to the queen?"

"She hasn't done anything to the queen," Rose responded, groaning. "The witch has earned an elastic lashing by way of her own defeated curse. I have seen the rebounding action in my visions."

Garrett stared at the younger princess, not knowing what to say. Her assessment was accurate, but he wouldn't tell her as much.

"Regardless of your insight, I must keep you both safe. I gave my word of honor to your father and mother that I would care for you if ever they could not. We must leave this prison."

Rose lowered her book to her lap. She didn't think to question his authority, but she wasn't aggressively natured like her sister. She rose from the bed, book in hand, and approached him. "I'm ready to leave this prison. Assist us then, and escort us from this place."

"Unfortunately, we must separate," he told them, raising

his hands in appeal. "Rose, you will depart with Theodore. He knows where to take you. It is planned."

As always, Ruby was difficult. She placed her hands on her hips once more while Rose placed her precious book inside the folds of a handbag. "You will not take my sister any place where I shall not be. We must remain together."

Garrett shook his head, and ran his hands through his hair. He didn't have time for willful temperament. "Ruby, two separate paths equal two directions for the queen's guard to search. I must make it difficult for you to be found."

Rose appealed to her sister. "It's all right, Ruby. The gods will keep us safe, and I have faith that Scarlett will see it so—I have foreseen the end."

Ruby let out an exasperated gasp. "Rose, you simple child. No one foresees the future."

"It's never an exact divination, but I do feel certain that…"

"Just stop. I don't believe it."

Rose shook her head and passed by her sister. "You're too stubborn. Let's leave, Theo. I'm tired of this place. My sister rants from early dawn to late at night. It doesn't matter that I know the truth of the queen's evil and Scarlett's innocence in the crime. I've attempted to share this truth with my sister, but Ruby knows everything and won't listen to a word I say."

Garrett regarded Ruby in earnest. "It doesn't matter. We must leave, Princesses. No one knows when the queen will recover from her ailment and send her guardsmen. We must take advantage of her weakness before your escape is not possible."

"He's right," Rose whispered. "I see the possibilities

toward a cutting end myself. The queen is through with mercy. I suspect she'll take a liking to a huntsman's blade, or a similar weapon of sharpness."

Ruby's face took on a distressed countenance. She growled and stomped her foot. Garrett was grateful when she progressed toward the door and grasped the handle. "Let us leave, then. I'll not have my pretty neck bludgeoned by the likes of the witch's swordsman. His aim is never true."

"Don't speak ill words, Ruby," Rose whispered. "The queen's spies hide everywhere."

Ruby opened the door and stepped from their prison into the corridor. "Frankly, Rose, your talk of divinity and recollections of past and future events, grows tiresome, but I'll miss you all the same. Be a gentleman and escort us to safety, Garrett Morris."

Garrett watched Princess Ruby descending the staircase, seemingly heedless of the dangers that lay ahead. Perhaps it was better for her mental well-being that she didn't know the dangers they could soon face, as the journey they were about to take through the mountains would not be an easy feat.

Garrett wasn't a praying man, but it seemed appropriate to appeal for help from a power higher than men could reach: "May the gods have mercy, and assist me to keep this young, obstinate woman safe."

Thank you for reading *The Scarlett Mark.*
If you enjoyed book one of *A Reign of Blood and Magic,*

your honest opinion of this fantasy novel matters to this author. Please review this book on your favorite book site, review site, blog, or your own social media properties, and share your opinion with other readers.

A sincere *thank you* for taking the time to write a review!

A Reign of Blood and Magic, Book 2
A Medieval Romantasy
The Ebony Queen

**A Queen's quest for supremacy.
A Royal family threatened by vengeance.
A Solomonic triangle is their means to destiny.**

Seeking revenge, Queen Cynara signs a blood contract with the devil Daemonis to gain new powers and enable her to conjure the highest level of Solomonic magic. Using an invocation spell, she shadows three princesses movements and tests her circle's potential in the king's forest, a forest *the people say* shelters evil. The action inters Ruby to a dark fate, binds Rose to the sea, and threatens Scarlett in a place that should earn peace, not further harm. Not even a god is safe from the queen's sorcery.

But power comes with a price and unbeknownst to Cynara, the devil has a secret strategy. When a blood moon eclipses the night, Cynara invokes her magic in the king's forest.

Will her quest for supremacy prevail, and how might it challenge the current King Lowell, *The Ebony Queen's* own son?

Contact Abby Lane

If you would like to learn more about Abby or her novels, visit her website at abby-lane.com. Here you can read excerpts from her books, linked reviews, blog posts, as well as discovering her professional affiliations and accreditation.

Abby enjoys hearing from her readers. If you'd like to contact the author, send her a message at: abby@abby-lane.com.

FOLLOW ABBY ON SOCIAL MEDIA

facebook.com/abbylane.author

instagram.com/authorabbylane

amazon.com/author/abbylane

bookbub.com/profile/abby-lane

goodreads.com/abbylane

About the Author

The author of several novels in genre fiction, Abby Lane admires the many ways myths, fairy tales, and fantasy connect us to our inner child. She credits Disney's *Sleeping Beauty* and George R. R. Martin's *Song of Ice and Fire*, with inspiring her love of story-telling. She appreciates the corridors of medieval history and in particular the Tudor period. She has visited the United Kingdom, touring many castles in her pursuit of story, having a special affinity for Anne Boleyn and King Henry's court. Abby shares her life with her husband and adores her adult children, including two special grand pups named Bella and Arya. When she isn't at her home in Calgary, she's admiring the ocean at her cottage in Maple Bay.